The kids were enough…

Claire had neither the time nor the inclination to complicate her life any further. So she would simply ignore the ridiculous, simmering attraction she felt every time Logan Matthews came into view. Instead—like any good neighbor—she'd do her part to establish a polite, somewhat distant relationship.

Not a problem. She'd earned the furtively whispered nickname her former employees had given her. Any Frost Queen worth her crown could easily control errant emotions.

And when she succeeded, she wanted an Oscar for Best Actress of the Year.

* * * * *

"A family under siege. Forbidden love. Courage and compassion. *Her Sister's Children* captures the imagination and touches the heart. Roxanne Rustand's distinctive voice charms and captivates."
—Vicki Hinze, bestselling author

Dear Reader,

Each autumn for decades, as the leaves start to change and the air turns crisp, my family has headed up to Lake Superior's North Shore. The steep cliffs, fragrant pine forests and wild beauty of Superior are unforgettable. What could be better than sitting around a campfire at midnight, with a wash of stars overhead and the sound of waves rushing against the shore? As children, my brother and I loved every moment we spent there, and now my own children love it just as much. We always hope Superior will grow fierce while we're there, and send waves exploding against the cliffs.

I hope you'll enjoy this story about a woman who leaves her urban life behind to take on the challenges of raising her sister's young children in just such a place. The enigmatic man next door creates even greater challenges for her—especially when painful secrets from the past are revealed.

If you'd like to write, I would love to hear from you. My address is P.O. Box 2550, Cedar Rapids, IA, 52406-2550. Thanks so much!

And Mom and Dad—thank you for all the wonderful trips north, and for the beautiful memories. No childhood could have been better!

Roxanne Rustand

HER SISTER'S CHILDREN
Roxanne Rustand

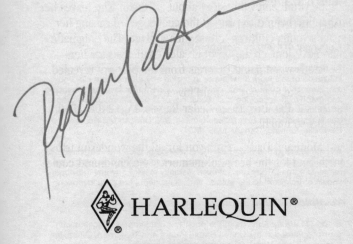

◆ HARLEQUIN®

TORONTO • NEW YORK • LONDON
AMSTERDAM • PARIS • SYDNEY • HAMBURG
STOCKHOLM • ATHENS • TOKYO • MILAN • MADRID
PRAGUE • WARSAW • BUDAPEST • AUCKLAND

ISBN 0-373-70857-2

HER SISTER'S CHILDREN

Copyright © 1999 by Roxanne Rustand.

This edition published by arrangement with Harlequin Books S.A.

Visit us at www.romance.net

Printed in U.S.A.

Many thanks to Leigh Michaels, Kylie Brant, Diane Palmer,
Kathie DeNosky, Chelle Cohen, Lyn Cote, Monica Caltabiano,
Shelley Cooper, Suzanne Thomas and Julia Mozingo. And
special thanks to Rob Cohen. You've all helped
my dreams come true!

CHAPTER ONE

IF SHE'D KNOWN about the snake, Claire would have thought twice about leaving New York.

Jason's two-foot albino corn snake slithered sedately across the kitchen floor and coiled itself into a neat, flesh-colored pile at the base of the refrigerator. From unwelcome experience, Claire knew Igor would bask in the warmth of the motor indefinitely—to avoid northern Minnesota's early-September chill, no doubt.

The children's dog or cat napping there would have an altogether different—a more *domestic*—effect on the room. But Gilbert, the elderly poodle, always took off for the farthest reaches of the old Victorian house whenever Igor managed to escape his guaranteed-escape-proof reptile cage. And Sullivan, emitting Siamese yowls to rival any civil defense siren, had found her usual refuge on top of the cupboards.

Claire had developed an aversion to snakes as a child, but she'd never argued over Jason's ownership of Igor. She'd tried to make every concession possible in hopes that Jason would feel welcome and happy. Nothing had worked.

A car door slammed. Heavy footsteps marched up the concrete walk. With a sigh, Claire remembered her days in New York as assistant personnel director of her father's electronics firm. After four weeks of strangers knocking at her door at all hours, mountain-high piles of laundry and a phone jangling from morning till night, her familiar world of deferential employees and maid service was rapidly gaining appeal. Her parents' wealth had never bought happiness, and her rise in the company had been her father's dream, not hers, but there had been some definite advantages to having money.

She'd made her decision, Claire reminded herself with a rueful smile. She'd welcomed the challenge of taking in her late sister's three children, although she had serious doubts about ever adjusting to their pets. So now she could dwell on her problems or view her new career as an exciting challenge. Here at Pine Cliff Resort she could finally succeed on her own merits, away from her family's influence. And after losing their parents in a car accident six months before, the kids needed her, not a nanny. Nothing mattered more than giving them the best possible life. She loved them too much to settle for less.

A sharp knock on the door echoed through the room. Smiling at an older woman staring at her through the screen, Claire crossed the gleaming vinyl floor. "Can I help you?"

"I'm Mrs. Rogers," the woman announced in a

two-pack-a-day baritone. A cloying odor of heavy perfume and stale cigarette smoke blew in as Claire opened the door. "I have reservations."

The decibel level of Sullivan's yowls rose.

Though built like a woman who could clear timber and slay bears before breakfast, Mrs. Rogers drew back in alarm. She leaned to one side to peer suspiciously past Claire. "Where's the manager?"

Suppressing a chuckle, Claire ushered the older woman into the small entryway and turned to the rolltop desk by the door. She ran a finger down the names in the reservation book. "I'm the new manager. Is cabin three okay?"

The woman shook her head and tapped the toe of her shoe against the floor. "When I called in June, I was promised the end cabin, as always. Check your book again."

Claire dutifully rechecked the reservation book. "That one will be open tomorrow, but three does have a lovely view."

A heavy, disapproving silence hung in the air. "We stayed in three once. My Henry, rest his soul, said the bed didn't have enough support—" With a sharp intake of breath, Mrs. Rogers stepped backward, her eyes widening.

Apparently, she'd seen Igor. "Anything else?" Claire asked sweetly. *A companion for your cabin, perhaps?*

Handing the speechless woman a pen, Claire snagged a set of keys from the strip of Peg-Board on the wall and silently thanked Igor for cutting short a potential tirade. Until a month ago, Claire had fired irritating people. Now she had to smile at them.

It wasn't easy.

After Mrs. Rogers backed out, key in hand, Claire lifted a bag of blueberry potpourri from a shelf above the desk, but decided that the delicate fragrance wouldn't have a chance against the raw scent of cologne still clouding the air. Frowning, she opened the three windows behind the claw-foot oak table, then watched the lacy white curtains dance high on the incoming breeze. The children deserved a clean, cheerful home, not one smelling like a nightclub at midnight.

She glanced over her shoulder at the clock above the stove. Two-thirty. Just enough time to finish cleaning the last cabin before meeting the school bus at the resort entrance.

For a moment, an image of the children's smiling faces and eager chatter warmed her heart. Maybe this time one of the kids would give her a hug. But Claire knew there was a greater chance for an August blizzard. The twins' subdued, sad-eyed compliance and their brother's veiled hostility hadn't changed since she'd picked them up in Minneapolis last month and brought them north. Brooke's will had given Claire the resort and custody of the children, but no legal document could guarantee an easy adjustment.

A second sharp knock at the door startled Claire. *Another pleasant guest, no doubt.*

She gave the snake a stern glance. "Stay!"

Motionless, with approximately the same dimensions and personality as a small pile of men's underwear, Igor stared back at her. He looked unimpressed.

Summoning her best innkeeper's smile, Claire lifted her chin and turned toward the door. A tall, broad-shouldered man in faded jeans and an ancient Nike T-shirt stood outside. His buff-colored jacket had the scent of fine leather. Backlit by bright afternoon sun, his features were cast in shadow, but Claire had an eerie feeling she had met him before. A shiver raced down her spine.

"Yes?" She moved a half step closer and looked up into the stranger's face.

Only he was no stranger.

Her heart stopped. Her breath caught raggedly in her throat. *Logan.* The past fourteen years had hardened the youthful beauty of his features, adding breadth and power to his elegant body. His hair had darkened to deep, sun-streaked caramel, but there was no mistaking those seductive deep blue eyes. Her pulse raced. Her knees wobbled. He was everything she'd remembered, only much, much more.

But this man was as safe as a plateful of nightshade or a midnight stroll in Central Park. He'd been the object of her first adolescent crush, then become the creature of her youthful nightmares.

And he had nearly destroyed her sister's life.

Suddenly aware she was staring, Claire lowered her eyelashes. She felt momentarily unable to speak. What did one say to the devil himself? And why on earth was he here?

The silence lengthened, grew awkward. After taking a steadying breath, she lifted her gaze and caught his expression of supreme frustration. "Can I help you?"

"I hope so." The boyish charm and humor of years past were gone, leaving a man who could glare the snarl off a rottweiler. "All I need is information. Can I come in for a minute?"

Claire considered the options of firmly dismissing him, or slamming the door in his face. The latter would be infinitely more satisfying, but—

Taking advantage of her brief hesitation, he reached out, opened the screen door and strode into the kitchen.

Claire pulled herself together—fast—and snatched the receiver from the phone on the desk. Her finger punched the first number of 911 before she had the receiver halfway to her ear.

Logan reached out, but she slid away and punched the second number. "Back off," she snapped.

He looked at her in surprise and held out his hands, palms up. "I was going to shake hands and

introduce myself. Are you always this edgy, lady?''
He managed a damn good expression of innocence.

"Of course not. People don't barge into my
house every day.''

"Believe me, I'm no threat.'' His voice was calm
and low, with the quiet reassurance one might use
with a frightened child.

Claire's finger hovered over the last number.
"Make one more move and I finish this call. The
sheriff will respond whether I say a word or not.''

"No need.'' He stepped away and slowly turned.
The tension in his body seemed to dissipate as he
studied the antiques and small paintings adorning
the lace-curtained room. "Someone has been
busy,'' he said with a trace of bitterness. "Brooke
was never one for the warm-and-welcoming look.
I'm Logan Matthews, her first husband. All I need
is the address and phone number of her executor.''

Claire stared at him. *He doesn't recognize me.*
Of course, fourteen years ago she'd been a child in
pigtails and cutoffs, and the effects of her passion
for French fries and hot fudge had been all too obvious. "Why do you want to know?''

"I've had remarkably bad luck trying to contact
members of her family in New York and Minneapolis.'' Logan ran a gentle hand over the surface
of the old oak cupboards, as if reliving a memory.
"My lawyer's calls haven't been returned and my
letters came back unopened. Not twenty minutes

ago, her mother's housekeeper hung up on me for the third time.''

''Must have been your gracious manner,'' Claire muttered under her breath, sending up a silent prayer of thanks that Brooke's children were the product of her *second* marriage. Once Claire got Matthews out of her kitchen, she would never have to see him again. ''Surely you can't think you were mentioned in the will.''

He gave her a look of complete disgust. ''Of course not. But Brooke died owning something that belongs in my family.'' He looked away and hesitated, as if considering how much to say. ''She won this half of Pine Cliff in our divorce settlement. She'd always hated the place, yet she refused to sell her half back to me at any price.''

Claire lowered the phone to her side, feeling continued reassurance in its cool surface under her fingertips. ''There must be other properties you could buy that are in much better condition.''

He moved across the room to the trio of windows overlooking Lake Superior. Bracing one arm high on a window frame, he silently stared out at the waves. Claire studied him in the bright sunlight. He had the face of an angel, but she knew his heart and soul belonged a lot farther south.

''I inherited this place from my grandmother years ago,'' he said at last. ''I just want a chance to buy it back.''

The faint note of underlying pain could not have

come from him. Not unless he'd decided to gain her sympathy. She remembered Brooke's tearful stories of how deceptive he'd been, how callous. But Claire was not the breezy, naive girl her sister had been. If he thought he could manipulate Claire Worth, he was dead wrong. She marshaled her coldest, most businesslike tone. "I'm her executor. Pine Cliff is not for sale."

Logan turned and studied her for a moment, his eyes reflecting dawning recognition. "Claire?"

"Right."

"Blond, but I don't see any other resemblance to Brooke." A hint of a smile tilted one corner of his mouth, although his eyes remained grim. "You were what, thirteen? Fourteen or so when she and I divorced? I can imagine what they told you."

"Enough," Claire snapped.

"I can see there's probably no point in discussion," he said slowly, his voice tinged with regret. "Brooke's version of the past must have been... convincing."

"It certainly worked for me."

"Are you planning to sell later on?"

"I'm planning to stay," she retorted. He stood there like a man in a TV commercial—muscled, sexy and altogether too appealing. Her sister had fallen for him almost overnight.

He lifted one eyebrow. "A little far from your social circle, aren't you?"

"That's not your concern." Some of his old charisma surfaced in a lazy half smile and a teasing glint in his eyes, but she was not taken in. The flutter of her pulse came from tension, not a response to the dark and smoky tone of his voice.

He glanced at the open reservation book on the desk, then gave her an incredulous look. "You're managing this place?"

"Yes."

"You won't last."

Exactly the sentiments of her ex-fiancé in New York, who had declared her incapable of raising three children and foolish for giving up her career. Of course, he'd been trying to protect his plan to become her father's protégé and heir. Claire felt the heat of anger rising in her throat. "I'd like you to leave."

Logan shook his head. "I should have recognized the Worth family wit and warmth right away." He walked to the door, hesitated, then dropped a business card on the desk. "Blood does tell."

"Out!"

His mouth curved into a faint smile, but no flash of humor showed in his eyes. "You'll be in serious country-club withdrawal by Thanksgiving. You'll be dying to sell. Don't bother with a real estate agent, just call me. You'll save time and won't get a better price."

As soon as he stepped outside, Claire shut the heavy oak door and rammed the dead bolt home, then moved to a window by the desk. After Logan's gleaming black Explorer disappeared up the lane, she sank into the creaky swivel chair at the desk.

The faint scent of sandalwood and leather lingered in the air, sending her thoughts flying back to the time when she had nurtured the world's most intense, embarrassing crush on this man.

As a teenager caught up in the throes of her first impossible romance, Claire had thought her older sister's boyfriend represented masculine perfection—tall, witty and handsome enough to compete with any teen idol. She'd lived for glimpses of his slow, easy smiles, loved the way his eyes crinkled at the corners and deep dimples grooved his cheeks. He'd always ruffled her hair and teased her, treating her like a kid sister.

Her lack of perception at the time still astounded her. Granted, she'd been an inexperienced young girl, but how had she missed seeing what the man was really like? In all her life, no one had ever fooled her so completely.

Shoving a hand through her short-cropped hair, she started to sweep Logan's business card off the desk and into the wastebasket, but his address caught her eye. She stared in disbelief. Matthews Architectural Associates, St. Paul, Minnesota. A local phone number and address had been written at the bottom. *The address nearly matched that of Pine Cliff.* Claire's heart missed a beat.

It was discomforting to know that one of her neighbors had a long-term grudge against her family, and a proven propensity for deceit.

CHAPTER TWO

"I DON'T like fish."

"Meat loaf. With baked potatoes?"

"No."

"Hamburgers?" Claire stared at the thirteen-year-old tyrant standing in front of her, trying to ignore the snake looped casually around his arm. From the defiant gleam in Jason's eye, she knew exactly why he held Igor—and why the creature managed to "escape" so often. Exasperated, she tried again. "Hot dogs?"

Jason shot her a look of utter disdain. "Our nanny *never* gave us hot dogs. Mother's orders."

Claire turned to the five-year-old twins, Annie and Lissa, who sat perched on matching stools at the breakfast counter like two wide-eyed owlets, silent and unblinking. "How about you girls?"

They stared at her, fidgeted, then simultaneously shot pleading looks toward their brother, who scowled back.

"Would you like to go out for pizza?" Claire cringed at her own desperate, pleading tone. The board members of Worth Electronics would die laughing if they could hear her now.

"Yes!" The twins spoke as one, their eyes lighting up with delight. Neither risked even a glance at Jason, whose sullen expression spoke volumes about their defection.

"Good." Claire pinned Jason with a determined look. "I'm starved, aren't you?"

Reluctantly, Jason returned Igor to his cage, then followed Claire and the girls outside. She could hear his feet dragging through the crunchy gravel and his occasional, long-suffering sighs. He took the rear seat of the Windstar as always, where he slumped in stubborn silence.

Buckling her seat belt, Claire looked over her shoulder. "Want to go exploring when we get back? We might see some deer."

Jason slid farther down in the seat and scowled. "I have homework," he said flatly.

"The first week of school?"

"Lots of it. I'll need to come straight—" he faltered over the word as if it tasted of vinegar "—home."

"What do you think, Annie and Lissa?"

The little girls exchanged worried frowns. "Are there any bears?" Annie asked, wrapping a blond curl ever tighter around her finger. "Jason says there's bears."

"I haven't seen one," Claire said, her voice firm. "And if we do, I'll chase that old bear away. I hereby declare Pine Cliff off-limits to anything that has sharp teeth and growls."

"There *are* bears," Jason muttered darkly. "Especially at night. I've heard them trying to get into the trash cans. And there are wolves, and foxes, and coyotes."

"All at Pine Cliff? The place is busier than I thought. They'll have to start making reservations." The twins rewarded her with tentative smiles. Jason didn't.

Driving down the long lane toward the highway, Claire resolved to make it through the fourth chapter of *Parenting: The Challenge of a Lifetime* before falling asleep tonight. There had to be some clue, some nugget of information in that book that would help her.

"It must be hard, moving away from all of your old friends," Claire ventured as she pulled to a stop at the junction of the resort entrance and the highway. "Want to invite someone up from Minneapolis, Jason?"

"Who'd wanna come up here?"

"Your best friends?"

"Yeah, right."

Lissa leaned forward in the middle seat. "Mother doesn't—didn't allow that. 'Cause we're too noisy."

Claire's hands stilled on the steering wheel. "Didn't allow what, sweetie?"

"Friends over. 'Cept when just the nanny was there."

The child sounded dead serious, but envisioning

happy-go-lucky Brooke as a stern mother took more imagination than Claire could muster. She hid her surprise behind a teasing tone. ''You guys aren't noisy in the least. How about it, Jason, would you like to invite someone up for a weekend?''

At the boy's stubborn look of indifference, Claire sighed, waited for a semi to pass, then pulled out onto the road. How did one reach a troubled, grieving teenager? She'd made some progress with the twins, but Jason rejected every effort she made. *Time heals,* she reminded herself. *I won't give up on him.*

As she drove, she found herself watching the mailboxes along the highway. With luck, Logan's would be much farther away than the scrawled address on his business card indicated. She breathed a sigh of relief as the numbers on the boxes rapidly descended past his. Neither his name nor house number appeared. Perhaps she'd misread his address.

It didn't matter. The North Woods was a vast, rugged area. She and Logan might never run into each other.

One thing was for sure. If she noticed him first, they would never meet again.

TWO HOURS LATER, Claire parked the minivan back at Pine Cliff. The children, stuffed on pepperoni pizza with double cheese, had been quiet all the way home.

"Who's ready for a good hike?" she asked, automatically hitting the door locks after everyone clambered out of the vehicle.

She looked down at the key in her hand, then scanned the vast forest rimming the resort on three sides. The endless expanse of lake to the east. The quiet felt almost overwhelming. This wasn't exactly New York, where thieves stripped cars in minutes, and an unlocked vehicle might as well bear an engraved invitation on its hood. Where the continual sound of traffic and anonymous crowds blended into the white noise of familiarity. Loneliness and a sense of unease streaked through her as she pocketed her car keys.

Then she focused on the single row of fifteen cozy cabins hugging the shore, each flanked by a guest's car. Gulls cried overhead and waves splashed. It wasn't quiet, not really. She glanced at the children. And she certainly wasn't alone.

"Why did we have to come up here?" Jason muttered, kicking a chunk of gravel across the lane. His chin lifted in sudden challenge. "Why didn't we go to New York?"

Because I'm going to save you three from the lonely childhood I had. You're going to have a real family.

Claire's own mother and father had abdicated their parental duties to domestic employees long before their divorce when she was twelve. Brooke, by then a college freshman, married young and never again came home. Claire had landed in an exclusive boarding school she'd hated from the first day.

And now, back in New York, her obstinate father was determined to see his only grandson follow that Worth family boarding school tradition, though Claire had already made her opposition clear. The battles ahead defied description, but a buffer of a thousand miles would at least limit most of those battles to phone and fax.

She searched for an excuse. "You couldn't have kept your pets in New York, honey. No animals were allowed in my building."

Jason's chin went a notch higher. "Coulda snuck 'em in."

"You don't know the doorman." Claire rolled her eyes. "He must have been a secret agent in a past life."

"Minneapolis, then."

Darting apprehensive glances at Jason, the twins edged closer to her. Claire could guess what they were thinking. Until Brooke and Randall's will was located and their tangled estate settled, the children had stayed at their maternal grandmother's gated property in Wayzata. They were probably remembering endless hours of proper behavior and dutiful silence in that cold and lonely place.

"We'll have more fun living up here, don't you think?" Claire asked. Conflicting emotions raced across Jason's face. *Fear?* Surely not. She gave all three children a dazzling smile. "So, shall we go for that hike?"

With a snort of disgust, Jason turned on his heel and stalked to the house. After a moment of indecision, the girls each took one of Claire's hands and they started down the lane.

There was a sharp nip in the September air, hinting at the change of season that was coming. Claire breathed deeply to inhale the crisp, sweet fragrance of pine. To the left, early-evening sunlight sparkled across the gentle waves of Lake Superior.

She laughed aloud with sheer delight. The twins looked up in surprise.

"Isn't this beautiful?" She smiled down at them. "I've never seen a northern Minnesota fall. The *Herald* says we'll be seeing the best autumn colors in years."

Both girls nodded silently and walked beside her, kicking up puffs of dust with their matching pink Nikes. When they passed the last cabin, Claire dropped to one knee and gave them both a hug. They instinctively stiffened at her touch, but she held them close for a moment before rising to her feet.

"Well, girls, where should we go next—down the shoreline? Or toward the highway?" She lowered her voice to a conspiratorial level. "We might see some deer in the woods."

Annie dug her toe into the gravel. "I never saw a deer, 'cept in a zoo."

"Then let's look, okay?" Claire reached down to take little hands once more.

They turned up the mile-long lane toward the highway. Ancient pines towered high above them at either side, leaving scant space for grasses and wildflowers at the edge of the road. Beneath the dense, dark skirts of the trees stretched an endless carpet of bronze and amber pine needles. The muted sunlight and heavy incense of evergreen reminded Claire of her favorite European cathedral, its vaulted expanses hushed into reverent silence.

"This is lovely. Do you like it here?" Claire asked.

The little girls tightened their hands on her own, but they didn't reply. In their entire month with her, they'd never said a word about their parents' deaths, or about the many changes in their lives since that awful night. She'd yet to see them display the grief they must be feeling.

Should she bring up painful topics? Wait until they did? She wanted nothing more than to help them in any way she could.

They spied a meadow, just beyond a line of pines standing like sentinels along the road, and moved quietly to its edge.

"This looks like a perfect place for fairies, doesn't it?" Claire whispered.

Annie nodded, her eyes wide and solemn. "I bet they dance here at night."

They stood in silence for a while. The earthy

scents of cold, damp moss and fallen leaves reminded Claire of her college years away from
home—of hayrides and fire-roasted hot dogs and
homecoming games of the past. She wondered if
the somber girls were even aware of their surroundings.

"You can talk to me about anything," Claire
said softly, giving their hands a gentle squeeze.
"Are you feeling sad? Will it help to tell me?"

Lissa dropped her head lower, but Annie looked
up with eyes filled with such haunting pain that
Claire drew a sharp breath.

"T-telling makes you cry. If we m-make you—"

Lissa jerked her hand away and spun around to
face Annie. "No! Don't say!"

Dear God. What did I do wrong? Claire cursed
her own inadequacy. She dropped to her knees,
drawing the little girls into a snug embrace. "Lissa.
Annie. Tell me what's wrong."

Lissa glared at Annie, clearly issuing a silent
warning. Annie stared at the silver ballerina appli-
qué on her sweatshirt, then sniffled and rubbed her
nose against her sleeve. "If we talk about M-
Mommy, you cry. If we make you s-sad you
might—you might—" Small hiccuppy sobs shook
her fragile shoulders.

Claire pulled the girls even closer. Her heart shattered. "I love you so much," she murmured, her dam-

nable, betraying tears welling hot and heavy against her eyelashes.

"See, see what you did?" Lissa's voice rose to a shriek. She flung a small fist at Annie, but Claire gently caught the blow in midflight.

Annie, like a stoic saint awaiting execution, had remained deathly still within the curve of Claire's arm, ready to accept her sister's punishment. Her voice, whispery soft, came indistinctly at first, then a bit louder. Complete resignation framed every word.

"You might send us back to Grandmother and Great-grandmother if we make you sad."

Curse those women. Claire's coldly aristocratic grandmother and mother were cut from the same cloth. No wonder her father had escaped to New York years ago. She could imagine them telling the girls, "Crying does not help. Sit up and eat your dinner" without so much as a pat on the shoulder. Heaven only knew how many times her own childhood emotions had been ignored. It had been a bad mistake to let the children spend any time—let alone five months—in that house.

The twins searched Claire's face, as if sure their only refuge would now collapse in ruins.

Claire stroked their corn-silk hair and gave each a gentle kiss on the cheek. "If I cry, it's because I'm sad for you. I'm sad for me, too. Your mother was my sister. It's okay to cry."

Annie snuggled closer, her tear-damp face

pressed against Claire's neck. Lissa wavered, her big blue eyes probing Claire's expression.

"You'll always have a home with me," Claire added softly. "Cross my heart." She considered for a moment, then added with a smile, "At least until you're grown-up and ready to fly. Deal?"

"D-deal," they said in unison.

Annie and Lissa snuggled deeper into her embrace, like two starving waifs finding unexpected salvation. A primal rush of tenderness surged through Claire. There was nothing she wouldn't do to keep these children safe.

From just ahead came the unexpected clank of metal against metal. The rusty screech of a gate hinge. Claire lunged to her feet and scanned the surrounding forest, which suddenly seemed dark. Menacing. There were several other properties along the lane leading to the resort, but none of them included homes, and she had yet to encounter any of the owners. A feeling of vulnerability washed through her. She'd been foolish, walking so far with the girls this evening.

"Let's turn around," she murmured. "It's getting late."

They had walked just a few feet when Claire heard another unexpected noise—the soft rumble of an engine. She whirled around. A dozen yards away, a black Explorer slipped out of the trees and onto the road, angled toward the highway.

She stopped dead and stared. *Logan Matthews.*

The vehicle also came to a stop, backed up a few feet, changed direction. Headed their way. Her pulse speeding up, Claire reached for Annie's and Lissa's hands.

The truck pulled up a few yards away. Its smoked-glass passenger-side window slid down a few inches. "I don't mean to be unpleasant, but I don't allow resort guests on my land," he said.

Claire couldn't see Logan clearly in the shadowed depths of the vehicle. Its darkened windows and the deepening twilight apparently prevented a clear view of her. The window began to glide upward.

Motioning the girls to stay behind, she crossed the road in two long strides, then braced one hand against the door and rapped sharply on the glass. Her career had taught her how to deal with men— and cowering before this one would be a major mistake. Bullies never expected strength.

"We're not guests. And I believe you're on *my* land, Matthews."

"Claire?" His door opened, then he slowly unfolded himself from the front seat. Facing her from the other side of the truck he stared at her for a long moment. "I didn't recognize you in this light—" he looked down at the girls, who had followed her across the road like ducklings "—and with children."

His eyes were shadowed with old anger and dark secrets, but pure male interest glimmered there as well. Another man, another time…and her shivery inner response might have pushed her into the next step of a tentative relationship. But this was Logan Matthews.

"*Three* kids, actually," she pointed out, sure his interest would wither. "The teenager is at home."

He gave her a knowing look, as if he understood exactly why she'd elaborated, then grinned at Annie and Lissa. They hid behind her.

He gestured toward the path she and the girls had followed from the meadow. "The surveyor's stake is hidden in those weeds."

Claire stiffened. "I—I'm sorry. My original tour of the property was brief and in the rain. I thought the line was another twenty-five yards down." A sudden thought chilled her. "Do you live out here?"

"Yes. I designed my house years ago, but didn't get around to building it until this summer. By next spring, I'll run my business from up here."

As an architect he could do his work almost anywhere, she supposed. Which meant he would be practically underfoot every day of the year—a constant reminder of Brooke and her family's deep bitterness over the past. Her heart sinking, she scrambled for an appropriate response. "You and your wife must have a lovely home."

"No wife," he said. "I try not to repeat past mistakes."

She couldn't let him get away with that dig at

her sister. "Women throughout the world can sigh with relief."

Logan threw back his head and laughed, his teeth gleaming white in the faint light. "Touché, Guinevere."

The sound of his laughter and the ring of his old nickname for her sent memories cascading through her thoughts. She studied him once more. He'd aged well—his eyes crinkled with laugh lines when he smiled, while a surprising hint of early gray at his temples added a touch of dignity.

"Look," he continued. "It's just the tourists I discourage. I don't mind if you three wander on my land while you're still up here."

"Still up here?" Claire's mellow thoughts turned to dry ice. "I certainly was naive years ago. I always thought you were a more perceptive man."

A corner of his mouth tipped upward. "I am."

"Then you realize the kids and I aren't going anywhere. We'll be happy at Pine Cliff. It's a perfect place to raise a family."

"You'll get bored. Or scared, surrounded by these deep dark woods. Trust me."

Claire didn't try to hide her look of astonishment. "Interesting choice of words there, Matthews. *Trust.* Brooke certainly discovered the value of *trust,* didn't she?"

"I'd say that lesson was mine. And it isn't one I care to remember." He pensively stared toward the meadow, a muscle working along his jaw. His gaze shifted back to Claire. "I do have a few good memories, though—of a sweet young girl in pigtails who told me her secrets, who said I was her Prince Charming. She said she would mar—"

"I was barely a teenager." Claire felt warmth rise in her cheeks. "A young girl's imagination takes wild flights."

"I can imagine." He winked at the twins, then looked up at Claire, his eyes grave. "I'll give you a deal. Twenty-five percent above the market value for your half of Pine Cliff. You and your children can even stay in that house until spring, if you like."

She hid her surprise. "All that for a struggling resort?"

"Not everyone has life handed to them on a silver platter," he said softly. "This place means something to me. But I don't expect you to understand."

"You think—" He was the one who didn't understand. Claire cleared her throat and started over. "If you only knew."

His smile turned cold and cynical. "Choke on that silver spoon, did you?"

Startled, she stared up at him, caught between irritation and hysterical laughter at his assumptions. "We were discussing the property. It won't happen, but I'm curious. If you did have all of Pine Cliff, what then?"

"The buildings will be bulldozed."

He spoke as if it were going to happen. Claire looked at him in disgust. "High-priced condos?"

"Just wildlife and trees."

"Lovely idea, Matthews. But I'm not selling. This place provides my income. I left New York under rather hostile circumstances and I'm not going back."

"You could apologize—to your father, right?"

He *had* changed. One easy smile and he could still turn her knees to aspic, but his youthful determination and charm had darkened to an unfortunate blend of stubborn and aggravating. "That's not even a remote possibility."

He glared at her. She met his dark, cold gaze without flinching, and suddenly she saw beyond his anger. She saw old pain, coupled with remnants of grief. The emotions were gone so quickly she thought she might have imagined them.

The world seemed to shift under her feet as she began to see the past in a different light. What really happened between Brooke and Logan all those years ago—could he have been as cruel as her sister had claimed?

Endless boxes of Brooke's possessions filled the attic of the Pine Cliff house. Perhaps they held clues to a truth far different than the version of the past she'd always heard. As soon as she could find the time, Claire would start looking for answers.

Annie tugged at a belt loop on Claire's jeans. "Gotta go," she mouthed urgently. *"Now."*

"Come on, girls." Claire gave them each a re-assuring smile and turned to leave.

"I'll be back," Logan said, his voice soft and low.

From the corner of her eye, she watched his truck vanish down the road, leaving a faint haze of dust in the air. Leaving an odd sense of emptiness in her heart.

The woods fell silent. Shadowy pines now loomed above like dark and dangerous creatures of the night.

"Let's get home and see if your brother has done his homework." Claire gave each child's hand a squeeze, keeping her stride calm and steady.

All the way back, she wondered if she'd really seen that hint of pain in Logan Matthews's eyes.

JASON SCRAMBLED UP onto the rough shelf of granite jutting out into Lake Superior, and turned his face into the cold breeze coming across the water. Aunt Claire and the girls would soon be back from their walk. The smell of buttery popcorn might fill the kitchen. Gilbert would be at the door, begging for a walk. But Jason couldn't go back. Not yet.

Waves spanked the rock face beneath his feet, then were sucked back out into the lake with a squelching sound, like wet sneakers. Above, a dozen or more seagulls drew lazy circles in the evening sky.

They were waiting for handouts—a piece of

bread, a chunk of hot dog—but he hadn't had time to raid the kitchen. He'd been in too much of a hurry. Escaping the house had been more important than bringing something for his birds. He'd simply had to get away; he couldn't stand the feeling of being watched. The whole house seemed like a creature with a thousand eyes, watching. Waiting.

With his whole heart, he wanted to believe that *they* hadn't followed him up here and that he was safe. But it wasn't true.

He'd seen a familiar gray car cruising slowly through town, and the same car had pulled into the resort yesterday. It had stayed at the far end of the lane for a few minutes, then slowly drove away. *Was that them?*

He'd heard strangers' voices arguing that awful night last spring, but hadn't seen the men's faces. Ever since, he'd held his breath whenever he saw strangers.

The sight of that car at Pine Cliff had made his heart stop.

If you go to the police, these guys will come after you and your sisters. His father's last words played through Jason's thoughts once again, an endless litany of warning that still stole hours of sleep and kept Jason's nerves on edge.

If he'd been brave, he could have stopped what happened that night long ago. If he'd been stronger, he and the girls wouldn't have lost everything that mattered.

He stared out across the water to where the sky and lake melted together in shades of gray. He wished he could ride the breeze like one of the seagulls overhead. He'd fly away from this place, away from the pain and sadness that sat on his chest like a two-hundred-pound bully.

The weight made every breath an effort, made his feet feel like lead. Worst of all, he knew the feeling would never, ever go away. Not until it was too late for all of them.

Sinking to his knees, he welcomed the sharp edges of rock that bit into his skin. At least this pain was something real—something he could control.

Alone, far from Pine Cliff, he lowered his head and on a soul-deep, shuddering sigh, his hot tears began to fall.

CHAPTER THREE

LOGAN STOOD at the glass wall of his new house and stared out at the whitecaps crowning Superior's gunmetal-gray waves. The windows stretched twenty feet skyward, providing a spectacular view of the most scenic length of shoreline between Duluth and the Canadian border.

But it wasn't enough. The Worths' greed and anger had divided Pine Cliff years ago. He wanted it all—the only real home he'd ever had, the land his grandmother and great-grandparents had cherished.

He wanted to get on with his life.

It should have been easy, stopping by Pine Cliff today for the executor's address. He'd figured the Worth family wouldn't care about Brooke's property in northern Minnesota. A handful of quaint cabins and an old Victorian house were hardly their style.

Finding Brooke's little sister there had been a complete surprise. She was grown-up now, well educated in her family's unique brand of arrogance and temper. Except she didn't quite fit the Worth mold. He'd seen the way she kept a loving hand on each of her daughters. Beneath the superior tone and air of control, she apparently had a gentle heart—a distinct aberration in the Worth family gene pool.

Meeting her again had set off warning bells. Maybe it was the contradiction of her tousled, touch-me mass of blond hair and her steel-cold stay-away voice.

Logan sank into the beige leather couch facing the fireplace and reached for the Wickham Towers file. He'd brought the new project—a proposed shopping center and office complex—to work on while up north. Back in Saint Paul, his partner, Harold, was managing the office and the regular accounts. For a few moments he stared at the hypnotic dance of flames curling through the stack of pine logs, then began to flip through the file.

But he was unable to focus on work. An image of Claire answering her door jumped into his mind. At the time his heart had hit his ribs with a thump, his skin had warmed and tingled. He hoped she hadn't noticed his reaction. Feelings like that had no place in a business transaction. Especially not with a Worth.

Claire might be a loving mother, but a woman related to Brooke couldn't have much more depth than a mud puddle in August. Hell, after the first good nor'easter sent waves crashing into the cabins, she and her kids would be heading south. She'd be gone by mid-November, easy.

Satisfaction radiated through him like a swallow

of hot coffee. So why did he feel this odd twinge of regret?

With a soft curse he launched himself to his feet and surveyed his surroundings, resolutely studying the features of his new house. Redirecting his thoughts.

The design was free and open, the exposed pine beams of the ceiling above as rugged and solid as the surrounding forest. But the place felt even less like a home than his austere office back in Saint Paul. Damp smells of plaster and paint, and the sharp chemical scent of new bedroom carpeting up-stairs filled the air. The stark white walls were ster-ile and cold.

He needed a decorator to hang bright prints on the walls, to do whatever it took to make the place seem like home.

Home. Closing his eyes, he remembered the be-loved Victorian at Pine Cliff and the glowing warmth of fine old oak and well-worn comfort. Its gables and turrets and fanciful cornice draperies had fascinated him as a child. Very different from this new place with its space and light and freedom from memories, both good and bad. Here he'd find the solitude he needed.

But right now, he needed fresh air.

After sliding open a patio door, Logan stepped out into the brisk evening air, sauntered across the deck, then descended a circular sweep of redwood stairs leading to the granite shelf below. It felt so good, so *right,* to be back at the lake, at the place he'd longed for these past fourteen years.

A brisk wind, raw with the threat of rain, ruffled through his hair, beckoning him to the edge of the cliff. The past filtered back in scents and in sepia-toned images. The sweet fragrance of long-past campfires and melting marshmallows, fragile wild-flowers and warm chocolate-chip cookies. His grandmother's vein-knotted hands, knobby with arthritis. Gentle, loving.

His mother and the raw stench of cheap booze.

The past no longer mattered. He'd grown up, worked hard, established a successful business. But sometimes, in the dark of night, he remembered that frightening evening long ago when his mother had thrown his clothes in a grocery sack, grabbed his hand, and hauled him out to a car where yet another one of her "boyfriends" waited. "Your grandma will take care of you," she'd said, reeling closer for a sloppy kiss. "I'll come after you in a while."

He'd been left like yesterday's trash on the steps of Pine Cliff that night, and his grandmother had raised him from that point on.

He never saw his mother again.

A squadron of fat white seagulls swooped low overhead. Their piercing cries were as evocative of his childhood as the scent of lilacs, his grand-mother's favorite perfume.

With keen eyes, constant hunger and an abiding love of handouts, the gulls were like feathered watchdogs, loudly announcing the arrival of any potential food source—any prowler—along the shore.

They swung lower, disappearing behind the sheer granite face, then shot upward, screeching with obvious disappointment.

Someone was on the shore below.

Irritation surged through Logan. The drive and shoreline were posted No Trespassing. Courteous hikers were fine, but some built bonfires, toasted marshmallows, then left behind crumpled food packages, grocery sacks, beer cans.

Moving to the other side of the cliff, Logan looked over the edge. Saw nothing.

He stalked along a narrow ledge, brushing aside the tangle of wild raspberry vines curling over the old trail. Ahead, aeons of winter ice and battering waves had pried away small chunks of granite, leaving irregular steps. With a growl of impatience, he caught the familiar handholds and descended to the rocky shore below. An avalanche of pebbles skittered underfoot, ringing against the rocks like a handful of marbles.

A small figure crouched at water's edge, half hidden under an outcropping of rock. A young boy with a damp Minnesota Twins T-shirt clinging to his bony frame, his thin arms curled tightly around his knees. He didn't move when the frigid waves licked at his sodden tennis shoes. Even at a distance, with the sound muffled by the slap of waves and raucous seagulls above, Logan knew the boy was crying. The scene was an eerie vision of his own past.

"Hi there," Logan called out as he approached.

The boy stiffened. He rose slowly, but didn't turn around. Hiding the tears, no doubt.

"Are you okay?"

He nodded silently.

"Is your family along here somewhere?" Logan continued, keeping his tone friendly. "This area isn't very safe."

The boy nodded again. His face averted, he started across the water-slick apron of granite at the base of the cliff. Two steps later his feet shot out from beneath him. With a small cry he fell, then gripped an ankle with both hands and threw his head back in a silent expression of pain. Surely he would begin crying in earnest now. Instead, he was oddly quiet.

Hunkering nearby, Logan offered an encouraging smile. "Can I get your mom or dad? Where are they?"

The kid was older than he'd guessed from a distance, probably middle school. He had a defiant tilt to his chin and a stubborn glint in his eyes despite the tear tracks trailing down his cheeks. That hint of rebellion triggered even more memories of Logan's adolescence.

"Is your family along the shore somewhere?" he asked again.

The boy stared at the ground.

"What's your name?"

No response. A stiff, rain-laden gust of wind came off the lake. The boy suppressed a shiver.

"Cold?"

"No." His voice sounded subdued. His thin shoulders started to shake.

Raindrops peppered the shoreline. Across the water, a wall of advancing rain turned sky and lake charcoal.

"Come on, fella. Let's get inside. You can use my phone."

Staring out at the advancing storm, the boy balked. Then he reluctantly stumbled to his feet.

"Don't worry, kid. I'll help find your parents and get you home before you freeze." Looping an arm around the boy's shoulders for support, Logan turned toward the series of narrow, ascending ledges leading to his house.

The boy whimpered, sagged after the first step. "I can't!"

"Want some help?" Logan waited until the child gave a grudging nod, then gently swung him up into his arms. "This is rough going down here. I'll set you down as soon as we're on level ground."

His face pale and clammy, the boy murmured some sort of indistinguishable protest, then melted into boneless surrender, his eyes closed. Logan's heart caught for a beat, until he saw the narrow chest rise and fall in steady rhythm. A little hot chocolate and a blanket would help until a parent showed up.

The child's weight felt good in his arms, filling Logan's heart with an unfamiliar surge of protectiveness. *Probably just some latent, universal parent-mode kicking in,* he thought wryly as he picked his way over the slippery rocks, though heaven knew when he'd ever hold another child in his arms. He sure as hell wouldn't risk another marriage, and he'd never have a child without one. His own childhood had taught him that. Deep regret washed through him at the thought.

By the time they reached the house, sheets of icy rain obscured the landscape, plastering Logan's shirt and jeans against his skin. The child had burrowed closer to Logan's chest for protection, and their shared warmth felt as deep and essential as the beat of his own heart.

At the door of the house he stopped. "Think you can stand?"

The boy nodded vigorously, but when he stood up he carefully avoided bearing weight on his injured ankle. "Thanks," he mumbled, ducking his head.

Logan pushed the door open. "Let's get you out of this rain, bud." Inside, he kicked off his wet sneakers and ushered the boy into the kitchen. The white cupboards and bleached-oak flooring had once appealed to his preference for wide, well-lit spaces, Logan thought as he glanced around, but the effect was nearly as cold as the weather outside.

"Phone's there," he said, pointing to the wall next to the curved breakfast bar. "I'll get you a towel and a dry shirt."

When he returned, the boy still stood at the kitchen door, a wary look in his eye. "I don't bite," Logan said, tossing him a blue bath towel and a faded Saint Olaf College sweatshirt.

The boy wrapped the towel around himself and shivered into it, his lips blue against his white face. If he didn't catch pneumonia after this, it would be a miracle.

"Called your parents yet?"

A flare of something—rebellion again?—turned the boy's cheeks pink. Poor guy. When Logan met this kid's mother, he would damn well tell her about the dangerous cliffs along the shore. Logan's own mother hadn't been any better; she'd never given a damn, either.

Logan reached for the phone. "If you won't tell me your name, I'll need to call the sheriff. Someone must be worried about you, and a doctor should see that ankle."

"I'm J-Jason." A look of anguish filled his eyes. "Please—*please* don't tell—"

He crumpled before Logan could reach him. The sound of his head hitting bare oak flooring echoed like a cannon shot in the vast emptiness of the house.

CLAIRE FRANTICALLY pulled open the massive oak and leaded-glass door, then rushed into the kitchen. She'd gone down the shore both ways, then followed the paths she'd shown Jason just days before. There'd been no sign of him. Her fears had intensified with every step.

After a last glance outside, she snatched the receiver and began dialing the sheriff's office. Again. *Why hadn't a deputy arrived? Or the sheriff?* The entire National Guard standing in her kitchen with muddy boots would have been a welcome sight. Her cold-numbed fingers fumbled over the last number. Punching the reset button, she redialed with a vengeance.

Annie and Lissa sat at the claw-foot oak table, their milk and chocolate-chip cookies untouched and their faces reflecting her own concern. Jason had never been out past nightfall. The forest and shoreline were dangerous in the dark. One false step—

"Hello?" Claire gripped the phone tighter.

A sharp rap at the door jerked her attention away from the receiver. *Jason?* With a prayer on her lips, Claire dropped the phone, raced across the room and flung open the door.

Omigod.

A gray-haired officer stood there, short and rumpled, with a belly the size of Hennepin County and a glaze of exhaustion in his eyes. After surveying the room, his gaze snapped back to Claire. "Deppity Miller, ma'am. Anyone missin' a boy?"

Measured footsteps crossed the porch behind him. It was Logan, holding a limp figure in his arms. *Jason*—his eyes half-closed, his skin pale as flour—wrapped in a red plaid blanket.

Claire's heart faltered, then picked up a rapid cadence that made the room spin. She sprinted out onto the porch. Her hands flew lightly over Jason's arms and legs. "Dear God, is he all right?"

"Hold on. You're going to embarrass the kid to death." Brushing her aside, Logan strode into the kitchen, then lowered Jason into a high-backed chair between the twins. He kept a steadying hand on the boy's shoulder.

Crimson flooded Jason's cheeks when he saw the five pairs of eyes trained on his face.

"He's fine, ma'am, just a bump on the head and a sore ankle." The deputy gave Jason a hard look. "Been trespassin', I hear."

Logan looked up at Claire as though she were barely worth feeding to the seagulls, but the steely glint in his eyes faded when he finally spoke. "The shore by my place isn't safe—"

"People come up here, and have no idea of the dangers. Think they can just let their kids run," the deputy cut in. "The shore is no playground for unattended youngsters."

Logan scowled at the deputy. "I think Mrs....

Miss...Ms. Worth must realize that by now.''

Surprised and thankful for his support, Claire ignored the veiled rebuke in Logan's tone. ''I had no idea that he would go roaming like that.'' She pulled an afghan from the back of the chair and smoothed it around Jason's shoulders, then took his cold hands in hers and bent down to search his face. ''Honey, why were you over there? I've been worried sick!''

When Jason tipped his head and didn't answer, Logan silently dropped his hands back onto the boy's shoulders. The gesture of masculine support touched Claire's heart. ''He seems so groggy. What happened? Was he unconscious?''

From behind her, she heard the deputy's impatient snort. ''Sounds like he might have fainted, and then bumped his head when he fell, but he's been plenty alert. Couldn't get a word out of him, though.''

''He must have been scared,'' Claire protested, eyeing Jason's pale face with concern. ''We're taking you to the hospital, honey.'' She wanted to hug him fiercely, but knew he would jerk away. Tears prickled behind her eyelids.

Angling her face to hide her emotions, she moved to the sink, where she filled a measuring cup with water, then set it in the microwave to heat. After he had a hot cup of cocoa and a deep, warm bath, she would take him to the emergency room to check out his bumps and bruises. Maybe he would talk to her after the men left.

She spoke without turning around. "I can't thank you two enough for bringing him home."

"You're damn lucky he made it back," Logan said sharply. "Some of those cliffs drop a hundred feet, and in heavy rain it's hard to see out there."

Claire glanced at him in surprise. He'd defended her against the deputy, yet now he echoed the man's criticism?

She lifted a box of instant cocoa from the cupboard, hesitating just long enough to temper her reply. "I'm deeply grateful for your help, believe me."

She opened a packet with a sharp jerk that sent a puff of cocoa mix into the air. "Would you like some coffee or tea?"

"No thanks." Logan said, giving Jason's shoulder a gentle squeeze. "You okay now, kid?"

Jason jerked his head in assent.

"Then I'll be—"

"Coffee would be nice, ma'am, it's a long way back to town," the deputy interrupted. He dragged two chairs away from the kitchen table. "Good to meet the new neighbors. Right, Matthews?"

A low growl rumbled from beneath the table. Gilbert rose from his spot at Jason's feet, his teeth bared.

The deputy sidestepped, taking the chair farthest

away. "Uh…nice pooch, there. You'll need a good watchdog out here."

Logan raised an eyebrow as he took the chair next to Jason. "High crime rate?"

"Nope, but off-season we're down to the sheriff and me, and this is a mighty big county."

Logan frowned. "So response times…"

"Depends on the circumstances. If we're at the far end of the county, could be an hour or more. Otherwise, maybe twenty minutes." Miller shrugged. "Population can't support a larger staff, but usually there isn't much going on."

Claire suppressed a shudder. *An hour?* Coming from New York, she had no problem imagining a few dozen frightening scenarios as she finished preparing Jason's cocoa and then offered a tray of coffee and fresh ginger cookies to the men. "Cream or sugar?"

The deputy creamed his coffee to a pale tan. "How do you all like it here?" He rocked back in his chair and took a long swallow.

Annie tore her gaze from the man's badge and straining shirt buttons. "I'm scared of bears. We got a nice man next door, though."

She extended one sticky finger toward Logan, nearly poking his arm. He looked down in surprise and she grinned back at him, her eyes sparkling. "You brung Jason home."

A muscle jerked in Logan's cheek. "Yes— well—he shouldn't be out with a storm brewing."

Watching Logan's sudden discomfort, Claire wondered what he'd been up to all these years. It didn't appear he'd had many conversations with children. Especially children who looked at him with such total admiration.

Years ago, had she looked at him that way herself? He'd been just twenty-two or so at the time, and as an awestruck fourteen-year-old she'd thought him handsome and wonderfully mature.

The deputy cleared his throat. "I'll check up on you now and then." Folding his hands across his belly, he gave Claire a broad I'm-your-guy wink. "You never know what's out in them woods."

She had no interest in any relationships right now—especially with an elderly deputy who eyed her like his favorite dessert. "Mr.—"

"Wayne, ma'am."

"Thanks, but we'll be fine."

He twitched, patted his hip pocket. "Pager just buzzed me. Gotta go."

Logan lifted his cup a notch higher in farewell. "Pine Cliff is safe tonight," he murmured as the screen door slammed. "In town, I heard the county deputy was in an accident. Miller's retired, but the sheriff brought him back for a few weeks."

She gave him a dry look. "That isn't very reassuring."

"No one seems too concerned. The off-season population up here is really sparse."

Fingering the slim gold bracelet she always wore,

Claire stood at the back door and watched the tail-lights of the patrol car fade into the darkness. She hoped Deputy Miller wouldn't entertain any romantic thoughts about her.

And then, without warning, the image of the deputy faded and one of Logan appeared in her mind's eye. Tonight he'd arrived on her doorstep with Jason in his arms, like some old-time western hero. She envisioned him leaning against a door frame, tall and rugged, an unbuttoned oxford shirt revealing the hard, muscular curves of his chest and the flat ripple of muscle across his belly. A streak of dark hair disappeared into the unbuttoned vee of his jeans. His dark, sensual gaze drew her closer. Closer—

A dark Mustang pulled to a stop under the yard light. Claire blinked, refocused her thoughts. Residual adrenaline and fear had to be taking their toll. Nothing else could explain her unexpectedly sensual thoughts and the ridiculous longing that now sped through her veins.

Back to business, she reminded herself sharply. Standing straighter, she watched the occupants of the car climb out and converse at the end of the sidewalk. More guests. She turned away from the window. "Jason, I need to take a quick look at that ankle."

Crossing the kitchen, she knelt beside him, gently propped his foot in her lap and started on his wet, tightly knotted shoelaces. From the corner of her eye, she saw Logan rise and finish his coffee in one long, slow swallow, then turn to leave.

"Don't worry, my ankle's okay," Jason mumbled. "Mr. Matthews gave me an ice pack, and called some doctor."

Claire looked at Logan. "You talked to a doctor?"

He shrugged. "He didn't sound too concerned, but a trip to the ER wouldn't be a bad idea, just to make sure."

He paused at the door and gave her a brief smile, then scanned the room, as if memorizing each detail. The lights shadowed the angles of his lean face and sparked gold highlights in his hair, while his navy ski jacket emphasized the bulk of his shoulders and narrow waist.

A ripple of deepening awareness started low in Claire's belly and unfurled into something akin to desire, a stunning echo of the errant thoughts she'd banished moments ago.

And something more—she felt a sudden longing to know him much better.

This is simple physical attraction, she sternly told herself. *Nothing more.* If she repeated it often enough, surely she would begin to believe it. She had to—there was too much at stake.

His hand on the doorknob, Logan glanced back at Jason. "Take it easy, kid. And listen to your mom from now on, okay?"

Jason's quick grin faded at the word *mom.* "Yeah, sure."

A tentative knock sounded at the door. Logan pulled it open, revealing a middle-aged man and woman whose faces were sallow beneath the bright porch light.

"I need to register," the man wheezed. He lifted an inhaler to his bushy mustache and looked expectantly at Logan through the screen door. "We have reservations. The Sweeneys?"

Logan ushered them inside, then drew close to Claire and lowered his voice so only she could hear. "Country clubs back home, or this? Ought to be an easy choice." With a smile at the couple hovering in the doorway, Logan left.

So they were back to that—opposing camps, with opposing goals. Claire gave the newcomers a bright smile of welcome. "I'm Claire, the manager," she said in a ringing tone, extending her hand. "I know you'll enjoy your stay. I can't imagine ever living anywhere else!"

The Sweeneys smiled in response. Through the screen door, she saw Logan continue down the stairs, though one of his shoulders twitched.

Sorry, fella, she said under her breath. *There isn't a person on earth who could make me leave.*

THE OLD PRIMER-GRAY Chevy was perfect. Parked a couple dozen feet off the road between some pines, it blended invisibly into the shadows.

Drumming his fingers on the cracked dashboard, the driver eyed the house and then shifted his gaze back to the hulking passenger sitting next to him. The guy wasn't very bright, but he had the muscle and skills of a back-alley street fighter. And he had just as much to lose. "Ain't gonna be hard. Once the lights go out, we can get in and be real quiet."

"But—"

"We've got to find the invoices and that tape."

"But they're *home*."

"That woman and her kids are *always* home, dammit. We don't have much more time."

"They've got a dog."

"It must be deaf. It didn't bark when we went through the shed last night," Hank snapped.

"What if that deputy comes back?"

"He didn't see us." Hank uttered a foul curse. "Just do what I say and *shut up*."

At a sudden motion on the porch they both froze, and watched as a tall, powerfully built man strode down the sidewalk, then drove off.

"Who the hell was that?" Hank muttered. If he was the woman's boyfriend, he might be back. *Damn.* "C'mon, Buzz, show time. Let's check the back windows. I want to know how we'll get in later."

He eased his car door open and slid out. Buzz shoved his own door open and followed him toward the house.

Voices reached them from an open kitchen window, barely distinguishable over the sound of waves hitting the shore.

"Am not!"

"Yes, you are, Jason."

"Not! I won't go!"

Silence. And then, "There'll be a bigger scene if the ambulance comes here to pick you up."

"Ambulance!" A long pause, then a sullen, "You wouldn't."

"Want to bet? We need to make sure you're okay. That bump on your head—"

"It's nothing!"

"I want a doctor to check your ankle."

Come on, kid. Cooperate. Hank stopped abruptly, thrust a hand against Buzz's chest. A middle-aged couple strolled into view at the far end of the lane. *Damn.*

A few minutes later the woman and all three kids came out of the house, then climbed into a minivan parked in the driveway. Maybe things were looking up after all. An emergency room meant hours of waiting.

And hours of freedom to search the house.

"Let's go," Hank growled. "If this doesn't work, we'll have to scare her off, or force her into cooperating and risk being identified."

"But—"

"You want one of our old *pals* coming after us? Or for her to go to the cops with Brooke's evidence? What's better—death or prison?"

At the look of naked fear on Buzz's face, Hank gave a harsh laugh. "That's what I thought." Motioning to him, Hank slipped through the shadows to the back door of the house.

Three hours later, as they heard the minivan return and pull to a stop outside the house, Hank punched a fist against an attic wall and swore. *Nothing.*

Time was running out. Had the Worth woman already found the evidence? Hidden it? With a jerk of his chin, he signaled Buzz. They both sped silently down the stairs and out the back door.

They'd have to return another night. If she was real lucky, she wouldn't get in the way.

If she wasn't, she might just have to die.

CHAPTER FOUR

SHE'D BEEN SURE no one could ever make her leave Pine Cliff, but by noon the next day Claire was ready to admit defeat. Almost. Two of the next night's reservations canceled. The Sweeneys had demanded two cabin changes, first because the "blinds let in too much light," and next because their second cabin was "too close to the lane." And Igor was once again contentedly curled up in front of the refrigerator.

"No, I don't offer sick leave. This is a twenty-hour-a-week job. Seasonal. Part-time." Holding the receiver farther from her ear, Claire winced at the applicant's petulant response. "Yes, I know you can make more on tips at a restaurant."

After hanging up, she slashed through the ninth name on her list and rubbed the tense muscles at the back of her neck. The advertisement for cabin help and general maintenance had run in the *Duluth Herald* for weeks. She hadn't come close to finding a suitable employee.

The phone rang before she got to the back door.

"Pine Cliff, Claire Worth speaking," she said automatically.

"Ms. Worth? I'm one of Randall's former business partners. We're missing some records from the past two years."

"I'm sorry, but I can't help you—"

"We've got to get them back...need 'em for taxes." The voice raised a notch. "We figure those records would have been in his desk at home. Uh...his wife did some of the books."

Brooke? "Look, Mr...." Claire paused, waiting.

"Bob. Bob...Johnson."

"None of that was sent up here. All of Randall's business records were turned over to the estate lawyer and accountant."

"They don't have what I need. I'll come up this weekend and help you look. I've got to have those records."

Claire bit back a sharp reply. "Then you'll have to talk to the lawyers, because I have nothing of the kind. And you'll certainly not be going through his personal effects."

Resisting the urge to slam the receiver down, she hung up and headed for the door, thankful that she'd had nothing to do with the business aspects of the estate.

Randall's choice of business partners didn't surprise her at all.

"YOO-HOO! Ms. Worth!"

Straightening, Claire dropped a sponge into the bucket of pungent disinfectant at her feet and rubbed the small of her back, then stepped out onto the pine-planked deck of cabin five. A deep breath of fresh air helped slow the spinning sensation in her head.

Mrs. Rogers scuttled down the lane bordering the cabins, one hand waving above her head. She looked like a broken-winged duck coming in for a rough landing.

"Anything wrong?" Thankful for a moment's respite, Claire took another cleansing breath and wiped away a stray tear. Cleaning was certainly hard on the nose and lungs.

The older woman pulled to a stop a few feet away, sniffed, and frowned. "What are you— Never mind. Come quickly—the laundry building!"

A vision of the commercial washer and dryer going up in flames filled her with disbelief and horror. Claire ripped off her yellow rubber gloves, dropped them at her feet and broke into a run. "Fire?"

Mrs. Rogers huffed along in slow pursuit. "Flood," she wheezed.

Flood? Oh, God. Claire skidded to a halt in front of the small building.

Thank goodness she'd left the double doors open to the morning sun. And thank goodness, Mrs. Rogers had seen the problem.

The washer was still chugging along. Frothy water spewed from its base, and had already flooded the entire laundry area. An island of dirty sheets and towels stood marooned in the middle of the floor.

Mrs. Rogers caught up, panting with exertion. "Quite a mess, eh?"

"I can't believe this."

Squinting against the sunlight angling across the lake, the older woman studied the situation. "Looks like a whopper of a repair bill to me."

"Great." Claire grimaced. More money—just what she didn't have. She'd already dipped into her savings to replace two cabin roofs and repair the old furnace in the house. With projected winter cabin rentals at a dangerous low, she couldn't afford any major problems.

She reached around the door frame, fumbled for the fuse box and cut the power to the building before stepping inside.

The flooring was uneven beneath her sneakers. Though the water hadn't yet flowed out the front doors, it was at least six inches deep through the center of the room—and very, very cold. Claire shuddered, imagining spiders and other crawly refugees clinging to the bits of laundry lint and debris floating past her ankles. Gritting her teeth, she sloshed forward to unplug the machine and turn off the water supply behind it. Claire turned to face Mrs. Rogers, who was standing in the doorway.

"It's going to take a lot of mopping," murmured Mrs. Rogers, a sympathetic expression on her face. She started to turn away, but stopped, putting both hands on her broad, paisley-draped hips. "By the way, dear, have you ever done much housecleaning?"

Claire felt a twinge of embarrassment. *No, I've been a princess all my life. Until now.* "Why?"

The deep, rasping laugh of an inveterate smoker echoed through the small building. "Most people *dilute* their cleaning chemicals, dear. Check the directions on those bottles."

Watching Mrs. Rogers trot toward her cabin, Claire groaned. A business career had not prepared her for this. Cleaning. Laundry. Book work. And most important of all, the children. Without help, she would have endless days and very short nights.

A quick survey of the room revealed no extra-large, heavy-duty mopping equipment. The dainty pink sponge mop and bucket waiting for her in cabin five would be as effective as using a teaspoon to shovel a Minnesota snowdrift. Worse, the pile of laundry was now slowly floating piece by piece toward the perimeter of the room.

Moving here had been a mistake. One huge, impossible mistake. Claire closed her eyes and prayed for a miracle. Why had she ever thought she could handle all of this—?

A footstep sounded against the slab of pavement at the door. Claire turned to speak, expecting a cabin guest, but her words died in her throat.

In the doorway stood a grizzled old man, worn and bent, wearing grease-stained overalls loose as clown pants. Claire thought she detected the smell of alcohol, but there was no denying the distinctive smell of unwashed male.

"Name's Fred Lundegaard. I worked at Pine Cliff most all my life. Tried the sunshine down south, but missed the pines and this ol' lake too much, so now I'm back." He grinned and lifted a hand, his broad gesture encompassing the laundry-room mess and the resort grounds beyond. "And it looks like I'm the answer to your prayers." With that, he walked toward the washing machine, a determined look on his face.

AN HOUR LATER Claire stood at her desk in the kitchen, handed a receipt to the middle-aged couple checking out and prayed they couldn't hear the string of oaths coming from the laundry building where the old guy was tackling the washing machine.

"I'm so glad you enjoyed your stay," Claire said brightly.

The woman smiled as she glanced around the entryway and into the kitchen beyond. "Lovely place. Have you thought of turning the house into a B&B?"

"It would be perfect," Claire agreed. "But with three kids and their pets we're a bit too noisy."

Stepping back through the door held open by her husband, the woman nodded. "Probably true. Actually, I did hear footsteps outside our cabin last night. Probably games of hide-and-seek in the dark?" She reached up and touched her cheek, looking apologetic. "Not that it bothered us, of course."

"I'm sorry, I'll certainly check into it right away," Claire murmured, waving goodbye.

The children had all been in bed and asleep by nine-thirty last night. Hungry raccoons had to be the culprits, she decided, slipping the last of the breakfast dishes into the dishwasher. They'd already shimmied through the windows of the boathouse and pried open the door to the laundry building. Luckily those buildings held little that could be damaged.

Pensively tapping the edge of the counter with a forefinger, she considered her next move. Finish cleaning cabin five...run into town for groceries...finish mopping up the laundry building...

A sharp clang, followed by another string of oaths, came from the building at the far edge of the lawn.

Fred. Allowing the old fellow to "show what he could do" with the washing machine had been a mistake. If he got hurt...or made the situation worse...

Claire dashed down the porch steps and across the front lawn, shading her eyes against the laser intensity of the sun. Sunglasses. She needed to find her extra pair of sunglasses packed somewhere in the mountain of boxes, furniture and whatnot piled in the attic of the house.

For the hundredth time, she cursed the delay in New York that kept her from being present when the movers arrived. So far she'd uncovered three half-filled wastebaskets from her high-rise in New York, but she had yet to find all of her possessions. To make things worse, the large number of boxes that had come out of Brooke and Randall's condo was now mixed up with her own.

Lost in thought, Claire rounded the closest corner of the laundry building. Her face hit a solid wall of fur.

The impact sent her staggering against the building. An iron-hard appendage grasped her arm. Pulling back with every ounce of her strength, she screamed.

Bears! Annie and Lissa were right.

The grip on her arm gentled, released. Even as she spun away, the furry object took shape.

It was Gilbert, the kids' poodle. Held securely in Logan's arms. Neither dog nor man looked pleased.

"Oh, dear. Excuse me!"

One hand over her heart to quiet its mad gallop, Claire stared in disbelief. It took a moment to catch her breath. "Uh...like our dog, do you?"

Logan bared his teeth, but didn't smile. Gilbert bared his, as well, but from his sheepish canine grin to his drooping tail, he was the picture of embarrassment. His captor simply looked aggravated.

"He moved over to my place," Logan said in a low, dangerous tone. "You were going to make sure none of your kids—or your pets—strayed."

Claire wondered if anyone had ever laughed at him—and if so, whether they'd lived to tell about it. The sight of him—a towering, glowering man gripping an amorphous mass of dog hair—tested her ability to maintain a straight face.

"He was here just a few hours ago. What makes you think he's moved in?" Her momentary alarm fading into giddy relief, she sagged against the broad white planks of the building and lifted one eyebrow for effect. "Brought his suitcase, did he?"

Logan snorted. "He likes garbage. He chases seagulls." Glaring at the dog's damp, unclipped coat bristling with twigs, leaves and pine needles, he added, "He belongs at *your* house."

"He would have come home eventually."

"Have you ever spent an hour listening to irate seagulls?"

"You could have told him no."

"He thinks it means bark louder. Keep him at home, Ms. Worth. I don't like this dog. He doesn't like me."

Logan put the dog on the ground and crossed his arms. Gilbert obediently sat. His innocent gaze fastened on a distant object, he began sidling back toward Logan's legs, his front paws moving inch by inch.

The most spunk the old poodle ever displayed

was at dinnertime, when he escalated to a faster shuffle to reach his food. And now, like an oversize gray mop, he was lying upside down across Logan's shoes. A limp, pink dishrag of a tongue hung out one side of his mouth. "I can see he's quite a fireball."

Logan cleared his throat and gave Gilbert a pained look. "He was a lot more...energetic at my place."

Claire nodded gravely. "I'm sure. How did you get him back here?"

"I tried to lead him. He planted his rear on the ground and wouldn't move. I tried to bring him back in my car. He wouldn't get in."

She remembered all too well the battle Gilbert waged over getting into her van in Minneapolis. She'd had to make a fast trip to a discount store to buy a portable pet carrier. "So you—"

"I carried him."

Claire grinned. Laughter bubbled up her throat. Jason had told her about the tortuous path leading to Logan's house—over a quarter mile of boulders, brambles, steep climbs and narrow ledges. The man was nothing if not determined. He might deserve every sore muscle he'd have tomorrow, but for some inexplicable reason she wanted to give him a hug.

"Look," Logan continued, giving her a narrowed look. "I've been thinking about the conversation we had a few days ago." He reached down to pry several prickly strands of bramble vine from his faded jeans. "We don't need to be adversaries. All I want is a chance to buy back my family land."

Claire's smile faded. "I'm sorry, but—"

"Wait. Just listen." Logan reached out and touched her arm, but withdrew his hand as if he'd touched something hot. "I've talked to a couple of Realtors up here. I'll give you fifty percent over the appraised value of the land. You could stay in the house until spring, rent-free. And you can let the cabins go empty."

"What?" Claire stared at him. He was offering more than the land was worth, being too reasonable. He must want it really badly.

"Fifty percent above the value," Logan repeated. "For that you could buy another resort in better condition, if you're set on this kind of life."

Claire's thoughts raced. Her recent frustrations were almost enough to make her agree. The money would be good. She could begin an easier life for her new family in another place far from New York. But trusting Logan Matthews would be as foolish as trying to swim across Lake Superior in November. And, as she swept her gaze across the sapphire and diamond waves on the lake and the cozy cabins lining the shore, she realized she couldn't walk away from Pine Cliff. "This land was Brooke's."

"She got half of the property that had been in my family for generations," Logan countered. "Yet she hated being up here, and she never set foot on the place after our divorce. She hired a manager and left before the ink was dry on our settlement.''

''You make it sound like she came out like a bandit.''

''Didn't she?''

We all paid dearly. A sense of loss flooded through her as Claire remembered their father's shock over Brooke's impetuous marriage after dating Logan less than six months, and his anger when Brooke came to him for help in ending it six months later. After a sudden rebound marriage, she completely broke off all contact with the family. Without that first ill-starred marriage, perhaps everything would have been very different.

Claire gave him a determined smile. ''Like I told you, this is a great place to raise the kids. It's also now my sole source of income.''

Logan's expression darkened. A telltale muscle in his cheek jerked. ''Okay, how about you *manage* this place until next spring? Keep it open—earn a salary. Not that there's much business over the winter. And you'd still have the money from selling. How could you do better?''

By owning it myself. If the stories were true, this man had married her late sister to get at the family money, yet hadn't honored his wedding vows. Even if Claire were broke and desperate, loyalty to Brooke precluded the possibility of selling the property back to him.

''I won't uproot the children again. Not now, not

next year." She drew herself up to her full height. "They need a permanent home, and this place is safe and secure. Losing their—"

"Hey, Miz Worth?" the grizzled handyman called out as he rounded the far corner with a piece of black hose in his hand. "Thought I heard someone back here."

"Did you find the problem?"

"You got any enemies?"

Logan studied her with intense interest. "Well, do you, Claire?" he murmured.

His voice vibrated across her skin. She felt the hairs rise at the back of her neck, sensed the sudden tension and heat of Logan's body, just inches from her own. His long, tanned fingers flexed at his sides. *Enemies? Only you, Logan.*

"None I can think of," she shouted to Fred. "Why?"

As the old man got closer, he held up the length of hose. "This was cut clean in two. And this wasn't no accident, Miz Worth."

CHAPTER FIVE

THE VOICE SOUNDED familiar. Logan turned around and stared in disbelief. Fred Lundegaard, in all likelihood wearing the same set of tattered overalls he'd worn fourteen years before, stared back at him with equal surprise.

The moment of stunned silence broke when Fred's face lit up like a kid's on Christmas morning. "I heard you were back, boy!"

Fred dropped the length of hose and strode forward, his arthritic gait less steady than in years past. His craggy features had blurred a little, as if he'd softened with age.

Logan met him halfway and extended his hand. Brushing aside the offer, Fred gave Logan a bear hug followed by a couple of bone-jarring slaps on the back.

"I knew you'd be back someday. I knew it," Fred chortled, stepped back to give Logan a once-over. "About time."

"Too long," Logan agreed, feeling his face shift into the unfamiliar contortions of a real smile.

Claire joined them and looked from one to the

other, clearly mystified. "Old friends?" she asked, tucking a blond curl behind her ear.

In jeans and a soft pink sweater that molded to every curve and plane from neck to ankles, she could be mistaken for a college student. But her cool voice was that of a person accustomed to being in charge. A surprising and all-too-interesting combination, Logan decided.

"This boy tagged along behind me when he could hardly reach my knees." Smiling broadly, Fred looked at Claire over the top of his wire-rims. "His grandma owned this place, you know."

"So he says. You worked here?"

"Twenty-three years for Sadie, and after she passed on, six months for Logan and Brooke when they took over. Clear up through their divorce—" Fred shot a quick glance at Logan and cleared his throat, then suddenly became absorbed in an all-out search through his grease-darkened pockets. Finally withdrawing a round metal tin, he turned away to slip a wad of tobacco inside his cheek.

Old Fred had seen and heard it all, Logan thought wryly. Every step of the biggest mistake Logan had ever made. Hopefully, Fred had forgotten the details—or had sense enough to pretend he had.

"Yep, that Brooke was one crazy woman," Fred continued. "She—"

With a sharp, dismissive wave of her hand and a look that could have melted granite, Claire broke in. "What were you saying about enemies?"

Logan had no doubt that the Worth family had collected its share over the years. He walked over to where Fred had dropped the hose and picked it up. Running a finger along each edge, he walked back and handed it to her. "Sharp knife, I'd guess. Doesn't look like the act of a friendly person to me."

Staring at the stiff black plastic in her hands, her eyes widened. "But, why? I don't even know anyone up here."

That same errant lock of blond hair fell forward. She impatiently shoved it behind her ear, then stilled. She turned first to Fred, then to Logan. "Any ideas?" she asked evenly.

Her voice had turned even more businesslike. It didn't take a Dick Tracy to guess that the two of them were prime suspects, but it didn't matter what she thought. All she had to do was sell him Pine Cliff and move away. "Not a clue. Fred?"

Fred shook his head. "Who knows? Just came north last night."

The little girls, who had been playing in a sandbox at the other edge of the lawn, came to stand at Claire's side. They edged closer until each pressed a cheek against her Levi's-clad hips.

"Bears?" one of them asked, toying nervously with a strand of silvery-blond hair.

Claire's voice warmed fifty degrees. "No bears, Annie. The big washing machine broke." She looked up at Fred. "How is it going, can you fix it?"

"I 'spect so." Fred rubbed his whiskered chin. "With Logan's help. How about it—want to help a guy out for old time's sake? I'm not quite as limber as I used to be."

The last thing Logan wanted was to make it easier for Claire to stay. He'd done all he needed to do—dropped off the big hairball, made his generous offer, discovered that Claire Worth was a stubborn fool. The day wouldn't be improved by dredging up bad memories with Fred—and Fred apparently remembered quite a few.

But now, the two little girls were staring up at him with total admiration, as if he could solve any problem on Earth. The damn dog, again lying heavily across his feet, was looking at him with the same expression. Even Fred looked hopeful. Only Claire appeared eager to have him leave, which made the decision easy. "Sure. Got the tools?"

Grinning, Fred clapped him on the back once more as they all went into the building to survey the damage.

As they worked, Fred rambled on, reliving memories of the great storms he'd seen from this shoreline, the heyday of the shipping era that kept the lights of distant ships crossing the lake's horizon throughout the night. Entranced, the girls stood quiet as mice. Fortunately, Fred didn't discuss Brooke.

Logan was barely listening; his thoughts kept straying to Claire. She stood to one side, with a protective hand on each of her daughters. Her actions reminded him of a mother hen, even though she looked like anything but. Tall and slender, her long legs were flattered by the slim cut of her jeans. From time to time, she looked at Logan, then Fred, then back again, as if assessing each of them for criminal tendencies.

"Might as well see what else we've got here, 'long as it's away from the wall," Fred muttered, delving deeper into the washing machine's motor. "None of this looks very good."

One of the girls edged forward, until she was breathing down Fred's neck. The other one crowded in for a better look, apparently fascinated by the array of greasy motor parts and pieces laid out on the old tarp.

"Girls," Claire said quickly, shooing them toward the door. "This isn't much fun in here."

Both of them balked and looked pleadingly at Logan.

"If you cooperate, I'll—" Logan thought back to his own childhood play along the shore "—show you where to find agates."

"Agnettes?" The bolder one, now with grease on her shorts and a smudge across her cheek, gave him a hopeful look. "Today?"

Logan looked over her head at Claire. "I've got

a decorator coming out tomorrow. But maybe after she leaves?''

''We'll see.'' Claire's voice was firm. ''Meanwhile, let's keep out of the way. Want a push on the swings?''

''But, Aunt Claire,'' Lissa whined, trailing behind Claire and her sister as they headed for the swing set. ''We just wanna see.''

Logan looked up from the transmission in his hands. Lissa's parting words echoed through his thoughts and hit him like a sucker punch. *Aunt* Claire? These weren't Claire's children. They were Brooke's.

Brooke must have remarried the moment she was free. During the divorce she'd accused Logan of running around, but she'd been the one breaking their vows. Even when he'd still been trying to save their marriage, she had been planning to end it.

He sat back on his heels, stunned. They'd both been way too young, but how could he have been so blind? A cascade of aching emotions rushed through him.

If Brooke had been the woman he'd thought, his life could have held such joy. He might have had years of laughter instead of anger, love instead of bitterness and his damnable, consuming desire for retribution. He might have been a father, instead of a wary loner avoiding permanent relationships.

Those three kids could have been mine.

TWO DAYS LATER, Claire stood on her front lawn and had to admit her first impressions about Fred had been wrong. Last night he'd accepted her invitation to supper, and had appeared at the door bathed, shaved and sporting a fresh haircut. Any man who could hold little girls on his knees and enthrall them with stories for two hours straight couldn't be all bad. Even Jason had opened up to him. Deciding to offer Fred a job had been as much the children's idea as it had been hers.

Today he looked like a different man. She'd told him his employment would depend on a makeover based on soap and a firm promise to stay away from the bottle.

His greasy, ill-fitting work clothes were gone, replaced by new navy coveralls with crisply cuffed sleeves. He shifted uncomfortably, reaching up out of habit to adjust the tattered overall straps that no longer hung over his shoulders. Finding them absent, he scratched at the back of his neck where a stiff label probably irritated his skin. "Well," he demanded. "Will this do?"

"You look wonderful." Cleaning cabins and light maintenance work would be the easiest labor he'd had in years, Claire guessed, studying his time-worn hands. "Are you ready to start?"

"You betcha." His eyes gleamed with satisfaction. "It's good to be back. Been away too doggone long."

Claire reached out to seal their bargain with a

handshake, then gave him a piece of paper. "The Sweeneys have a slow drain, for starters," she said. "Can you do any plumbing?"

"No problem." He studied the neatly typed schedule, tipped the bill of his cap and sauntered toward an old golf cart laden with cleaning supplies.

With luck, her problems with cabin cleaning and general maintenance were over. If he did the job right—and if he stayed. For extra encouragement she'd offered him supper on weeknights plus a smaller cabin, rent-free, figuring the loss of rental income would be offset by the security of knowing he'd be close by. He'd declined the cabin with a vague comment about a sister's place and some old buddies in town.

Fred drove the cart up to her and pulled to a stop. He pushed back his cap, rubbed his forehead, then snugged the cap down tight as if he'd given a matter great thought.

"You oughta invite that boy to dinner one night, ma'am." He gave her an expectant look.

"Boy?" Claire chose to be obtuse. The thought of Logan glowering at her across the dinner table was enough to give her a case of anticipatory indigestion.

"He's a lot different now from what he was." Fred pinned her with a look that could have cut glass. "I hear he's had a damn hard time of it, over the years. More than he knows. I'd say he deserved a lot better.''

''Yes, well—''

''Ran into him in town this morning,'' Fred continued blithely. ''Told him how the girls have been talking about him and all...and I sorta invited him over.''

''*What?*''

''Well—you always make supper anyways.''

''You invited him?''

Fred shrugged and gave her a broad grin before turning back to his cart. ''You invited me, but I'm going to my sister's place. Be the same number of people for you to feed.''

Speechless, Claire watched him drive off. It had never occurred to her that Fred might invite a guest. Well, he'd simply have to uninvite this one.

In truth, she probably did owe Logan dinner. He'd spent three hours working on that dinosaur of a washing machine and had refused payment.

He'd also revealed a side of himself she'd thought long gone. With a streak of grease on his cheekbone and smudges covering his white Polo shirt, his good-natured banter with Fred had been a revelation. He still had his wry sense of humor, despite recent evidence to the contrary. And without a doubt, he still possessed the easy charm that could fill a woman's head with sensual daydreams.

When she'd thanked them both for doing the repairs, he'd given her that familiar grin and said,

"That's what knights are for, Guinevere," and her heart had started to melt.

Enough of that, she thought now. She would definitely avoid those foolish daydreams and not do any more melting in his presence. But she should repay her debt.

Turning back to the house, she suddenly wondered what it might have been like to meet him without the rocky past between them. Even with their history, she'd been all too aware of him from the first moment he'd appeared at Pine Cliff.

And she would've sworn he'd been just as aware of her, at least for a moment. He'd stared at her, met her gaze. She wasn't the only one feeling the heat between them. Magnetic. Dangerous. So powerful that her pulse raced and every nerve ending in her body quivered.

From both the house and the nearby laundry building, the shrill jangle of extension phones ringing in discordant stereo jarred her thoughts. Claire strode back to the laundry building, reached inside the door and fumbled the receiver off its hook.

"Pine Cliff."

"This is the counselor at Rock Point Middle School—"

Claire twisted the spiral phone cord around her fingers. Her heart sank deeper with every word the woman spoke. *Attitude. Poor adjustment. Rebellion.*

Hanging up the phone she leaned against the

door frame, trying to decide how she would handle this.

Jason barely spoke to her as it was, backing away from any attempts at friendship like a feral puppy—wary, half-willing to approach, then shying away in full retreat. And always, there was his air of rebellion.

She'd hoped he was adjusting well at school, that he could find normalcy and friendship in the routine of schoolwork and next-desk buddies. Obviously, that hadn't happened.

Nose-tickling scents of bleach and hot-dried linen wafted from the laundry area behind her. A light breeze fluttered through her hair, cooling her sun-warmed face. Familiar sensations. Comforting.

After she and her pint-size James Dean finished their next discussion, she might need all the comfort she could get.

AGS. BI.

Claire read the crayoned scrawl forward, upside down, held it up to the late-afternoon sun. Finally, she cracked the code. The little scamps had finished their after-school snacks with unusual speed. They must have labored over their note as soon as she stepped out of the house to get the mail.

"Jason? Jason!" Claire searched the house upstairs and down, calling his name, but only the hollow echo of her voice answered. He'd been here a minute ago, too. All three jackets were missing. Logan Matthews would love this.

Leaving a Back in Ten Minutes sign on the front door, Claire swung a wool sweater over her shoulders and headed for the shoreline. Had the kids gone looking for agates on their own? A scan of the area from a high crag by the boathouse revealed only a trio of ducks floating serenely near shore, and a squad of bosomy seagulls stationed far out on the water.

They've gone to Logan's. She could only guess at his joy when her three charges pounded on his door.

Luckily, they hadn't got much of a head start. Maybe she could catch them before any damage was done. Claire moved along the boulders, slippery granite shelves and narrow trails along the shore, her wet sneakers slipping, unseen bramble vines clawing at her jeans. Winded and damp, she finally passed a large No Trespassing warning marking the division between Logan's property and hers.

From her low vantage point at the water's edge, she stared up at the soaring peaks of his house. Her mouth fell open in surprise at its sheer size and scope. He'd designed a masterpiece. Anyone with that eye for balance and form would walk a red carpet straight to success. Matthews had done well for himself. Very well.

Acres of glass faced the water, promising spectacular views from every room. The log construction blended seamlessly with the towering pines surrounding its other three sides.

On the broad, wraparound deck, her missing children sat at a patio table sipping some sort of beverage. Logan was nowhere in sight.

"Oh, God," Claire breathed. "They've made themselves right at home. The man will explode if he sees them."

By the time she scaled the steep granite face, the kids were munching on a snack, oblivious to her approach. And by the time she'd climbed the long flight of steps and reached the deck, they were sitting back in their chairs, like satisfied, round-tummied kittens. Logan, looking like a hawk among the litter, was seated with them.

"There's an easier way up," he said, idly twirling a straw in one hand. He leaned back, one long leg hooked over the other, one arm draped over the back of an empty chair. The look in his eye was anything but casual. "Decide to search for your missing kids?"

Claire sensed his head-to-toe assessment of her was instinctive, a purely masculine evaluation of a new woman in his territory. Normally, she would have felt insulted. Instead, she felt far too aware of him. His long, sleekly muscled frame. His aura of strength and restraint, the hum of dark sensuality just beneath the surface.

Claire studiously shifted her gaze to the children,

who were beaming at Matthews as if he were an action hero come to life. "Why did you take off like this?" She gave each child a stern look. "You know Mr. Matthews doesn't care for company. I made that clear last night. Jason?"

"It's no big deal." His gaze slid away. "The girls couldn't come alone."

"Girls?"

"He 'vited us." Lissa's lower lip pouted forward. "Said so. Remember? To find agnettes."

Annie slid down in her chair. "We left you a letter."

"Ah, yes. The letter." Claire repressed a smile. *Ags. Bi.* Incredibly informative, that. "But you must *ask* me if it's okay. And you must never, ever leave without letting me know. Come on, guys, we'd better leave Mr. Matthews to his—uh—work."

Logan rose to his feet in one fluid movement, looking taller, more intensely masculine than he had before. His expression warmed when he spoke to the children. "We'll go find those agates another day." He gave Claire a much less friendly look. "If that's okay."

Jason scuffed a sneaker against the redwood planking of the deck, affecting an expression of bored indifference. The note of hopefulness in his voice gave him away. "Fred said you were coming to dinner tonight."

"Yes...well, maybe another time."

His true feelings were very clear, but the excitement on Annie's and Lissa's faces would have turned iron to mush.

"You're certainly welcome to join us," Claire murmured. She was sure he wouldn't accept—which was just fine with her, but the kids would be hurt by his vague rejection. She made sure he caught her challenging look. "I know how much you enjoy our company. Perhaps tomorrow night would be better?"

"Fine." He gave in with grace, with an easy grin for the children, but the flicker of emotion in his eyes told her he would rather eat lye.

Despite his unenthusiastic response, Claire's heartbeat hitched a little. She'd managed some truly awkward dinner meetings in the past. She could handle one evening with him. "At seven?"

"Fine."

The girls smiled at him as if he were a favorite uncle. With luck, they would become more perceptive with age. "Can you all thank Mr. Matthews for his hospitality?"

As soon as they did, Claire herded the children to the steps of the deck. At the edge she glanced at the wall of windows to her left. Her mouth dropped open. She leaned against the glass and cupped her hands at her eyes to cut the reflection.

The interior of the house was stunning. Glass soared a good twenty feet skyward. Inside, a wide staircase curved upward to what might be bedrooms, while the main floor was open and airy as a sunlit beach. A drafting table stood near the windows. Rolls of blueprints fanned like a modernistic flower arrangement from the tall copper pot at its feet.

Yet, despite tastefully casual furniture and beautifully finished parquet floors, nothing inside beckoned her with promises of warmth and comfort. It was a showplace, not a home.

"What do you think?" he asked, leaning a shoulder against the glass and studying her expression.

"It's...impressive." She looked at him from the corner of her eye, wondering if the cold interior of the house reflected the personality of its architect, or if it inadvertently revealed an emptiness in his life that he'd never filled.

Stepping back, the toe of her sneaker caught against an uneven board on the deck. With a sharp cry she teetered at the edge of the step. Logan's arm shot forward but before he could catch her, she grabbed the railing and saved herself.

"You'd better be careful," he said, still close to her, his voice a low rumble in her ear.

Claire stared up at his face. An unruly lock of hair curved over his forehead, begging to be swept back. Silvery highlights sparkled in his eyes.

"I—I'm usually the most careful person you'll ever meet," she said.

He watched as she and the children left the deck

and started home with Jason leading the way. Until the moment they left the broad shelf of granite for a path through the trees, she felt Logan's eyes on her back. Without a backward glance she knew he still stood in that same spot on the deck. She would have given a hundred shares of AT&T to be privy to his thoughts.

She'd also like to know what the children saw in him. He certainly didn't seem like the type to toss footballs or tell funny stories. He seemed tolerant, if not a bit wary, of them.

Still, a workable relationship was beginning. And as a good neighbor, she would do her part to establish it as polite and somewhat distant. The ridiculous, simmering attraction she felt was simply something to ignore. She had neither the time nor the inclination to complicate her life any further.

Not a problem. She'd *earned* that furtively whispered nickname her former employees had given her. Any Frost Queen worth her crown could easily control her errant emotions.

And when she succeeded, she wanted an Oscar for best actress of the year.

SOMEONE WAS KNOCKING at the back door.

Claire eyed the bedside alarm clock. Twelve-thirty? Late-night arrivals had awakened her twice during the past week, but this was ridiculous.

With a yawn, she burrowed deeper under the

covers, savoring the warmth held by her down comforter and heavy flannel sheets. *Go away. Just go away...*

In New York she'd had a doorman and an intercom to screen visitors. Now, managing Pine Cliff meant she had to open her door to strangers every day. *But not after midnight, for heaven's sake!* Tomorrow she would order a much larger sign for the highway entrance: No Registrations after 10:00 P.M., with a skull and crossbones added for good measure.

The knocking deepened to the pounding of a heavy fist against the wood. A flicker of fear raced through her.

Ridiculous. It was probably just the reservation that had failed to show up earlier—the retired pharmacist and her two sisters, who came up every year for the fall colors. Maybe they'd had car trouble on the way.

With a groan, Claire slid out of bed and hoped fervently that the blankets would remain toasty long enough to welcome her return. All three children had electric blankets, but she'd thought down would do. So much for the cold-weather apparel of ducks.

Wrapping herself in a heavy chenille robe, she scuffed into a bedraggled pair of bunny-faced slippers and headed downstairs. She hugged herself against the chilly air in the kitchen. After ordering that sign, figuring out the monstrous furnace in the basement would be next on her list.

Leaving the security chain fastened, Claire opened the heavy oak door a few inches. "Can I help you?" She stifled a yawn. And then she caught her breath in surprise.

There wasn't an elderly lady out there. There was a man, who stood with his shoulders hunched. Stamping his boots on her porch, he touched the low bill of his baseball cap in greeting and jiggled the handle of the locked screen door with his other hand. "'Bout froze out here!"

Claire recoiled. Studied him intently. The wire mesh of the screen door, made nearly opaque by the dull glow of the dim light over the stove, hid his facial features, but he spoke deliberately, his words slurred. *Oh, Lord. Was he drunk?*

"Made reser-reservations, but me and my buddy slowed up a bit goin' through Duloop—" he paused, considering. "Duluth. Great place."

He *was* drunk. If she tried to send him on his way, he might raise a ruckus on the porch—and both the sheriff and his deputy could be a good hour away. If he cooperated and left, she'd be sending a drunk back out on the highway, where he might kill someone.

Reaching for the key rack by the door, she forced a smile. "You can have cabin five. Just come up in the morning for the paperwork when you're, ah, less tired." She slipped him the key and relocked the screen door, but he didn't turn away. "Is there a problem?"

He raised his head and looked her in the eye. "Do I have a problem?" He gave a harsh laugh. "Not anymore, sweetheart."

He moved so fast, she almost didn't see it coming.

The screen door burst open, its handle falling to the concrete landing with a sickening clatter. Claire screamed, threw her weight against the inner door.

A thick, hairy arm shot through and caught her with the speed of a striking snake. He shouldered his way in, the safety chain snapping under his assault. He clamped a meaty paw over her mouth before she could scream again.

"Shut up," he snarled. "You and me need to have a little talk." His nylon-masked face loomed closer. The smell of bratwurst and stale beer on his breath made her stomach lurch.

She tried to twist out of his grasp, then kicked at him, aiming high. The blasted bunny slippers softened her effort. He didn't so much as flinch.

Fear sliced through her. *If the children woke up and came downstairs—* She struggled to draw breath.

The lights all around grew hazy, indistinct. Waves of dizziness washed over her. A floating sensation, curiously light, lifted her from the floor.

From somewhere at the bottom of a deep, dark well, a voice growled, "This is her, right?"

And then everything grew black.

A WOMAN SCREAMED. Something screeched across a floor. The sounds of struggle stampeded through his brain.

His nightmare was back. Jason whimpered, tunneled under his covers.

A door slammed.

His heart hammering against his ribs, Jason furtively looked out from beneath the blankets. The old poodle still snored softly at the foot of the bed. "Gilbert!"

The dog twitched in his sleep, his paws running in place. Lame for an hour after every nap, he wouldn't be much help.

Forcing himself into action, Jason tiptoed into the hallway. He held his breath until his lungs caught fire.

Silence. Eerie, total silence.

Claire's door wasn't really wide open, he told himself, her bed wasn't empty. But her door felt real under his shaking fingertips. The floor felt cold beneath his feet. This was no dream.

His heart pounding in his throat, Jason slipped silently down the stairs, paused cautiously at the kitchen entrance. By the back door, a skinny circle of gold gleamed in the dim light. Claire's bracelet—the one she never took off. Her good-luck charm, she'd once said.

Jason hesitated, then crossed the room and reached down to pick it up. Next to it was one small, red drop. *Blood?* He pulled back in horror, fought the urge to run, to hide. Willing his rubbery legs to move forward, he crept toward the windows.

Two dark, hulking figures stumbled down the lane. Dragging someone in white, they awkwardly moved toward the cabin next to the supply building, then disappeared into the inky shadows.

A sob burst from Jason's constricted throat. *Aunt Claire.* The terrifying nightmares of the past year spun like a tornado through his head. *No!*

He grabbed the phone, punched 911. Shouted the address into the receiver—then choked on the huge sob rising in his throat when a calm, male voice said, "Stay on the line—"

He fought the impulse to slam the receiver down, shifted from one foot to the other. *Hurry!* How long could this take? What if the sheriff and deputy were busy somewhere else—far away?

Jason dropped the receiver on the counter and bolted to the back door. Snatching his jacket from a nearby hook, he jammed his feet into his Nikes and stepped into the cold. Scanned the area for movement.

Staying on the grass, he ran with every ounce of strength he possessed. At the far edge of the property he hesitated, stared at the ink-black forest. Someone could be in the darkness at this moment, waiting for him. He had no choice. The sheriff might not make it in time, but there was someone else who could.

With every stride, Jason prayed that Logan was home.

CHAPTER SIX

"DON'T DO THIS," Claire said quietly, staring at the two surly drunks blocking her escape from the cabin. *Control. Stay in control.*

Dark nylons stretched over their faces gave them an alien look, the semisheer fabric blurring their features. They hadn't suddenly decided to use a convenient woman. They'd planned ahead. That thought terrified her more than their size or stench of cheap beer and stale sweat.

"Let me go. You guys can sleep it off, and I— I'll forget this ever happened."

"Believe me, sister, you won't forget." He leaned forward on ham-size forearms, his belly flattening against the table. "Unless you decide to finally cooperate."

"Finally?" Claire gasped.

"You have something we need, and we don't have time to waste."

Stunned, Claire stared back at him. The phone calls. The former partner? But the voice had sounded very different on the phone—muffled, indistinct.

"If you're after any of Randall's business records, there aren't any here. None!"

"You're a liar. But I bet we can make you wish you'd been honest right off the bat."

The younger man shifted his weight and darted a nervous glance at the door. "Dammit, G—"

"Hank." The look he threw his companion suggested an imminent and traumatic loss of front teeth if the guy said another word.

Fear slashed through her at the unspoken exchange.

"If you take it a might easier this time, Buzz, I'll bet she holds up longer 'n the last one." Hank slid a look toward Claire.

Revulsion twisted her stomach. In this little pine cabin, with red gingham curtains and cheerful doe-and-Bambi prints on the walls, she stood face-to-face with her worst nightmare. She drew back, pulling a chair in front of her. Until now she'd kept her fear under control. But there were two of them, twice her size. She didn't have a prayer.

"Come on, babe, let's party." Hank yanked off his navy T-shirt, exposing a sweat-glistened chest covered with tattoos and a belly the color of lard.

An obscene smile split Hank's face. "She's gonna play games, Buzz. You always like that."

He reached forward. Claire shoved the chair at him. He hurled it behind him, where it crashed against the wall.

This couldn't be happening. The dry taste of fear

turned her mouth to cotton. She stepped back without looking away from his face. "L-look, my husband's dead. I don't usually tell people." She hoped fear had washed the color from her cheeks. "I've got it, too."

Hank halted. "Huh?"

"AIDS. I could have kept quiet and—" Claire choked on the words "—had fun, but then you'd have a death sentence, too."

She watched him for a response, praying he would think twice. Her heartbeat thundered in her ears. Every cell in her body quivered, dissolving her muscles into jelly. Straightening, she shook off her terror. *I can do this.*

Buzz moved out of the shadows and faced her from across the room. "She is sorta sickly-looking."

"You should have seen him." Willing tears to her eyes, she did a quick estimate of Hank's size. "That six-foot, two-hundred-pound man was eighty pounds of pure misery when he died."

"Hank?" Buzz's voice rose.

"She's lying. And once we get done with her, we're gonna take a little trip up to her house. We got things to do."

Terror crashed through her at the implication. *The children?* She tried to remember her train of thought. Tried to stall. "H-how do you think AIDS spreads? Carriers look healthy for a long time."

A sneer curling his upper lip against the filmy

nylon over his face, Hank grabbed her upper arms and jerked her against his chest. "Didn't work, sweetheart. I've been watching you, and you are damn easy prey."

Claire twisted her head away, but he grabbed her face with one hand and jerked it back. His ragged fingernails bit into her skin. "Got your attention?" He fisted one hand in her tangled hair. "Where are Brooke's files?"

The incongruous words didn't register. *Brooke's files?* Until leaving home, her sister's greatest concern had been over what shade of nail polish to buy. *Files?* "I have no idea what you mean."

Hank twisted a handful of her hair tighter. "I'm in no mood for games. Talk, or I'm giving you to Buzz."

From the corner of her eye she saw Buzz stroke his groin. She had to make her move. *Now.*

Wrenching herself free, she tipped a chair in Hank's path and raced for the door. Grabbed at the doorknob, twisted it hard. The cool metal felt like salvation under her fingertips. *Free!*

Burly arms snared her from behind, hauled her backward. Buzz shoved her into the center of the room, where she skidded and fell.

Behind them, the doorknob jiggled violently. A deep male voice, blessedly familiar, rang out. "Claire? Claire?"

"Aunt Claire?" The sound of small fists beat a tattoo low against the door.

Logan, with Jason.

"After I finish with them," Hank sneered, "you belong to us."

Claire shot a glance toward the door, then swiveled toward Hank. In an instant, hope changed to horror. He aimed a gun, fitted with a silencer, at the door.

"Don't! Oh, please," she begged, reaching out to him in supplication. She lowered her voice to a whisper. "I'll do anything, just let them leave. I'll tell you anything—anything you need."

Hank shoved her back with one fist and clicked the safety off. "You're sure?"

"Claire? Are you in there?" Outside, a heavy object crashed low against the door once, twice. A pause followed, and then the door shook from a greater blow.

"Logan! Stay back!"

Millimeter by millimeter, Hank's finger squeezed the trigger back. "If you're smart, you won't say anything about those documents. You'd be the third person to die over them," he growled. "Now tell him you and me are getting it on in here, and you don't need no help."

Logan wouldn't believe her. And if he broke in, this man wouldn't hesitate to shoot. She had to do something. Fast. Her eyes fastened on Hank's gun hand.

She launched herself at the weapon, shoved it away. The gun exploded. A flash of heat scorched her cheek. A stinging scent burned her lungs as she fell.

The door burst open with a thundering crash. Hank's massive bulk twisted above her, slamming her to the floor beneath his weight.

Lights sparkled behind her eyelids.

She felt a desperate need to draw breath—and then Hank's crushing weight disappeared. Instantly she heard the powerful impact of a fist, the sickening sound of splitting flesh.

Hank fell facedown on the floor. Buzz flew against the far wall of the cabin. And when she tore her gaze away from them and looked up, Logan held the gun pointed at Hank's chest.

Claire struggled to force air back into her aching lungs as she levered herself onto her forearms.

"Aunt Claire?" Jason peered around the door into the cabin, his face ghostly white.

Drawing a deep, steadying breath, she surveyed him from head to toe. "Thank God, you're okay—"

"I called 911 before I left home," Jason announced, his voice wavering. "The sheriff will be here any minute."

"Good job, kid." Logan glared at Hank and Buzz. "Except you were supposed to stay back at my house. See this gun? You could have been killed."

Jason edged into the kitchen, sank to his knees and touched Claire's face with one trembling hand.

"I couldn't stay there. I had to come and see if you were okay."

Claire scooted back against the cabinets and drew him into her arms. "Oh, honey," Claire murmured into his hair. "Thank you."

He awkwardly pulled away, his cheeks scarlet. "Wasn't anything," he mumbled.

Logan gave Jason a look of approval over his shoulder. "She's lucky to have a man like you around."

"I sure am." Claire breathed. "You're a real hero, Jason. Now let's get back to the house and check on the girls."

Jason scrambled to his feet. "I'll go myself."

Claire hesitated, as a dozen frightening scenarios whirled through her thoughts. At the house, she would spend every moment imagining Hank and Buzz had escaped.

"I'm not a kid." Jason gave her a pained look. "It's okay," the boy said, and slipped out the door.

Claire rose gingerly, then stepped out onto the cabin's narrow deck. She watched Jason as he sped down the lane and through the pool of light at the door of the house, then dashed safely inside. A moment later he waved from the girls' bedroom window and disappeared.

She went back into the cabin.

"Let's get these guys under lock and key." Logan jerked his chin in the direction of the small bathroom and gave Hank a less-than-gentle prod with the toe of his shoe. "Move!"

"Stupid bitch. With luck you would have jumped into my line of fire." Hank pinned Claire with a look of pure hatred, then lowered his voice to a whisper only Claire could hear. "I'll get what I came after or someone else will. Don't even imagine that you'll ever be safe again."

"Move," Logan growled. "Now."

Hank retched, spat blood and stumbled into the bathroom. Buzz sidestepped after him, never taking his eyes from Logan's face. Logan shoved the door shut, then wedged a chair under the handle.

A deeper awareness of Logan's masculine size and power flooded her senses. He was invincible. He'd taken on two men to protect her. Her intense, elemental response startled her.

"Don't even think about trying to get out," he said quietly at the bathroom door. He turned to Claire, his expression still grim. "What did he mean, 'line of fire,' Claire? Did you do something stupid?"

"Not...exactly."

"You could have been killed," he said flatly.

His voice was calm, but his eyes betrayed him. Residual fear, she realized with astonishment. He'd been unafraid to risk his own life, but he'd been deeply afraid for hers.

"Hank pointed his gun at the door. You and Jason were on the other side."

Logan stared at her. "My God, Claire. I couldn't have lived with myself if he...if you got..."

Claire shrugged helplessly. "Exactly."

Logan paced the floor with long, angry strides, obviously fighting a desire to rip open the bathroom door, haul her attackers outside, and tear them both apart.

Finally, he pulled to a stop in front of Claire. "Did they—did they hurt you? If they left so much as a bruise, I want to know."

Claire closed her eyes against the sensations of fear and helplessness that washed through her.

He stepped closer, his expression softening to one of concern. He placed his hands gently on her shoulders and settled her into a chair at the table by the picture window.

"Tell me what happened. Going through it now will help you tell the sheriff later." His voice lowered. "I promise those bastards *will* answer for any—ah—pain they caused. Understand?"

He thought she'd been raped. And he was telling her that whether or not the law took care of this, her attackers would pay. As primitive as that promise was, a warm rush of comfort and security coursed through her. The rage in his eyes had melted into a look of pure compassion. An indomitable sense of honor burned there as well. A woman who married him would be truly blessed. The thought brought a lump to her throat.

And awakened fresh doubt in her heart. Claire thought back to Brooke's phone calls years ago, her desperation. None of her sister's tearful litanies fit the man Logan was today. Had he matured, changed? Or had he ever been the man Brooke claimed him to be?

"Well?"

A numb feeling expanded in her chest. Her surroundings faded as she forced her thoughts to that first loud knock on the door of her house. In a halting voice, she related the night's events.

Then suddenly, like a slap in the face, Hank's words came back. *Don't even imagine that you'll be safe again.*

Claire launched to her feet. "They wanted information." She strode to the bathroom door and raised her voice. "What did you want to know from me?"

Neither man locked inside said a word.

She slammed her palms against the door, then spun around and sank back into the chair next to Logan. "They—they said something about cooperating. Said we had to talk. About what? I'd never met these guys before!"

Logan reached for her hands. He felt so warm, so very warm and strong. When she began to shake, he drew her into an embrace. "It's okay now," he murmured against her hair.

"I—I'm sorry. I shouldn't be such a—such a—"

He pulled back and met her gaze, the blue of his eyes shaded indigo by the thick fringe of his lowered lashes. "It's okay to cry."

She sank against his chest, ashamed of her momentary weakness. Yet thankful for it, because it felt so right to breathe in his scent and his strength.

The night's terror released everything she'd held inside for six long months. The loss of the beloved sister she hadn't seen in years, the pain of watching three grieving children suffer. But no matter how good it might have felt to simply let go, she didn't dare unleash the tears threatening to fall.

There would never again be a place in her life for fragile emotions. Not with three children to raise, a business to run...and unknown dangers that might reappear at any time. Taking a deep breath, she drew away, feeling awkward and at a loss for words.

With one arm still curved around her, Logan lifted her chin with a forefinger and studied her face. "It's all right."

For a moment she let herself believe that Logan felt more than the need to comfort her. His tenderness made her feel...cherished. The night's events faded as heightened awareness swept through her.

But then reality descended like an anvil from above. She wasn't the type of woman that men cherished—her past had taught her that.

Logan was simply providing support. Reading

anything deeper into his actions would lead only to heartbreak.

''M-my first job tomorrow will be lining up estimates on security systems,'' she said, failing miserably at a breezy tone.

''That's a start.'' Releasing her, he leaned back and rested his elbows on the arms of his chair, his expression enigmatic.

With absolute certainty, she knew Logan would have gone to any length to protect her. Her family despised him, and he undoubtedly felt the same way about them.

But during those moments in his arms, she'd never felt more safe and secure.

CHAPTER SEVEN

WHEN DEPUTY MILLER arrived twenty minutes later, Claire forced herself to calmly recite her story in full detail. Logan had been right—going through the story a second time was easier.

Miller asked endless questions and wrote extensive notes after cuffing the two men and depositing them in the back of his cruiser. "I'll ask for a forty-eight-hour hold, but I'm not sure what the judge will decide," he said at last, closing his notebook. "If they have a clean record and a good lawyer, they could post bail and be released pending trial."

"*Released?*" A weak-kneed sensation of fear rushed through her. "What if they come back?"

"They'll each have to post at least twenty thousand dollars," Miller retorted. "Probably more like thirty. And they'll be first on our list if you have any more trouble. We'll make that real clear."

As Logan walked her back to the house, an image of Hank's pendulous, fish-belly pale stomach twisted her insides into a knot and sent a wave of nausea through her. She faltered to a stop and shoved her tousled hair away from her damp forehead with both hands.

Logan reached out to steady her. "You'll feel better when you get home. It's over, Claire."

Right. It was over. She would never tremble at another late-night knock on the door. See shadows coalesce into hulking forms twice her size. Or imagine Hank and Buzz lurking around the next corner.

And Lake Superior would be bone-dry tomorrow.

In truth, she might never feel safe again. The last vestiges of her wavering self-control nearly crumbled as other images returned—Hank's confident leer, the feel of his damp, meaty paw grasping her arm. Only her refusal to break down in front of Logan made her feet start moving again, one halting step after another.

When they reached the porch, Claire turned to face him. "I want to apologize for being so rude when we met. I owe you more than I can say."

Logan looked down at her, his expression somber. "You're alone here. Will the children be safe? Will you?"

"We'll be fine," she said, forcing a lightness she didn't feel. "Fred can install some simple window and door alarms. We'll be okay until I can have a complete security system put in."

Logan gave her a doubtful look. "I can stay tonight—on the sofa—if you're worried about being alone."

She considered his offer. After all that had happened, adult company would be reassuring, but there were just a few hours left until morning. "Thanks," she murmured, extending her hand. "Hank and Buzz are in custody. There's no need to stay."

The clasp of his hand around hers was all too brief. She resisted the urge to lean into his grasp, knowing that in the safety of his arms she might collapse into a trembling mass of emotion.

She paused, cleared her throat and resurrected a calm, businesslike tone. "Would you join us for supper tomorrow? As we'd talked about earlier? The ki—we'd all enjoy that."

"I don't think—"

The faint sound of crying drifted from the second story of the house.

Oh no. She should have hurried back to the house, instead of staying at the cabin. "Excuse me!" She ran up the four steps to the porch, threw open the door and raced upstairs.

Had the girls seen the cruiser's rotating beacons swirling bloodred smears of light across cabins and trees? Handcuffed men being taken away? She found the girls on Annie's bed, huddled next to Jason's thin frame. Their faces were wet with tears.

"Hi, kids," Claire said softly.

Logan came to the door, surveyed the situation and sauntered in with a gentle smile. "Everything okay?"

The girls snuggled closer together, looking as defenseless as baby rabbits. Annie hiccuped. Lissa sniffled.

"They woke up and couldn't find Claire, then saw I was gone. They were real scared," Jason said, awkwardly lifting an arm to rub his nose on his pajama sleeve. "I'm all they've got, now."

All they've got? Claire moved closer and swept them into an embrace.

But she knew Jason had been referring to their parents, their old home. Claire could offer her love, but he was right. He was all they had left of their immediate family. Fighting back a sense of helplessness, Claire rested her cheek against Lissa's silky curls.

Jason shivered. "What if those guys come back?"

"They won't," Claire said firmly. "We'll be safe."

"But what if they escape?" Jason turned to Logan. "Maybe you could stay with us, just once?"

"Guess you've been outvoted, Claire." Like the soft brush of velvet, Logan's low voice rippled over her skin. She sensed the warmth of his body behind her, imagined the steady beat of his heart. Suddenly she felt like a child herself, her fears and insecurities melting at the sound of his voice.

Annie lifted her head slowly, clearly exhausted and on the verge of sleep, and looked around with tear-filled eyes. Her unfocused gaze settled on Logan. "Daddy?" she whispered, her voice wavering with exhaustion. "My *daddy?*"

"No—" Jason began, grabbing at her foot.

She had already launched herself toward Logan's arms.

FIVE O'CLOCK in the morning. Logan shifted his weight slightly against the hard oak headboard, trying not to disturb the soft bundle of pink flannel and blond curls nestled against his chest. On the other side of the bed, all too close yet much too far away, Claire leaned against some pillows. Jason and Lissa, each cocooned in a down comforter, lay between them.

"Thanks, Logan," Claire murmured. "It was good of you to stay like this."

"No problem."

Faint moonlight whispered through the lace curtains, accenting her pale face and the lines of tension bracketing her mouth. Her eyes drifted shut, delicate violet smudging the fragile skin beneath.

The slash of pink across her cheek served as a chilling reminder of the moment she'd fought for Hank's gun, had risked her life to protect Jason and him.

He'd intended to crash on a sofa downstairs, but with Lissa clinging to him and the raw fear in Annie's eyes, he'd ended up staying with the entire family. He'd wanted to take Claire into his arms all night, but whether that longing for contact was to share comfort or to satisfy something far more primal, he tried not to assess. When had he begun to feel so protective about these children, this woman?

He shifted so he could study her profile. He'd seen how she'd struggled for control after the deputy left. A woman with less determination might have fallen hysterically into the nearest available arms. He almost wished she had.

Funny, how perceptions changed. He'd thought her to be a cold manipulator like her sister, a woman with a calculator in place of a heart. Now he knew he'd been blind.

Tonight he'd seen her gently touch a frightened child's cheek. Heard her murmur words of comfort that dried tears, and softly hum lullabies as the children tossed and turned. How much more different from Brooke could anyone be?

Annie snuffled, burrowed closer against Logan's chest. Her warmth and the steady beat of her heart against his filled him with other overpowering emotions. In sleepy confusion she'd called him, "My daddy!" Those two words, whispered with immeasurable love and joy, had nearly done him in. *Her daddy.*

He might have been, if Brooke's reasons for marrying him had included any thought of lifetime commitment. When he'd realized the three children were hers instead of Claire's, he'd felt a stiletto pierce his heart. The fiercely protective feeling of holding Annie in his arms drove it deeper, reminding him of what he'd missed all these years.

Brooke was dead, and he was alone. The cruel irony of it all was inescapable.

Feeling a subtle shift in the mattress, he broke free of the past and looked at Jason. The boy had finally settled into troubled sleep, his occasional muscle jerks betraying the effect of a frightening experience.

Next to Jason, Lissa slept with her head on Claire's lap. Claire gently brushed a strand of hair away from the child's face and smiled softly. "Brooke and her husband must have been so proud of these kids."

"I sure hope so." Logan stared into the darkness, wondering what it would have been like to have a family of his own. Had Brooke even realized what a blessing they were, or had she always remained a self-centered child herself?

His thoughts drifted. Maybe it was just the late hour and the intimacy of the darkness, but he found himself imagining himself with Claire, sharing with her the kind of hot, demanding passion that drove a man and woman over the edge. Savagely, he tore his mind away from the thought. She was traumatized. Vulnerable as a child. Thoughts of sex and sin were as appropriate as offering Whistler's mother a one-night stand.

"Think we could tiptoe away?" Claire whispered without opening her eyes. "You must wish you could get back home and catch a few hours of decent sleep.''

No. Returning to his empty house held little appeal. These moments were golden, filling him with unfamiliar peace. He held Annie just a little tighter, savoring her warmth. He didn't want to put her down. Not yet.

Moving by almost imperceptible degrees, Claire eased Lissa into a comfortable position on the bed, then stood up. She gave Logan an expectant look as she finger-combed her wild curls into place and scuffed her feet into a pair of slippers.

Stifling a sigh of regret, he repeated her subtle movements and lowered Annie to the mattress. The minute he released her, he felt bereft. Cold. He wanted to sweep the child back into his arms and hold her close.

Instead, he drew the covers over Annie's shoulders and followed Claire to the kitchen. The bright lights and gleaming off-white floor made him blink.

Claire shuffled to the center of the room and looked blankly around her as if she wasn't quite sure of where she was. ''I— Do you want—''

Logan pulled a chair away from the table and beckoned her closer. ''Sit down. It's my turn to make coffee.''

Looking grateful, she sank into the chair and crossed her trim ankles in front of her. Logan glanced at her feet and did an abrupt double take. She was wearing rabbits.

Claire started to speak, then followed his gaze and laughed. She extended one leg and wiggled a furry foot, her tentlike bathrobe parting to expose a slender ankle and calf. "Like my slippers? They're great for dusting hardwood floors."

He liked her gracefully sculpted legs a lot more than the slippers; her weary touch of humor even more. Everything about her was at odds with the cool career woman she'd been until tonight. What other surprises, other secrets did she hold?

"Cocoa or coffee?" Logan filled the coffee-maker with water, then fumbled through the cupboard overhead until he found both canisters.

"Coffee." She frowned. "But if you'd rather get home—"

"No," Logan retorted. Her words jarred him back to reality. He would go home soon, and they would go back to square one. Wary neighbors with opposing agendas. Each of them carried too many old wounds for anything to change.

He stared out into the darkness, arms braced on the edge of the sink, while the coffeemaker gurgled and spat, sending curls of amaretto-scented steam into the air.

"Thanks for everything," she said, once they were seated across the table from each other, cradling mugs of hot coffee in their hands. "For coming to my rescue. For helping with the kids. I—I didn't handle this very well."

"You did just fine." He took a slug of coffee.

Hell, staying hadn't been an altruistic gesture. He'd reacted with startling intensity to the weight and warmth of Annie's trusting embrace. She'd reminded him of things he'd lost, things he would never have.

Refusing to recall the other desires that had pulsed through him with Claire so damnably close by, he tossed out the first thought that came to mind. "Tell me about Brooke's accident—were the kids in the car?"

Closing her eyes as if offering a brief prayer of thanks, she shook her head. "No, but we weren't notified of the accident for three days. By that time the nanny had turned the kids over to the authorities." Her voice caught. "They were in a foster home."

"Jason didn't have any idea where you lived?"

"He didn't know anything about us."

Logan's heart twisted at the thought of the frightened young boy, suddenly alone. The little girls would have been terrified. "Not even your address?"

"He didn't even know we existed." Claire's knuckles whitened around her coffee mug. She thought back fourteen years. "My father was angry when she ran off to marry you. He was furious over the divorce. When she started dating Randall right away—" Claire halted, traced a finger around the rim of her coffee mug. "Dad and Brooke had a huge fight, and that was the last time she ever came home.''

''But surely with her second marriage, and the kids—''

''After she married Randall, I saw them just once, several years ago. But by then Randall was angry with the family and he didn't give her a chance to speak. None of us ever heard from her again.'' The bleak look in Claire's eyes conveyed far more than her words. ''We didn't even know about the children until after she and Randall were killed.''

''Sounds like the Charles Worth I knew years ago,'' Logan said heavily.

''It wasn't only our father who kept her away,'' Claire retorted. ''It was her husband.''

And a nickel could still buy a cup of coffee. What else did she refuse to see about her family? Logan gave Claire a grim look. ''You have no idea what your father can be like, honey. The Worth family dynamics are a frightening thing.''

''And you obviously haven't been hearing what I said.'' Claire's eyes sparked with anger, her mouth thinned. Getting to her feet, she stalked over to the sink and rinsed her coffee cup. ''We're both exhausted, and we're going to say things we don't mean. Perhaps you'd better go,'' she said, staring down at the cup in her hands. ''It's been a very long night.''

"You're right." Logan rose, cursing himself for being so blunt. "Take care of yourself, Claire."

"Thank you...for everything." She didn't turn around when he walked out the door.

At the end of the sidewalk he stopped and looked back at the house. Through the window he could see her still standing at the sink, her head bowed.

It was for the best if they kept their distance.

He'd be wise to remember that she was a Worth. Both she and his ex-wife came from a family where only Dow Jones stirred emotions. That Claire had turned out so much better than the rest of them was nothing short of a miracle.

But if he dared start a relationship with Claire, her family would try to destroy him for the second time. He was no longer a young, inexperienced college boy, and they would never succeed. But Claire would be caught in the cross fire. Claire would be the one who got hurt. No matter how much he wanted her, he could never let that happen.

He would not make the same mistake twice.

CHAPTER EIGHT

SHE WOULD NOT MAKE the same mistake as her sister.

Despite Logan's surprisingly gentle touch with the children and her own shattered emotions last night, he was a proven heartbreaker. A man capable of beguiling a woman until she abandoned common sense and tried to capture an impossible future with both hands. Claire had seen it happen to Brooke.

Surveying the jumble of boxes covering the attic floor, she resolutely shoved all thoughts of the previous night from her mind, but like waves against a shore they inexorably returned.

He'd spent the night in her bedroom. On her bed. Granted, he'd been dressed in Levi's and a faded sweatshirt, but he'd been there.

Fool that she was, she'd even begun to imagine what it might be like to fall in love with him. And to be loved by him in return—to be as cherished and protected as she'd felt last night. Even now those thoughts suffused her with warmth and made her heart feel two sizes too big for her chest.

She could only pray that he hadn't had a clue about her wayward imagination.

Whistling a mournful version of "The Sound of Music," Fred clomped up the attic stairs. The vibration of his footsteps shook a gauzy film of dust from the tie beams overhead.

Farther above, from the murky darkness of the steeply pitched rafters, came a whispery rustle. Bats. Nice brown hamsters that fly, she reminded herself, trying not to envision scalpel-sharp teeth and leather wings.

They eat mosquitoes. They eat mosquitoes...

"More trash?" Fred leaned against the handrail at the top step, wiping his forehead with the back of his wrist. From the bleary look in his eyes, he'd probably enjoyed more than a few beers with his buddies the night before. "Or should I start cleaning cabins?"

Claire hesitated. Maybe the repeated trips up the stairs were too hard on him, given his arthritis. He sure sounded out of breath. "Hmm...the cabins would be best. I haven't made much more progress up here."

With visible relief, Fred nodded and stomped back down the stairs, leaving her to deal with the ocean of sealed boxes. Between her own possessions and those of Brooke and her husband, there had to be a hundred or more cartons. Not to mention the jungle of old furniture, trunks and dusty odds and ends that must have been up here for years.

Oh, Brooke. A lifetime now sealed in impersonal

cardboard boxes stored in an attic. A familiar lump rose in Claire's throat. *We missed so much.*

As children, they had been too far apart in age to be great companions. Brooke had been tolerant, if not exactly overjoyed, over having a younger shadow. When Claire hit her awkward preteen years, they'd shared a few heart-to-hearts over midnight popcorn when Brooke came home on college breaks. Claire had treasured every moment.

Claire sighed. Just stepping into the attic had stirred memories and a grief she'd rather not face. She shouldn't have come up here today, not while her emotions still felt so raw and exposed.

Fred's footsteps halted at the bottom of the stairs. "Phone's ringing," he yelled.

"Coming." Relieved at the interruption, Claire nudged a few boxes to one side, then reached for the string dangling from the lightbulb overhead.

An unfamiliar shadow caught her eye. Her heart skipped a beat. Picking her way through the maze of boxes, she reached to turn on another light. And then another, moving more cautiously as she advanced.

An eerie feeling shot down Claire's spine. Curled icy fingers around her stomach. At least three—no four—boxes had been ripped open, the contents scattered. File folders. Loose papers. Books. Without a flashlight the labels on the boxes weren't clear, but none of the contents were familiar. Surely Jason hadn't been going through these things. The girls wouldn't have come up here. They'd be afraid to ascend the stairs.

From somewhere in the darkness came a whisper of movement. The crackle of paper. Claire lifted a hand to her face, held her breath. A rush of dark shadows streaked past her feet.

Mice? She shot backward, bumping her calves against an old end table, and fought the urge to race for the stairs.

But they were just—just harmless little mice. Slowly her heart settled back into its proper place in her chest. There would be a logical explanation for the opened boxes.

And logic precluded that an intruder would care about anything stored in her attic. Or did it?

First thing tomorrow morning, she had appointments with three security system companies. Within a week she would have written estimates to compare. Everything was under control, like always. She would call the local exterminators the minute she got downstairs.

The phone was ringing. Someone on the other end of the line was going to be really annoyed, if they were still there at all. Claire darted back to the stairs, turning off lights as she went. With luck, the caller would still be on the line. With more luck, the call would be for reservations. The cabins were still occupied thanks to the beauty of Minnesota's fall, but that would all change when winter hit.

Downstairs, she picked up the receiver lying on

the desk and flipped open the reservation book. But at the first hello, she would have gladly settled for someone selling life insurance or cemetery plots.

Her father's secretary gave her a chilly greeting, then a Chopin polonaise thundered in her ear while the call was transferred to his office.

"Come back to New York. You've surely had enough of that rustic life by now."

No greeting, no *I love you, honey, how are you doing?* Just the same authoritative voice she'd listened to all of her life. "Hello, Father, how are—"

"You can't possibly plan to keep my grandchildren in some godforsaken wilderness."

He'd probably glanced at his watch at least twice in the last thirty seconds, Claire guessed, and was now standing at his desk gathering folders for a meeting. Charles Worth had not wasted a minute in the past sixty-five years.

Claire's fingers whitened around the receiver. "We're doing very well."

"Well?" His voice grew icy. "You can't offer those children what they need. Schools—cultural advantages—"

"There are good schools here, and I can give them what they need—a home, and lots of love."

"You're an intelligent woman," he snapped. "Surely you can see they need more than that."

"Right now this is exactly what they need."

Her father continued as if he hadn't heard a word she'd said. "Nelson has done a study on private schools here. Sommers Academy in Massachusetts is best, statistically speaking. Jason will have every opportunity to advance his education and make the right friends. I can enroll him for January first. The girls would do well at Corbeil.''

''Annie and Lissa at *boarding school?*'' Claire had spent her entire childhood at such schools, but all she'd ever wanted was a real family—like the ones she'd read about in her favorite storybooks.

''Corbeil is a girls' day school here in New York.''

Claire's right hand grew numb from gripping the receiver too tightly. She switched hands and stretched the phone cord across the room, then sank into a chair at the round oak table. ''We aren't coming back.''

Again, he continued as if he hadn't heard a word she said. ''I can have Nelson make airline reservations for all of you in mid-November, so the children can settle in before the next school term.'' He hesitated, then said in a lowered tone, ''I only want what's best for them, don't you see? And for you. Your position in the company has been held.''

Remembering their last argument before she left New York, his imploring tone startled her. ''Thank you, but—''

''I've checked on Pine Cliff. You don't have the capital to keep it going. The manager who ran the place for Brooke didn't make a profit in four years. You belong back in the family business, where you have a future.'' His voice grew colder. ''It's a crime to deny the children all that I can provide.''

Something within Claire snapped. She'd had far too many years of orders. ''No,'' she said, taking a deep breath. ''Pine Cliff will succeed.'' She braced herself for the irrevocable rift her next words would cause. ''Brooke gave me legal custody of these children. She wanted them to have a normal family life, not years of boarding school. We aren't coming back.''

''We'll talk again, when you're less emotional.'' He hung up, not with surging anger, but with a neat, final click that dismissed Claire's opinions as if they counted for nothing.

He never listened. And despite that fleeting hint of vulnerability in his voice, he was certain he would win. She resisted the urge to slam her own receiver against a wall.

Minnesota hadn't been far enough away.

If she'd been determined before, she felt close to obsession now. She would make Pine Cliff succeed if it was the last thing she did.

And when it did, her father would finally have to recognize that she was much more than a genetic investment in his company's future.

THE REST OF THE DAY flew by. After cleaning three of the cabins herself and checking Fred's progress, she gave herself a good dose of depression by reviewing the resort account books. At three o'clock she remembered with a start that Logan was coming to dinner—and that she hadn't been to the grocery store in days.

What on earth would she feed him? Peanut butter à la jam? Frozen chicken patties coated with triple-bypass breading? The kids' favorite boxed macaroni and cheese?

After a half-hour search through the boxes marked Books, still piled in the living room, she found a cookbook promising "elegant but easy" recipes. Most were gourmet delights requiring ingredients like cream of mushroom soup and crushed potato chips, and included the helpful suggestion that the meal be served with wine and candlelight. Claire suspected that with a *lot* of wine, and *dim* candlelight, the recipes just might work.

Except she didn't have wine. And her candles were packed...somewhere.

Just as well. Romantic settings and culinary masterpieces would convey the wrong message.

Thank heavens for the package of boneless chicken breasts she'd found hiding in the back of the freezer. Logan deserved a decent meal.

She'd just started thawing chicken breasts in the microwave when the children came in the door. "Hi, guys," she said, wiping her hands on a paper towel. "Have a good day at school?"

All three looked tired and drawn. The girls' worried expressions relaxed when they saw her, though

Jason merely gave her a cursory glance before dashing up the stairs to his room.

"We were scared last night when you were gone," Lissa said, fidgeting with a pot holder on the counter.

Annie shivered. "Jason says there were bad guys here."

They'd spent the day worrying, Claire realized with a pang. She gave them each a confident smile. "They're long gone, and they won't be back. Are you two hungry?"

Lissa looked hopeful. "Cookies?"

"You bet. Chocolate chip." Claire took several cookies from the bear-shaped cookie jar sitting on the counter, then poured two glasses of milk. After setting everything out on the table, she gave each girl a big hug. "Do you think Jason wants some?"

"He went to get Igor," Lissa said. Both of the girls scooted into their chairs and reached for their cookies.

"How nice," Claire managed to say, trying to envision what her mother might have said if Claire or Brooke had brought such a creature to the table. "Mr. Matthews is coming for supper, remember?"

Annie set down her glass and looked up. Her milk mustache coordinated well with the spots of school-lunch spaghetti and purple poster paint on her pink sweatshirt. "He's nice," she ventured after finishing a mouthful of cookie. "Maybe he'll stay and read us bedtime stories."

"Mmm—probably not. I expect he'll need to get home before that." Measuring wild rice into a pan of boiling water, Claire frowned. Whatever her crazy, sensual thoughts about him, the children would only be at risk for disappointment if they expected an ongoing relationship with Logan.

"Mr. M-Matthews *could* tell stories," Annie repeated, turning to Lissa. "Maybe if we both asked."

"Stupid. Daddies don't have time." Lissa gave her an arch look. "They're too busy."

Annie's face fell. "But he isn't a daddy. So maybe he will."

Claire's breath caught in her throat as she reached for some spices in the cupboard. Then, resting her palms on the counter, she stared out at Lake Superior.

She'd seen their father only once—an accidental encounter at a gallery opening several years ago. Randall had possessed the oily confidence of a man who liked to make a quick buck, the slippery gaze of someone who'd learned to keep exits in view. Exactly in keeping with what her father's private investigator had reported about Randall's shady business dealings.

As soon as he spotted Claire, Randall had whisked Brooke out the door and into a waiting cab.

The well-masked bruise on Brooke's arm and the haunted look in her eyes had been a part of Claire's dreams ever since. She had desperately tried to make further contact with her sister, but Brooke and her husband moved several times, and their phone number was always unlisted.

The next time Claire saw her sister, Brooke lay surrounded by satin and mahogany and a nauseating profusion of cut flowers. She'd looked happier in death than she had at the gallery.

Almost certainly, Randall had been an abusive and controlling husband. Now Claire knew he hadn't been much of a father, either.

Lost in thought, she measured basil and garlic powder into a bowl of cream of mushroom soup and sour cream, then for the life of her couldn't remember if she'd already done so.

A screech of outrage echoed through the kitchen.

She turned in time to see Lissa give her sister a goading smile.

"He likes me best."

"Does not!"

"Does!"

"Hey, guys," she murmured, scooting Annie to a chair farther from her sister. "Need more cookies?"

Lissa's lower lip pouted forward. "No," she mumbled, pushing cookie crumbs across the surface of the table with her thumb.

Claire ruffled her hair. "If you're talking about Mr. Matthews, I'm sure he likes all three of you very much."

Wearing a plaid flannel shirt over a black turtle-neck, both tucked into his jeans, Jason wandered into the room. He poured a glass of milk and collected a handful of cookies, then plopped down in the chair farthest from Claire.

Only then did she notice two or three inches of Igor peeking over the crook of Jason's elbow. The snake's ruby eyes focused on her for a moment, then he withdrew from sight.

Claire's stomach fluttered. "Uh…Jason," she asked, imagining Igor making a quick slither across the floor to her feet. "Where is Igor now?"

Jason gave her a defiant look. "I've got him."

The creature certainly wasn't visible. Claire thought back to the few times she'd been able to catch Jason and give him a hug. Perhaps Igor had been hugged as well. Perhaps he *liked* her now. And when he got loose, he'd come right up to her to say Hello.

Shuddering, she grasped at the first topic that came to mind. "How's school?"

"Fine."

"What did you do today?"

"Nothin'." He directed all his attention on the pile of cookies in front of him.

She took a deep breath. "A school counselor called me, honey."

Fidgeting, Jason began picking up his cookies and casting furtive glances at the door.

"Can you guess why she might want to meet with me this week?"

Hooking one arm protectively around his midsection—supporting Igor, no doubt—Jason shrugged, gave her a wary look, then fled out the front door.

Claire sighed. Their relationship appeared to be back to square one—with an edge she couldn't quite identify. Mistrust? Fear?

And now there were problems at school to deal with. How could she help if Jason wouldn't even talk?

THREE HOURS LATER, Claire studied the dining room with an experienced eye. She'd started off with low aspirations for the meal, but a lifetime of proper hospitality would have filled her with guilt if she hadn't done something attractive.

Her late aunt's elegant Spode china and sterling silver gleamed against the dark blue tablecloth, reflecting like diamonds in the Waterford tumblers. The table setting echoed the view of Superior's sparkling indigo waves visible through the large picture window dominating the opposite wall.

Reaching over to adjust a delicate bouquet of wildflowers she'd picked along the lane, she glanced through the window. All three children were on hands and knees in the front yard, while Logan toed at the shrubbery flanking the sidewalk.

Even seeing him from this distance made her

pulse flutter, and she caught herself double-checking her appearance in the mirror above the sideboard.

Ridiculous. There had been lots of handsome, intelligent men back in New York. Witty, well-dressed men-on-the-rise in the family corporation who'd practically kissed her feet. But they'd been interchangeable; their polished manners and carefully orchestrated attempts at romance almost identical. Her brief engagement had been the most humiliating mistake of her life.

They'd all been after the president's daughter. Never really *her*. The memory still hurt. Ultimately, dining alone on Chinese takeout had held far more appeal than the thought of facing yet another fawning smile over lobster and Dom Perignon.

Logan would have stood out in that crowd like a panther among a litter of hopeful puppies. Lean and tall, he moved with a casual grace that spoke of a complete sense of confidence and control, not elevated ego.

She moved around the dining-room table and stood at the window, ostensibly to watch the children.

Logan bent to inspect an area where the shrubbery grew rampant, his shirt stretching across the well-defined muscles of his back and shoulders. A man who looked that good ought to be cloned.

I'm not interested, Claire told herself. But it was an outright lie.

She wondered what it would be like to kiss him.

She might as well wish to be empress of the universe or fit into size six shoes. Glancing ruefully at her size nines, she turned away from the window and adjusted a place setting a few millimeters to the right.

Logan would not be sweeping her into his arms. And she would not be plastering any infatuated kisses on his face.

She could have learned her lesson well enough with one former boyfriend—but fate had given her two more of them to drive the message home. She was an eminently resistible woman. Her former *status* had been intriguing, not her, and these days she was a struggling resort owner with three children and an uncertain future. Hardly an enticing commodity.

"I'm perfectly happy right now," she sternly reminded herself, giving the dining room a last inspection.

A platter of marmalade-glazed chicken and bright green broccoli steamed invitingly on the sideboard. Creamy garlic-and-basil wild rice and amaretto coffee filled the room with tantalizing scents. It would all be cold in moments.

She stepped out the front door. "Come on in, everyone. Supper's on."

"Can't," yelled Lissa, patting at the grass along the sidewalk.

Jason rose and jogged to the overgrown flower

bed bordering the front edge of the lawn. Ignoring Claire's approach, he bent over and swished his arms through masses of gold and scarlet chrysanthemums.

"What did you lose?" she asked, studying the grass at her feet for anything out of place.

"Igor." He twisted his head to shoot a sullen look in her direction. "Bet you're glad, too."

Actually—well, no, she admitted to herself. The distraught note in Jason's voice and bleak look in his eyes weighed more heavily than any aversion she might have to Igor. "Of course not. I'll help you look, okay?"

Fifteen minutes later, Jason sank sadly to his knees. "He's gone. I'll never find him."

Logan continued to scuff at the long prairie grass in the small clearing next to the yard. "Not likely," he agreed. "It's so cool out here he probably zipped down the first hole he could find."

"Maybe he'll show up tomorrow," Claire added, looking at Jason. "You might even find him in the spring."

"Yeah, right."

Jason's sarcastic tone hit Claire like a wet towel on a cold night.

Logan came up behind her. "Hormones," he said softly. "He'll turn human when he hits twenty."

"If I survive." Dealing with Jason was hard enough. Knowing Logan had witnessed her failure made it all seem worse. She turned back toward the house. "Jason loves Igor. I sure hope he finds—"

She found Logan's broad chest inches from her face, closer than she'd expected. The faint scent of sandalwood, the heat of his body, and his sheer size filled her senses. "I—I..."

Logan looked down at her, a wry grin lifting the corners of his sensual mouth. "Finding something we need isn't always easy."

The look in his eyes was anything but wry. Interest gleamed in those dark blue depths. His lashes lowered. His smile faded. Had the early-evening chill raised the goose bumps on her arms, or were they a response to the deep vibration of his voice?

Claire took a faltering step back. He was wrong. Finding what she needed at this moment would be *far* too easy, but it would be a mistake.

From the corner of her eye she saw the kids had stopped looking for Igor. They stared at her and Logan, their eyes widening with obvious fascination.

"Uh...I think Mr. Matthews is right. Igor is hiding. If we're lucky, he'll turn up later. Can we go in for supper?"

She glanced at Logan as she started toward the house. A whisper of sensation skittered through her. If ever she'd questioned her sister's abrupt decision to marry him, Claire no longer had any doubts as to the attraction.

Brooke hadn't stood a chance. She had prized

beautiful things, reveled in objects and experiences that delighted her senses. One smoky look from this guy and she wouldn't have thought to consider mundane things like compatibility or the concept of *forever*.

Logan shook his head, as if clearing his thoughts, then abruptly spun on his heel. "Come on, kids," he called out. "Time for supper."

Minutes later, they all sat at the dining-room table. The children cast nervous glances at the elegant table setting and shot warning glances at one another.

Claire eyed the limp broccoli and congealing marmalade chicken. The wild-rice side dish now resembled a plop of hardening concrete. Would it be better or worse if she tried to reheat everything? Her intimate dinner parties in New York had always been perfect, understated affairs. This was a disaster.

One could only plunge ahead. She shook a linen napkin into her lap. "Everyone ready?" she asked brightly, passing a platter.

Annie gave the marmalade chicken a suspicious look. "It's *orange*. Can I have a hot dog?"

"Manners!" hissed Jason, aiming an elbow at her side.

Annie dodged his blow and bumped Lissa's arm. Lissa's glass tipped, flooding the dark blue tablecloth with more milk than the glass could possibly have held. The glass itself scattered in gleaming shards across the darkening cloth.

Lissa, horrified, leaped to her feet and ran from the table. Her chair teetered wildly. Annie started to cry. Jason paled, looking as though he'd trade his new Nikes to be anyplace else.

The milk continued its inexorable progress—straight toward Logan's lap. Gilbert, asleep under the table, launched to his feet in belated response and began barking. Asleep on a chair in the corner of the room, Sullivan awoke and arched her back in disdain. Casting a look of utter contempt in Claire's direction, the cat stalked out of the room.

Jason and Annie both looked like deer ready to bolt. "I—I'm sorry, Aunt Claire," Jason finally ventured. "It's my fault."

Annie stared at the toes of her shoes. "Me, too."

"No harm done. Can you two go up and get your sister?" Jason and Annie raced away, clearly relieved.

"Nice evening," Logan said mildly, damming the approaching milk with several dinner napkins. He lifted one eyebrow. "And how is everything here at Pine Cliff?"

Claire stared at the scene before her. And then, from deep inside, a bubble of laughter forced its way past her constricted throat. "Actually everything is just fine, thank you," she managed to say, trying to shape her quivering lips into a prim smile. "We're so glad you could—you could—"

She burst into laughter. It couldn't be much worse, and she didn't care. Formality be damned. She wasn't a child in her mother's dining room, cowering with embarrassment. Her father—and his arrogant butler—weren't here to express their insufferable blend of utter horror and complete disappointment in her. She was free of them all. "Shall we give this another try? This setting is history."

With a bemused look, Logan studied her from across the table as he rose to his feet. No doubt, he'd had few dinner invitations turn out like this one. He'd be happy having an excuse to leave.

But his eyes twinkled, and laugh lines deepened at their outside corners. Sliding his chair in, he moved around the table, then looked down at Claire. "Thanks so much for a memorable evening."

She started to chuckle, but he lifted his fingertips to her mouth. "I mean it. Tomorrow my decorator is bringing things out for my house, but there's nothing she could do that would match the kind of home you are creating for these kids."

He took her hand within both of his own. She felt fragile, feminine. Protected. Warmth radiated up her arm and pooled in her chest. "Yes—well, we're not always quite this entertaining. Can I offer you something else?"

"I was hoping you would ask." His fingers tightened around hers, his thumb stroked her palm. Slowly.

In instant response, her toes curled inside her shoes and her skin tingled with new warmth. The sound of children's feet thundering down the hallway upstairs and the sodden disaster on the table faded away, leaving only the escalating beat of her own heart and the heat in his eyes.

A shiver—anticipation or fear—raced down her back. This was a mistake. Yet she couldn't have stepped back if someone had screamed "Fire!"

Logan's hands rose to her shoulders. A flash of panic speared through her. In a heartbeat she felt Hank's callused hands wrench her head around, felt his slack, wet lips against hers.

"I—I—"

"You're thinking of something that never should have happened. Of someone else. Look at me, Claire," Logan said quietly. He lifted one hand and stroked the line of her jaw, then traced the curve of her lips with exquisite care. "Lovely…"

Slowly, ever so slowly, he drew closer. Slanting his head slightly, his eyes drifted shut. His lips brushed hers once. Then again, sending currents of pleasure clear to her toes as the kiss deepened. His hands lifted to cradle her face, as if she were a rare and beautiful thing. She leaned toward him, wanting more.

Instead, he pulled back and studied her face. "Okay?"

Dazed, she stared at him and wondered if anything else had ever been so okay in her entire life. "Yes—"

A herd of galloping children raced down the stairs. He glanced at the table, then at her. "Is life always this quiet around here?"

"Always."

"The food will be fine," Logan said smoothly. "Jason and I could straighten up in here while you reheat it."

Claire edged away from him. "Er...yes. Good idea." Scooping up the platter and two serving bowls, she fled to the kitchen. Logan's soft chuckle followed her through the door.

In ten minutes, the dining-room table looked much more welcoming, with chestnut-colored place mats, ivory stoneware and *plastic* glasses. The children chattered endlessly as they ate.

Claire struggled to participate and relived that kiss at least a hundred times.

She shouldn't have kissed him. Wished he hadn't stopped. The kiss had left her feeling like warm pudding, without form or direction.

Several hours later, Claire punched the Power Wash button on the dishwasher, took two cups of decaf to the kitchen table and sank into a chair with a sigh of relief. Dinner was finished. The kids were finally in bed. The evening was *over*.

Except for the fact that Logan was still in her kitchen.

''Great dinner.'' He took a swallow of coffee. ''Second try went better.''

Savoring the warmth of her cup in both hands, she held it near her face. She'd made mocha almond this time, and its aroma soothed her senses. After tackling an incredible pile of dishes with Logan at her side, two rounds of bedtime rituals for three kids who didn't want to go to bed and hours of suppressing her inappropriate sensual thoughts, it felt good to simply sit down.

She looked across the table at Logan. He'd capitulated with a smile, in the face of Annie's hopeful request and pleading expression, and had read a half-dozen books to the girls. Even Jason had lurked nearby to listen, feigning nonchalance despite his obvious attention.

The fact that Logan's kiss had turned her world upside down and short-circuited her entire nervous system was something she simply needed to…forget.

Logan was a neighbor she'd probably run into often in the coming years. He was someone she could count on. She needed a good ally, not a man who would break her heart. Suddenly she remembered Brooke's tearful words. *He was so nice at first, everything I wanted him to be. But it was all an act. Then the lies started, and the late nights. The things he said to me…*

She studied him carefully, trying to find some evidence that Brooke could have been right. Was he putting on an act to gain her acceptance? Was he only trying to get her to change her mind about selling him the property? A thousand questions crowded Claire's mind. Maybe now she could find some answers. "Friends?" she asked, offering her hand across the table.

"I'll always want your land," he said solemnly.

"And you'll never get it."

Extending his hand, he chuckled. "We'll see."

Then he leaned back in his chair and glanced around the room, at the high ceilings and intricately carved moldings, the age-darkened oak cupboards and trio of windows looking over the lake. His expression grew somber. "After so many years it's good to be back. I can still see…"

His voice faded into silence. Was he remembering Brooke standing in this room, welcoming him at the end of a day? Brooke had been radiant, a natural flirt who drew admiring glances wherever she went. As her husband, Logan must have felt like king of the world.

He finished the last of his coffee in one long swallow and stood abruptly. Startled, Claire also rose, then followed him to the door. What on earth had happened?

At the door, he turned back to her, as distant as if his thoughts were a thousand miles away. "Thank you. It's been—I've enjoyed this evening."

This did not bode well for the start of a supportive friendship. "We did too, Lancelot," Claire teased.

He smiled, then reached out and gave her a quick one-armed hug, just as he had done long ago.

At the touch of his arm, she drew in a sharp breath. A desire to melt into that brief contact shot through her. *New rule. We'll definitely skip the hugs from now on.*

Logan must have felt something as well. His brief embrace relaxed. Tightened. Then he stepped back, nodded a brief farewell and walked out the door.

Friends, Claire reminded herself, watching him disappear into the darkness. She had a struggling business and three young children to worry about. They were her priority above all else. She already knew the results of investing in relationships. Moments of happiness never outweighed the dividends of deep disappointment in the end.

As mere friends, she would never enter the dark and dangerous world of passion and hunger, where her heart and soul would be inevitably shattered. There would be no risk. And friendships could last forever.

The warmth of that thought lasted less than fifteen seconds. Until the phone rang.

"Pine Cliff," she answered, automatically glancing at the Caller ID. *Pay phone.*

The only response was silence.

She hung up. The phone rang again. And again.

She left the receiver lying on the desk after the third time.

The caller never said a word.

LOGAN CURSED HIMSELF with every stride he took into the darkness. He'd left like a bat out of hell. No doubt Claire was wondering if he was completely sane.

If he hadn't gotten out of there, he might have said something foolish like "I want more than friendship, Claire."

And that would destroy the calm balance in his life, wreak havoc on the quiet and solitary existence he'd achieved.

With a Worth, those farewells could be downright lethal. It had taken months to clear his name of the false allegations Brooke and her father had made against him. With the credit cards she'd taken, Brooke had managed to destroy his credit rating and take his last dime.

Claire wasn't at all like her sister, but his years of wary solitude and noncommitment had taken their toll. What was it about this woman, these kids that had weakened his defenses?

Leaving the gravel lane for a narrow trail through the pines, Logan rationalized with every step. He thought of Annie and Lissa. Anyone would feel all warm and loving with those tykes snuggled close, smelling of bubble bath and shampoo. They triggered simple instincts for the perpetuation of the species, nothing more.

And Jason—the anger and hunger and loneliness in that kid were as clear as day. Added to the emotional chaos of the average teenager, he needed a good friend. The kid reminded Logan of himself twenty years ago.

The emotional pull of those three kids could be easily explained with logic. But there was nothing remotely logical about his ridiculous awareness of Brooke's little sister. Good God. Wrapping an arm around Claire's shoulders had jump-started his hormones over the one woman he should never want— and would never have. Following up on that surge of heat and desire would be the second worst mistake of his life. He would stay away from Pine Cliff until it was his once more.

Had Claire ever guessed the truth about his brief, misguided marriage to her sister? Not likely. It would have set her back on her trim little rear. He had no doubt she'd been well educated by the Worths about her sister's disastrous marriage to the kid with no name and less future.

It would be best to let the lies stand. Knowing the truth about Brooke could destroy Claire's relationship with her family forever.

And even a family like hers had to be better than no family at all.

CHAPTER NINE

EVER SINCE she'd been a child, Claire had always hoped to find a four-leaf clover someday. She had never, ever hoped to find a snake. The weak September sunlight warming her back did nothing to dispel the chill settling somewhere in the region of her stomach.

Apparently Igor had found a spot of sunlight that met his needs perfectly. Curled on the sidewalk in front of her house, he might have been a forgotten twist of manila rope.

At Claire's approach, he raised his head in her direction with languorous interest, then drooped it back over a section of tail—or neck—and went back to sleep. The subtleties of reptile anatomy escaped her, but one thing was certain: she had to capture this one.

The kids were at school. Fred had left for town in search of a new transmission for the riding lawn mower. There wasn't another person in sight. If only Logan would saunter into view just about now...

But if he showed up, she'd have more to deal with than Igor. The deep timbre of Logan's voice would send vibrations humming through her veins, and she'd feel herself warming from head to toe in instant response.

Cut that out! she told herself sternly, turning her attention back to Igor. She had a family to care for now. She didn't need anyone else to make her life complete.

And right now, she had the power to make one member of that family a much happier kid. The chance would be lost if she didn't move fast.

Gritting her teeth, Claire took a tentative step forward. Then another. Despite the cool air, perspiration dampened her palms and welded her sweatshirt to her back. She was an adult. This was merely a— a pet. Jason carried him around all the time. Recalling Jason's sad expression at breakfast helped her step a few inches closer.

"It's you and me, Igor," Claire whispered. "Why couldn't you be something fluffy?"

Muttering a quick prayer under her breath, she darted across the lawn, snatched a small bucket by the laundry building, then cautiously approached Igor once more.

"Here boy," she urged, holding the bucket near him. Igor lifted his head when the rim of the bucket scraped against the concrete walk. Then pulled back. How on earth did one herd a snake?

Closing her eyes, she reached out with one trembling foot to nudge him into motion. When she opened her eyes, he was heading straight for the overgrown flower garden. Luckily, the cool air had slowed him to the speed of refrigerated honey.

With a groan of frustration, she darted ahead of him, planted the bucket in his path, and pushed him—or most of him—into the bucket with the side of her foot. The part in the bucket started to flow up and over the other side.

"Oh, Lord!" Grabbing the handle of the bucket, Claire took off at a run for the house, keeping one eye on her captive and praying fervently that Igor would stay put. If she made it into the house, at least he'd be safely inside.

The rocking motion of the bucket slowed his progress. Moving faster than she'd ever thought possible, she raced through the kitchen, up the stairs, and skidded into Jason's room. With a relieved sigh, she poured Igor into his cage and slid the door shut.

I did it. Giddy with relief, she flopped backward onto Jason's bed. Igor. Bats in the attic. Creeps appearing at her door. Crank calls. At this rate, she wouldn't be surprised if she found alien invaders camping on the front lawn.

Propping herself up on her elbows, she scanned the room. Spotless, as always. The neutral beige-and-cream plaid wallpaper, blue vertical blinds and matching bedspread were uncluttered. A neat display of Jason's beautifully intricate pen-and-ink drawings was thumbtacked to the bulletin board over his desk. Save for the drawings, it might have been a hotel room for all the evidence a thirteen-year-old boy lived here.

Had he always been this way, or did he still feel that living with her was just another temporary stop on his way to somewhere else?

The only personal item on the oak desk was a framed eight-by-ten of Jason and his mother standing by a sleek sailboat.

Claire rose and moved across the room to take a closer look. With her heavy blond mane lifted by a lakeshore breeze, Brooke looked so young, so fragile.

Why did you have to die? As she stared at her sister's face, familiar dampness weighted Claire's eyelashes and threatened to spill over. If they'd only had more time, maybe they could have grown closer someday. *Why didn't you ever come home again?*

Even as she repeated the old litany, Claire knew the answer. As she'd told Logan, their father had been upset over his and Brooke's precipitous, youthful marriage and sudden divorce, furious when Brooke started dating Randall so soon afterward. After they eloped, she cut all ties with her family, and Charles Worth never again spoke Brooke's name.

If Logan had been a better husband, that first marriage might have succeeded—and Brooke might still be alive.

Claire's gaze drifted to the young Jason in the

photograph. There was such strength in his jawline and that determined chin—so similar to the generations of Worths whose portraits still hung in Father's study back in New York.

She angled the photograph toward the sunlight. The camera lens revealed what Jason's rebellious attitude now masked. Sensitivity, humor. Even a youthful promise of sensuality in the way he looked up through his long, dark lashes. It wasn't hard to imagine teenage girls competing for his attention.

He had eyes like Logan's, Claire realized with a start. The same unusual deep blue rimmed in black, the same heavy fringe of lashes. She gave a self-deprecating chuckle. Of course, Brooke's eyes also had been blue.

Just not quite *that* blue.

Could Logan have been Jason's father? Shaking her head, she studied the photograph closely, trying to remember the tumultuous events surrounding Brooke's divorce. Had it been in fall or winter? She'd been away at boarding school when it happened. Surely a bitter and angry couple on the verge of divorce would be engaged in verbal warfare, not last-minute passion that could create a child.

Impossible. Foolish thoughts, nothing more.

After carefully replacing the photograph on Jason's desk, she headed outside to finish hanging the new gingham curtains in cabin fifteen. By the time the children flew into the kitchen after school, she'd finished the curtains, checked in three sets of guests and had answered the phone four times.

Throughout the afternoon, other faint similarities between Logan and Jason continued to nag at her. *All just your imagination,* she told herself, watching the kids walk up the lane.

But from the moment they came in the door, she found herself staring at Jason. Was Logan Jason's father? she asked herself once more. It was certainly unlikely.

Brooke would never have kept such a secret from the child's rightful father.

Or had she?

THE POSSIBILITY still tumbled through Claire's mind hours later as she tried to start a campfire on the shore. The log-cabin arrangement of the kindling at her feet looked workable. It wasn't. Each small flame faded to a wisp of smoke in seconds.

Crossing the pine logs one way, then another, she surveyed her efforts with disgust. The twins, approaching with a picnic basket held between them, and Jason, carrying a cooler, would be here in seconds. Where on earth was Fred?

A chilly evening mist along the shore sent ghost-like fingers of fog curling up through the jagged rocks and cliffs. Below, waves splashed against the granite with a metronome-steady rhythm, then drew back and disappeared into the low-lying fog.

A perfect night for roasting hot dogs and sipping

hot chocolate around a fire. *If* she could get the fire started.

Jason dumped the cooler at her side. "It won't work," he announced. "You don't have the kindling right."

With a surprising air of assurance, he rearranged the stack of pine and coaxed a small pile of bark chips until they caught fire. In moments flames surged skyward into the night. He glanced at Claire and shrugged, trying to be cool about his success, but the corners of his mouth trembled upward into a triumphant grin. "Scout Camp."

Claire laughed. "Time well spent. Someday you'll have to teach me."

Pine sap sizzled and snapped, sweetly perfuming the air. With a look of satisfaction, Jason added several logs. The golden warmth danced shadows across his face and chased away the chill on her own. Bending into the welcome warmth with her hands outstretched, she studied the boy from across the flames.

Despite his youth, there were facets of his appearance and bearing that hinted at the handsome man he would become. None that resembled Logan, Claire reminded herself firmly, rubbing her arms against a sudden chill.

Discovering Igor's return had sent him into a crazy war dance and whoops of joy. He'd even turned to hug Claire, though at the last moment he'd offered her a fumbling handshake instead. She smiled to herself. He was at that first awkward threshold of maturity.

Lissa broke Claire's reverie by tugging at her jacket sleeve. "I'm hungry! Fred says he'll be here in a minute. Can I help?"

Smiling at Lissa's familiar leapfrog conversation, Claire bent to search through the basket. She produced a handful of metal hot-dog sticks and a package of hot dogs, handed one of each to the children, then laid out the rest of their supper on a folded blanket. "Don't get too close to the fire, kids."

Their faces glowing in the amber shifting light, Lissa and Annie held their hot dogs above the flames. They were completely engrossed in their endeavors.

Jason propped his stick against some rocks and walked to a lower spot along the granite shelf, jumping back a step when a stronger wave splashed high enough to catch his sneakers. He stared down the shore. Looking over his shoulder toward Claire, he pointed south. "I bet that's Logan way over there. See—out on those rocks?"

Claire stood and joined Jason. Far in the distance, a ghostly male figure stood on a promontory, fog swirling at his feet. In the twilight, he might have been just a figment of her imagination.

"Could we invite him over for hot dogs?" Jason pleaded.

She nodded, and Jason took off down the shore like a deer.

''Mr. Fred!'' Annie's hot dog wobbled danger-
ously into the fire. ''You brung chips.''

Wearing a battered peacoat, Fred shuffled down
the small bank separating the lawn from the stretch
of granite overlooking the lake. ''Gonna lose that
dog,'' he warned, setting a box of potato chips on
the blanket.

''We left Gilbert at the house,'' Lissa piped up.
''He likes to run away and that makes Mr. Matthews mad.''

Across the campfire, Annie's hot dog slid off her
stick—just as Fred had predicted—and into the fire
with a burst of soaring, snapping flames. Her lower
lip trembled.

''Come here, sweetie, I'll help.'' Claire patted a
smooth rock next to the one she sat on and lifted
another hot dog from the picnic basket. Annie
joined her, and soon had a roasting fork loaded and
back above the fire.

Hunkered down next to Lissa, Fred surveyed the
shoreline. ''Jason off exploring?''

Claire gestured to the south. ''He saw Logan
along the shore and went to invite him to our cook-
out.''

Fred nodded his approval. ''How're you two get-
tin' along?''

''He's…'' Claire hesitated, probing carefully at
her feelings. Her doubts. ''He's a good neighbor.''

Fred threw his head back and guffawed. ''Now
there's quite an assessment.''

From behind her, Claire heard pebbles skitter across the rocks. Footsteps drew closer. She shifted to look over her shoulder. "Jason?"

Logan stepped into the circle of campfire light and immediately felt its welcome heat. Another type of warmth radiated through him as he looked down at the little girls watching their hot dogs with intense concentration, then at Claire and his old friend Fred, who had apparently just shared some sort of joke. Fred's cheeks were as rosy as a Santa's. Claire's eyes sparkled with humor.

The intimacy of the scene—this small group of people around a glowing campfire, the crackle and hiss of burning pine, the lulling splash of waves a few yards away—made him feel as though he'd stepped into a Norman Rockwell painting.

Jason tentatively offered him a hot-dog-tipped stick and Fred motioned to a log across the fire from Claire. "Last chair," Fred said with a wink.

Logan found himself moving into that scene wondering whether he should've stayed home and grilled the rib eye thawing in the refrigerator. Should've kept his resolution to stay away from Pine Cliff until he owned it once again.

He liked being alone, dammit. The peaceful silence of his house and the wild beauty of Superior's windswept shoreline were perfect for a man who prized solitude. He didn't need anyone to make his life complete. Especially the woman sitting across from him.

Fred moved over and threw an arm around Logan's shoulder as soon as he sat down. "Good seeing ya, kid."

A twinkle danced in Claire's eyes. "Nice of you to come over. Jason thought you'd like some company."

She probably could see just how much. Forcing his shoulders to relax, he gave her a level look. "Jason was insistent."

From the corner of his eye, Logan saw the boy shift uncomfortably. Chagrined, he added, "And I was glad to come."

"I can tell." Claire gave him a wry look before turning to the little girl at her side. "Finish telling us about your day, sweetie."

Without physically moving, the little blonde seemed to withdraw inside herself. Apparently she was the shy one, Annie. Lissa talked faster than jets flew, and could barrel through thirty topics at the speed of light.

"What was the best thing you did today?" Claire prompted.

"The worst was those people with the hair."

"What?" Claire looked taken aback.

Lissa made a face as she leaned over to grab a hot-dog bun. "The people in cabin eight with the funny clothes and scraggly hair. They're mean. They told us to go away and not come back."

"The Sweeneys?" She looked up at Fred, a militant gleam in her eye. "Have you seen any of this?"

"Just old hippies, I'd say. Keep odd hours, don't seem friendly. Can't say as I've seen 'em cause any trouble, though."

"Why would they come here if they don't like the lake?" Jason added, around a mouthful of hot dog. "Their shades are pulled all day. Even the ones facing the shore. Weird."

Reaching up to tuck a lock of hair behind her ear, Claire looked thoughtful. "Maybe they just aren't used to children."

"They don't *like* kids." Lissa poured catsup over her hot dog until it dripped from both ends. She gave a satisfied sigh and took a big bite. Catsup dribbled down her chin and onto her sweatshirt. "Oops."

Annie and Jason laughed. Claire shook her head. Apparently accustomed to drips and spills, she fished a plastic bag from the picnic basket, produced a wet cloth and began mopping up the red splotches trailing down the child's clothes.

"We like the grandma in the other cabin, though. She's nice," Lissa said.

Glumly, Jason shoved another hot dog onto his stick. "If she ever stops talking."

"That would be Mrs. Rogers," Fred chortled.

"She's a widow, and I'd guess she's lonely." Claire tossed the washcloth back into the picnic basket. "She's staying all month, so we're getting to know her quite well."

"So it seems." Logan reached for some chips and fixed his hot dog. Claire handed him a can of Pepsi.

"I found some opened boxes in the attic," she murmured. "Have any of you kids been up there?"

Annie and Lissa looked startled at the thought. Annie shuddered. "We never go up there."

"Nope," Jason said, his gaze fixed on the flames licking at his hot dog.

He stared at the fire for another few minutes without looking up. "Honey, you're certainly welcome to go up there anytime to look for your things," Claire told him. He didn't acknowledge her words by so much as a nod.

The murmur of small talk continued, then drifted into an easy silence as everyone turned their attention to their meal.

The crackling fire and the smoky aroma of sizzling hot dogs sent Logan's thoughts drifting back to his childhood. With his white-faced old retriever on one side and a campfire on the other, he'd spent countless nights in this same place staring up at the heavy sweep of stars overhead. He felt the same sense of peace now as he had then.

Sensing someone watching him, Logan looked up. Half-hidden in the flickering shadows, Jason sat alone. The expression on the child's face suggested that he was not finding that same peace.

The kid was probably still grieving over his parents. Missing his home, and his friends. It was tough, leaving an entire life behind. Logan knew that all too well.

Claire shook open a plastic sack and dropped her paper plate into it, disrupting his thoughts. "Trash, everyone," she said, passing the bag to Lissa. "Then it's bedtime."

The night was much colder when Logan rose and stepped away from the fire. He felt as if he'd stepped out of a snug embrace. In the distance, a dog burst into sharp barks and fierce growls.

"Gilbert and his bats," Claire said with disgust. "He must think they're planning to steal the silverware. Guess we'd better head back before he has a heart attack."

She stood up slowly and stretched, then rubbed the seat of her trim jeans. Then she started tossing odds and ends into the picnic basket while Logan doused the fire. "Next time, we're bringing lawn chairs. Right, Fred?"

Fred grimaced as he awkwardly rose. "I'm too old for this. Give me an electric blanket and I'll consider it." He glanced at Logan. "You come back, now."

Claire nodded at Logan, not quite meeting his eyes. "You're always welcome." Turning, she urged the drowsy twins to their feet.

He watched them all head up the lane. At the edge of the lawn surrounding the big old Victorian,

Claire waved goodbye to Fred, then herded the kids up the sidewalk and into the house. Fred waved back, climbed into a battered pickup and drove down the lane toward the highway.

Alone on the shore, Logan watched the lights come on, room by room, and imagined the bedtime rituals taking place inside. A hot bath for the twins. Bedtime snacks. Storybooks. Would the kids pile onto Claire's bed for stories, as they had the night of Claire's attack, when he'd stayed until daybreak? He felt his world tip off center and wondered if his life of solitude was as perfect as he'd thought.

The exterior of the house hadn't changed in all these years. Logan could still see his grandmother limping out onto the porch with her cane, even detect her faint scent of lilac if he closed his eyes. But inside, the house was now foreign land.

A family was being built there—stengthened by the love and commitment of a woman who would never walk away.

For a moment, Logan allowed himself to dream.

CLAIRE KISSED the twins good-night, then stepped into the hallway and closed the door partway. All three children had been good about bedtime. The cool night air and toasty campfire had mellowed them into docile strangers who sank willingly into bed. Nightly campfires, come blizzard, sleet or rain, might be something to consider in the future.

Gilbert thumped his tail on the kitchen floor as

she entered, clearly happy for her company. "I'll bet you set those bats on their ears, old boy." His tail thumped harder. "Mrs. Rogers will be here in a few minutes to baby-sit, and then I'll take you out for a walk."

Pouring a cup of lukewarm coffee, she settled down at the kitchen table with the resort account book and uncapped her pen. Gilbert crossed the room and rubbed his fur against her jeans.

The pages blurred before her eyes. Claire yawned, stretching her arms high overhead. Ten o'clock, she noted, glancing at the clock above the stove. Back in New York she'd be starting the paperwork filed neatly in her briefcase. The night was young everywhere else on the planet but here.

She cleared her throat, took a long swallow of coffee and tried again to concentrate. Her thoughts strayed back to the evening. To Logan.

Restless, Claire shoved her pen away. She couldn't concentrate. It was too early for bed. At the sound of Mrs. Rogers's sturdy footsteps clomping up the sidewalk, she dashed upstairs to peek in on the sleeping children, then tiptoed back downstairs.

The older woman had settled at the kitchen table with a needlework magazine and big mug of coffee. "Thanks so much for stopping in," Claire said, shrugging into her mauve down jacket. "I feel better knowing someone is here while I take Gilbert out—even though it's just for few minutes. I usually take him out while Jason's still awake.''

''No problem. I'm quite the night owl myself. Take your time.''

Claire grinned and ushered Gilbert outside. ''Come on, buddy, let's go for your last walk.'' He froze on the top step, then walked pressed against her leg. ''Some guard dog you are!''

Twilight had melted into total darkness, save for one fog-shrouded light above the laundry-shed door and the security light at the far end of the lane, where incoming cars had to take a sharp left or risked an intimate embrace with a stand of pines. She'd nearly missed that turn on her first visit.

All of the cabins were dark—except for the one just past the boathouse. Some sort of dark material covered the windows. A thin slice of light gleamed under the door. Reaching down to keep a steadying hand on Gilbert's collar, Claire sauntered past. Odd, there already were curtains and vertical blinds on all the windows. Why would the occupants cover the windows with blankets?

A thump came from inside the cabin. The soft screech of a screen door. From the corner of her eye, she saw two forms struggle out the door with a large rectangular object held between them. Her heart rocketed north and lodged at the back of her throat. *Hank and Buzz?*

Taking deep breaths, Claire forced herself to relax. Willed her heart to slow down. Of course, those two were in jail. These people were the Sweeneys. Eccentric, but harmless. And they were paid up through the end of the month.

They didn't appear to care about the usual guest activities, though. Most people went hiking or sight-seeing, or hunted agates along the shore. Claire walked past the cabin and then, cloaked in the misty darkness, she stopped and turned.

A hushed oath and stern rebuke were the only words she heard as the couple shoved their load into the back seat of the car parked a few feet from the cabin. They both climbed into the front seat and then pulled their doors shut—almost.

Claire slipped behind the sweeping branches of a pine as they drove away so slowly their tires barely crunched against the gravel. Belatedly, Gilbert growled.

What were these people doing? Once past the sharp turn that marked the start of the cabins, they switched on their headlights, slammed their car doors and sped up.

Wishing the cabin's windows weren't so well covered, so she could peek inside, she gave Gilbert a pat and continued down the lane.

There had to be a logical explanation. They were filling their cooler with ice at the twenty-four-hour grocery store in Cascade Falls, maybe. Or taking the cooler in for a late-night ice-cream run. Who on earth would consider doing anything illegal under the eyes of so many other cabin guests? Tomorrow she would stop by for a visit and lay her ridiculous thoughts to rest. Ever since Hank and Buzz had attacked her, she'd imagined danger lurking in every corner.

"Come on, boy, we've been gone long enough." Suddenly, Gilbert whined and launched himself into the darkness ahead.

"Gilbert!"

The dog didn't look back. In a split second, he disappeared into the night. Claire looked ahead with disgust. The dog was senile, barking at the bats he saw every night and taking off after nothing. Could a twelve-year-old poodle develop Alzheimer's?

She turned toward the house. She'd been gone too long already, and Gilbert must have taken care of his business by now. She'd check on the kids again, then make some coffee and try losing herself in a good book.

A soft whine from somewhere behind her stopped Claire in midstride. "Gilbert?" she whispered.

Silence. Maybe a branch had snagged his collar. Or he was hurt. Goose bumps rose on her arms. The night felt colder. She swallowed hard, her courage faltering as she imagined Hank and Buzz lurking in the darkness...slipping silently among the trees.

Nonsense. They're in jail. No one else is out here. Tomorrow the terrain would be as familiar as the back of her hand.

Taking a deep breath, she strode in the direction of Gilbert's whine. After another dozen feet or so down the lane, she heard him skitter along a bank and then heard his toenails clicking on granite. She turned toward the lake. "Gilbert?"

Gilbert bounded out of the mist and licked her hand, then wheeled and disappeared. "Gilbert, get back here!"

"Hello, Claire, it's just me." The deep voice rasped across her skin like the rough caress of a cat's tongue. Only slow. Sensual. "I didn't mean to scare you."

"*Logan?*" A flood of relief poured through her at the familiar voice. "I thought you'd gone."

"I started to leave, but…" He stopped speaking, and studied her for a long moment. "Are you okay?" he asked finally.

"I'm fine. I've just been a little jumpy tonight."

She became aware of his warmth, the sheltering breadth of his shoulders, the faint scent of his aftershave. Had she stepped closer, or had he? Perhaps it was an illusion created by the mist, and by the moonlight breaking through the clouds overhead.

He breathed her name so softly that his voice didn't penetrate the silence. She felt it in her soul.

Slowly, with infinite gentleness, he drew her into his arms, sliding his hands down to the small of her back. Bending, he rested his forehead against hers and took a ragged breath.

Emotion warring with logic, Claire stiffened as his hands drifted lower and settled over the backside of her jeans, but when his lips brushed her forehead, her bones started to soften. When he curved a broad hand at her nape and drew her into a kiss, his lips warm and soft on her own, her legs turned to hot fudge. If he hadn't been holding her, she would have hit the ground. Her blood had never surged with such fire at a mere touch. She'd never had to suppress an urge to rip the buttons off a man's shirt with her teeth.

With her *teeth?* The thought startled her into action. What in heaven's name was she doing on a deserted lakeshore with Logan Matthews? How many other women had he seduced with such charm, such an effective wounded-soul look in his eyes? Or was that just an excuse she held on to?

With each day, it became harder to remember why she should keep her distance. She would have to try a little harder—already she cared for him far too much. Claire spun out of his arms and faced him from a safer distance.

"Good night, Logan."

As if he'd expected her to bolt, he showed no hint of surprise. But then, such an innocent embrace wouldn't have affected him. He wouldn't share the hollow, strangely bereft feeling she felt at the sudden loss of contact.

Claire walked up the slope toward the lane without a backward glance. Gilbert wavered between

Logan and Claire, then moped along behind her. "Traitor," she hissed. "See if he buys you Super Sirloin dog food."

She was halfway up the sidewalk when she heard the telephone ringing. In the nighttime silence, the noise was enough to wake the dead. Or sleeping children upstairs and the guests in the cabins near the laundry building.

Claire rushed into the house and snatched the receiver. Breathlessly, she turned to hold the door open for Gilbert, then sank into her desk chair. Mrs. Rogers had dozed off over her magazine, oblivious to the noise.

A prickling sensation lifted the hairs at her nape as she said, "Hello?"

All she heard were several deep, slow breaths, then one sharp click as the caller hung up.

CHAPTER TEN

CLAIRE STARED at the receiver in her hand. The phone number of a local pay phone was displayed on the Caller ID. Oh, God, she'd managed to put last night's calls out of her mind. But they'd come from the same number.

Maybe someone was casing the place, making sure she wouldn't be home. The odd noises at night now took on new meaning. The damaged washing machine. The scattered papers and books in the attic.

And the night Hank and Buzz had attacked her.

The memories of those men and that night crashed through her. She could smell their stench of sweat and stale beer. Feel Hank's sweaty hands on her skin. Her heart picked up a staccato beat.

"You've got something I need, and you damn well know what it is," Hank had said. What had he meant? She'd never dealt with the man in her life.

Oh, Lord. Please let them still be in jail.

With trembling fingers, she dialed the county jail in Cascade Falls.

A dispatcher answered the phone. "The suspects

arrested out at Pine Cliff?'' Claire heard the woman shuffle through some papers. ''They were on forty-eight-hour hold and had their preliminary hearing this afternoon. They posted bond and were released.''

''What?'' Stunned, Claire sank into the nearest kitchen chair. Mrs. Rogers still snored softly in her chair on the other side of the table. ''I should have been notified!''

''We wouldn't have released them without letting you know.''

Claire twisted the telephone cord around her finger. ''No one called.''

''Wait a minute—'' Voices hummed in the background, then the dispatcher cleared her throat. ''George here says that they tried calling several times throughout the day but didn't get an answer. The deputy said he was going out this afternoon to tell you.''

Ice slithered down Claire's spine. ''And that would have been Miller?''

After a pause, the dispatcher cleared her throat. ''Yes, ma'am. I'm really sorry. We've been short-staffed, but this never should have happened.''

''Can you at least tell me who they were?''

''Gerald Thompkins and Willie Black, ma'am. Some high-powered Minneapolis lawyer came up and posted thirty thousand dollars bond for each of them. He took them back to Hennepin County pending trial.''

"How could the judge let them go free?"

"Unfortunately, that's how the system works."

Claire hung up the phone, her thoughts racing.

Hank and Buzz hadn't simply blundered down the lane to Pine Cliff a few nights ago, drunk and daring and full of themselves, too inebriated to consider the consequences of their actions. Hank—Gerald?—had been trying to get something from her with his talk about threats and secrets. Maybe Randall had cheated them on some business deal. Surely the two had headed back to the Twin Cities, exactly as the dispatcher said. Harassing her further would be just plain stupid so soon after arrest.

But they'd both looked broke, as if rustling up beer money would be a major feat. How had they come up with a good lawyer and that kind of bail?

She'd been uneasy all day, but now that feeling escalated at the speed of light. She looked at the open windows. The dry rustle of breeze-tossed branches outside could mask a prowler's approach. Anyone could slit a screen, curl a hand under the sash, then shove it open.

She shivered as she forced herself to walk calmly across the kitchen. With deliberate care she locked each window, pulled each shade.

The older woman shifted in her chair, opened her eyes, and yawned. "Oh, my. Did I fall asleep?"

"Just dozed off. Do you want to stay here at the house? I've got an extra bedroom."

"Land sakes, no. My cabin is only a little ways down the lane. I love walking at night."

"But it's so late—"

With both palms planted on the table, Mrs. Rogers hoisted herself to her feet. "If you're worried, you can send your dog with me for company."

Logically, there should be no cause for immediate concern, Claire decided. There were no pay phones at Pine Cliff. The nearest was in Wolf River, so the anonymous caller couldn't be anywhere close. Mrs. Rogers's cabin wasn't more than a hundred yards away. "Let me walk you home, okay? I'll leave Gilbert here, with the kids."

Claire locked the door behind them, made sure the elderly woman got into her cabin safely, then jogged back to the house and carefully locked the door for the night. Gilbert was still curled up on the rug in front of the sink when she walked in. He raised his head to look at her, then dropped it back down onto his paws. The house was still quiet.

Flipping off the lights as she left the kitchen, Claire glanced over her shoulder to double-check the back door. Locked, safe and sound.

Next to it stood a box containing new dead bolts for each door of the house and one for every cabin—Fred's first priority tomorrow morning. Soon she would be able to breathe a lot easier.

Gilbert still hadn't come upstairs by the time she'd changed and brushed her teeth. When he failed to come when she called, she sighed and went down to the kitchen.

He was definitely awake now. Standing motionless in the center of the room with the hair raised along his spine, he stared at her. ''Gilbert!'' she called, exasperated.

Gilbert whined, hung back, as if the distance to her side were an impassable stretch of quicksand. ''C'mon, you goofy dog.''

When she turned away she heard him bound across the floor. He lurched past her and thundered up the stairs, but at the landing he froze. Growling softly, he backed up a step. His growl grew deeper, louder.

Claire's breath caught in her throat. Gilbert was a bit deaf and not very bright, but even he had basic canine capabilities. *Were the kids okay?* Fear snaked through her as she took the stairs two at a time. By the top step, she'd had time for logic. No doubt, Gilbert had heard another bat blunder down from the attic.

At the upstairs landing she warily surveyed the baseboards in the hallway. Nothing moved—no little leather wings flapped helplessly against the floor, no small creatures looked up at her in terror. Gilbert growled again, his body stiff and his attention fastened on the far end of the hall.

The attic door stood ajar several inches, spilling a narrow apron of faint light across the hall.

How had she missed that when she'd been up

here getting ready for bed? A chill swept through her. There would be a good explanation, she told herself, trying to still the images her mind conjured. Maybe Jason had been in the attic, and had forgotten to turn off the lights.

Resolutely, Claire walked down the hall and pulled the door open wide. A half-dozen or more lightbulbs were spaced across the cavernous attic, but the dim wash of light illuminating the narrow staircase suggested only a few of them were on.

"Come on, Gilbert," she coaxed. "Keep me company."

The old dog looked up at her and whined, took another step back.

"Gilbert?"

With surprising speed, the dog spun away and scrambled down the hall, his toenails clawing furiously at the hardwood floor. Slipping and sliding, landing on his side twice, he barely made the turn into Jason's room. A sudden creak of bedsprings identified his destination.

Claire started up the attic stairs by herself, firmly turning her thoughts to events of the day.

Despite several frustrating guests, she'd kept things under control. The odd behavior of the Sweeneys—well—she'd keep an eye on them in the future.

By the top step Claire decided she'd done well so far, despite her father's dire predictions of failure. A capable, intelligent woman could do anything if she just used her head. Smiling to herself, she lifted her gaze to survey the attic.

It was all she could do to choke back a scream.

LOGAN FELT as if he'd taken a November dip in Superior when he walked into his house.

All the way home he'd wavered between frustration and an odd sense of relief. He'd moved too fast, wanting more of her than she would give or he should want. Hell, he shouldn't have kissed her at all, but somewhere in the moonlight and mist he'd lost his common sense.

Now he was back at his house—a structure as welcoming and warm as a mausoleum in Antarctica—wishing he were anywhere else. He'd told the decorator to select whatever would work, thinking she'd do a much better job of it than he would.

Big mistake. Her gaudy choices for adding ''warmth'' reminded him of framed bruises and blood splatters on the walls, while the new tabletop sculptures looked like aliens undergoing torture. First thing Monday, she'd better be here to collect every last item she'd brought, or it would all be out in the garage.

Logan considered his schedule as he headed upstairs to his office. Originally, he'd expected a few days of relaxation in his new home after straightening out any minor complications over buying Pine Cliff. He hadn't expected to encounter a stubborn Worth who refused to sell.

Much less one capable of tearing down his greatest defenses, making him want her with such unreasoning desire that he forgot the past. Long-term relationships without commitment were comfortable, familiar. Painless to leave. Things would never be that easy with Claire.

Settling behind the massive oak desk in his office, he firmly shoved aside all thoughts of Claire's soft arms curving around his shoulders, her lips melting beneath his own.

He studied his planner.

And still inhaled the light fragrance of peaches she'd worn tonight.

He ran a forefinger down a list of goals for the coming week.

And felt the warmth of her body against his own, her breasts pressed against his chest.

He picked up a pen and began to write.

Contact Hayward Heating Systems. Call the county building inspector.

Heat pooled in him. Low, insistent.

Check on the building codes in Blue Earth County.

His thoughts slid back to the vision of Claire's upturned face, her eyes dewy with wonder after that solitary, shattering kiss.

Logan slammed the planner shut and launched to his feet, then paced the floor.

Call the contractor in White Bear Lake...

He shook his head sharply, clearing away the

much more enticing thoughts of Claire that threatened to eclipse everything else in his brain.

Fortunately his partner Harold seemed to be doing well enough back in Minneapolis. The reports he faxed and his daily e-mails showed reasonable progress on their two largest projects.

Another couple weeks up here wouldn't hurt. He hadn't taken a vacation in years. In fact, if he waited a little longer, he might be able to settle a deal on her property. Hell. If he stayed, he'd have more time with *her*.

Staring at the wall of windows facing the night, he heard the rush of waves against the shore, but saw only the reflections of his office and himself. The man mirrored there in shades of gray looked like someone three days dead. Cold and alone.

Once, the thought of owning the rest of his family property had driven him, tantalized him. Promised a sense of victory and validation after far too many years. But now, his pending victory no longer seemed quite as sweet. Unexpected regret still lingered.

It had to be over his discovery of Brooke's children. Brave little kids, having to leave the life they'd known for a new one with their aunt. He had no biological or legal ties to the children, yet he felt some inexplicable bond.

But surely any man worth his salt would be affected by his ex-wife's young orphans.

Which explained his growing awareness of their

aunt, he realized with a profound sense of relief. The whole situation had upset his equilibrium, complicated his plans. It had been so simple until he'd met Claire Worth and those kids.

With a muttered curse Logan turned to his computer, pulled up the Wickham Towers file, and settled in for a productive night. Instead, the hours passed long and slow, in a languorous drift through the memories he'd shelved years ago and thoughts about the stubborn woman who stood between him and his dreams.

When the telephone rang at two in the morning, impatience spilled into his voice. *"Hello?"*

Silence. Followed by a quavery, "I'm s-sorry to call so late—"

"Yes?"

"I—I called the sheriff, but they say he and the deputy are going to be a while. I've got some trouble here—" he heard her take a deep breath "—and wonder if you could come over. The kids—"

"The kids?" Visions of flames or intruders sent him thundering down the stairs and reaching for his car keys with the portable phone still at his ear. "Claire—"

The phone on her end went dead. "Claire?" She didn't respond.

Slamming the receiver on the counter, he spun around and raced out the door. Halfway to his truck he pivoted and went back to retrieve the shotgun locked in a downstairs closet. Whatever the threat, he'd be ready.

Minutes later Logan slammed on the brakes in front of her house, parking at a crazy angle on the edge of the lawn. He reached for the shotgun. Without bothering to slam the door, he ran up the sidewalk.

The house was still standing. No fire trucks or ambulances crowded the lane. The cabins along the shoreline were dark. Only a few lights were on in the big old house. Claire stood on the back steps, hugging herself, her eyes huge in her pale face. Even from this distance, despite the bulky robe she wore, he could see her trembling.

Logan strode across the lawn. "Are you all okay?"

"So far."

He tried to keep the edge from his voice. "What's going on?"

Lifting her shoulders, she opened the screen door, motioning him to follow. The kitchen appeared untouched. A glimpse into the living room revealed no evidence of struggle.

"Dammit, what's wrong? Why did you hang up?"

"I—I heard a noise, and ran to check all the locks." With a finger to her lips, she crossed the kitchen and led the way up to the second floor. "Please—come upstairs."

At the top of the stairs, she stepped aside and

gestured toward the door leading to the attic, looking even more pale than she had before. "This way."

Logan walked past her and strode to the attic stairs. "There have always been bats up there, if that's what you're worrying about."

"In a manner of speaking." He could see her struggle to take control of herself. She stood a little taller, her voice level.

"So I raced over here to protect you from bats?"

"Not exactly," she said.

She followed him, her breath quickening against his back. At the top of the stairs he scanned the rafters for darting shadows.

Nothing moved.

"They aren't up there," she whispered.

"Of course. You *don't* have bats. At two in the morning, you suddenly realized this and wondered why?" He turned, prepared to dry tears and provide comfort.

The expression on Claire's face could have seared a sirloin at fifty feet.

"This is no joke, Sherlock." Lifting one slender arm, she pointed to the left. Her hand trembled. "Doesn't this seem strange to you?"

Strange didn't quite describe the sight of endless packing boxes stacked and strewn from one end of the huge attic to the other. At least a dozen boxes were opened, erupting with clothing and papers that flowed like lava across the floor.

"Interesting storage system." Then he followed her wide-eyed gaze lower. His stomach clenched.

A dozen small, bloodied bats lay on the floor.

They were dead, and they were laid out in two perfect rows.

"Did you—"

Claire shook her head vehemently. "I didn't touch them."

"Does Jason have a BB gun? Air rifle?"

"Of course not! He wouldn't do this." Glaring at Logan, she waved a hand to encompass the spacious attic. "It's not just the bats. Every box was taped shut. I've even resealed the ones we've been going through, to keep out the dust. *Someone* has been up here."

With a defenseless woman and her children in the house. Or perhaps she and the kids had been just outside, in clear view from the curved, eyebrow attic windows. The urge to shove a fist through the intruder's face made Logan clench his hands into fists at his sides.

Arranging those little gray corpses with such precision was not the act of an ordinary thief. Nor of teenagers on a cruel lark. Most people detested bats, assuming they were rabid and dangerous, and few people would handle them, much less arrange them with such exquisite care.

"Who had access to the attic today?"

Claire hugged her waist. "The kids. Fred. Me."

From beneath the bats, a small splash of bright

blue reflected the lights overhead. Logan leaned closer. It was a photograph. Soaked in blood. Logan's heart shot into his throat. "My God, Claire."

She moved closer, but he held her back with his arm. "Don't touch anything."

"What is it?" The defensive note in her voice had fled. Sensing her growing fear, he rose and spun around to catch her arm. She was staring at the exposed edges of the photo. Her face had turned as pale as death.

"It's of you and the kids."

"I don't *have* any pictures. M-my cameras are still packed away."

"Someone gave the picture to you?"

"No one!"

He tugged at one corner of the photo, then let it drop. "It's of you and the kids washing the dog."

Her eyes widened, her chin trembled. Logan pulled her into an embrace and tucked her head beneath his chin. For a moment she felt as lifeless as one of the girls' plastic dolls.

"We washed Gilbert late this morning for the first time. I didn't see anyone with a camera." Her voice faltered. "At first I thought Hank and Buzz broke in to retaliate, but they were just released this afternoon and returned to the Twin Cities. They couldn't have taken the photograph."

Logan tightened his arms around her. "Did the sheriff's office say when someone would get out here?"

"The dispatcher said that they're finishing up on a burglary at the south end of the county. One of them will get here as soon as he can, but if more urgent calls come in, who knows?"

Swearing under his breath, Logan rested his chin on her head. "I'm staying."

Claire gave him a shaky smile as she stepped back. "Thanks," she said finally. "You're a good friend. There's a guest room on the second floor—"

"I'll camp out in the living room," Logan said firmly, taking one last scan of the attic before starting down the stairs. "Just go on to bed. Ten bucks says you won't see a deputy until morning."

At the second-floor landing she stopped at a hallway linen closet and gathered some blankets and a pillow. "I do appreciate your offer," she said, starting down the stairs toward the main floor.

Following her, he studied the firm set of her shoulders, the determination in her stride. For someone who'd always been surrounded by household staff or high-rise security personnel, it had taken guts to move to an isolated place like this. Most women he knew would have been packed and gone after the first midnight cry of an owl.

When she turned at the bottom of the stairs, her oversize robe slipped off one shoulder, revealing a soft gown edged in some sort of frothy lace, with a neckline dipping beyond the bounds of innocence. Despite the robe, the faint glow of light from the kitchen accented her slender curves and long, long legs. Even disheveled, she was more provocative than any woman he'd ever seen.

In the living room, she put the armload of linens on an end table, glanced at the motley collection of furniture, then gave him a rueful smile. "You'll never be comfortable on that old sofa."

"Doesn't matter."

"And it's so cold down here—"

"I don't intend to sleep. I'd rather keep an eye on the place."

Without conscious thought, Logan crossed the room and settled his arms around her shoulders. *So warm. So smooth and soft.* His heartbeat quickened, thudded against his ribs. He expected her to pull away. Instead, she swayed into his embrace.

He cradled her head against the hollow of his neck. She fit perfectly there, like the final piece to a puzzle he'd given up on years ago. As the heated surface of her body aligned with his, her subtle, clean fragrance filled his senses. He bent his head, lowered his mouth to hers. A reflex, nothing more.

Until her mouth opened beneath his and she kissed him back. And then that gentle kiss wasn't enough.

"Get on upstairs before we do something you'll regret," he said, pulling her closer.

Regret? Her thoughts reeling, Claire stepped back and fumbled with the switch of a small lamp on the table by her hip. Soft golden light bathed the room, bronzing Logan's skin and darkening his hair to bittersweet chocolate. Any hesitance she might have felt dissolved as her senses absorbed the full impact of the man before her.

Perhaps it was just a trick of the lighting, but his eyes seemed to darken as he covered her hand with one of his own. "Good night, Claire." His deep, gravel voice lowered, wrapping around her like a velvet embrace. Powerful, yet infinitely gentle. "I promise, you and the kids will be safe tonight."

She stared into his lean, dark face. Time stopped. The room spun and faded like a carousel dissolving in heavy mist. All she heard was the steady beat of Logan's heart.

She remembered the night he'd sat up with Annie nestled against his chest. Saw him reaching out to Jason. Protecting her with his life. Realization slammed through her, sweeping away forever all of the lies she'd ever heard about this man.

Claire looked up at him, and when she saw the tender possessiveness in his eyes, her words came straight from her heart. "I—I need you."

"I'll be here, watching over you."

"Come up with me." Her gaze slipped to his hard, sensual mouth. Anticipation raced like wildfire through her veins. "Please."

He searched her face before finally taking her hand in his. His eyes darkening even more, he reached out and traced her cheek with his fingertips, then lingered over the curve of her mouth. Exquisite sensations flew through her, warm and sweet and intimate.

Perhaps just this once the angels would allow her a taste of heaven. She could pretend it was real and imagine it was forever.

Nothing had ever felt more right than the moment she stepped into Logan's arms.

CHAPTER ELEVEN

WHEN THEY ENTERED her bedroom, Claire quietly shut the door and locked it, then turned to face him with a haunting look of vulnerability and desire in her eyes.

He'd come to protect Claire and the children, not to seduce her, and after all she'd been through tonight, she needed a comforting presence, nothing more. But when her lips parted in silent invitation, he couldn't turn away.

She melted against him, soft and yielding, and when her sigh feathered against his shoulder, a surge of need rocketed to his very soul. It felt so right. Inevitable. As if some part of him had waited a lifetime for this moment.

A kaleidoscope of sensations spun through him when he lowered his mouth to hers. He felt as if he'd never kissed a woman until now. She tasted of sex and sin and sultry innocence. Of unexplored passion and long, hot nights.

A primitive sense of satisfaction and possession crashed through him on waves of heat.

Settling a hand against the delicate arch of her neck, he felt her pulse hammer beneath his thumb.

With infinite care he eased her robe off her shoulders, savoring each new millimeter of access to her—

Flannel?

He'd glimpsed her provocative, lace-edged neckline, but now he could see the rest of her gown— soft white flannel sprinkled with rosebuds and violets, a thousand tiny buttons from waist to neck. The effect couldn't have been more virginal if it had been a nun's habit.

Logan bit back a grin. "Just how many buttons are there?"

"I'm sorry—I never expected..."

The embarrassment in her voice made his heart turn over. "Honey, you could be in fatigues and army boots and I wouldn't want you any less."

She stared at him, her breath fast and uneven as he lingered with deliberate care over each button before flicking it open and descending to the next. He felt the heat of her body and the thud of her heart beneath the soft material. As the gown opened, he kissed each newly revealed bit of flesh.

Only a few more buttons. He moved slower, as if he might take until next week to finish. And dropped lower, to where his hand brushed the soft inner curve of her breast.

"*Logan.*" She drew in a sharp breath, her body arching into his touch.

He'd never realized flannel could be so provocative. It held her heat, molded softly to her body.

Gauzy material revealed, but this gown clothed her secrets, making his hunger more acute.

When he reached the last button, he hesitated, letting her anticipate. Imagine. Then he rose and captured her mouth in another kiss.

"You're so very beautiful." Her fragrances of citrus shampoo and lemon bath powder teased at his senses, evoking thoughts of sunlight and sweet promise.

A child cried out.

They both froze.

Again, a frightened voice pierced the silence. "Mommy? I need my mommy!"

Her eyes locked on his, Claire blinked and stepped back. "That's Lissa. I—I'm sorry. The kids still have nightmares, sometimes. About the accident. I have to go—"

"It's okay." Logan shook off the disorientation clouding his senses. "I'd better go back downstairs."

Claire nodded, then disappeared down the darkened hallway without a sound.

Stunned, Logan closed his eyes. In that brief moment she had opened up a part of his heart he'd thought closed forever; a place where caring rivaled passion, and where both could take off like wildfire—unstoppable, overwhelming.

More than anything else on earth, he wanted her back in his arms.

Since sleep was out of the question, he wandered through the darkened house checking windows, flipping on lights in empty rooms, feeling a pervasive sense of loss every step of the way. Deeper involvement would be a mistake for them both.

If he said it often enough, he might even believe it was true.

Before heading downstairs, he looked in on the children. Both girls were now asleep and snuggled under their covers, their hair pulled back in ponytails that spread across their shoulders like tumbled gold silk. When he stopped at the next room, he edged the door open a few inches and listened. Jason slept soundly. Logan smiled to himself, turned to leave, but something on the far wall caught his eye.

The pale hallway light streamed across a desk, illuminating the bulletin board that hung above it. Neatly arranged on the board were a half-dozen pen-and-ink sketches. Intricate castles and fanciful beasts, robots of impossible complexity in form and function. Logan whistled under his breath as he studied each drawing. The kid was talented. Extremely talented. He certainly hadn't inherited it from Brooke, so maybe Randall had been the one with an artistic bent.

Logan silently pulled the door closed, then went downstairs and checked the first-floor windows and door locks. He headed for the kitchen. After pouring a cup of decaf, he settled into one of the kitchen chairs, folded his arms over his chest and stretched his legs. At any suspicious noise, he could be on his feet in seconds.

With luck, he'd catch the intruder entering the house. The bastard would be sorry he'd come. And would damn sure explain why he had chosen to hit Pine Cliff.

Still, Logan's nerves vibrated with tension. Restless anticipation. He forced himself to relax. The sheriff would show up, sooner or later. A crew would arrive in a week or so to install Claire's security system. She would be fine.

After a last scan of the room, he willed himself to drift back into memories of the past.

But all he saw were images of Claire.

MORNING CAME on dog's feet—with toenails clicking across the vinyl flooring, scratching at the back door. Logan sat up with a jerk and glanced around. Lacy curtains lifted on a light breeze and sent pale coins of sunlight dancing across the room. Gilbert stood pressed against the back door, giving him a desperate look.

Logan crossed the room and let the dog out. "You don't earn your keep," he muttered, watching Gilbert amble sedately across the lawn.

The upstairs rooms were still quiet, though it was nearly a quarter of six and everyone would be awake soon. Logan tried to envision the confusion of children, clothes, breakfasts, backpacks and the arrival of the Wolf River school bus. It would be best to get out of the way before they awoke. Less awkward.

A few hours of counting sheep and regrets hadn't made things much more clear than they'd been last night. He'd wanted her—still did. Not just her body, though the glow of her skin in the moonlight and her luminous gray eyes would have tempted a saint.

It was more than that. An increasingly familiar warning flashed through his thoughts. It would be all too easy to fall victim to her wit, the touch of those gentle hands, the way she smiled at the kids with such total devotion. Or the way she could nail him with a sharp observation and a quick grin.

Luckily, he'd remembered why it was so important to stay clear.

Searching blindly through his jeans pockets for his truck keys, Logan's gaze strayed to the royal blue Twins jacket lying across the rolltop desk next to the door. Jason's, he guessed, reaching out to touch the smooth satin of one sleeve.

Peeking from beneath the edge of the jacket were the bright eyes of a worn pink panda. Annie's. Around the room, there was other evidence of the children who lived here—a stray purple sock, a refrigerator door camouflaged by crayoned pictures and memos from school. A tennis ball crammed under the overhang of a cupboard.

The place was clean. But there was evidence of

life, activity. The business of living with kids. Even with its occupants asleep, the house seemed to hum with life.

In a few minutes, Logan would be back at his own house, where the only thing that hummed was the refrigerator paneled in white to blend in with the kitchen walls. Hell. That house was no more welcoming now than it had been with exposed studs and skeletal rafters. It was a damn lonely place.

Logan looked out the window at Gilbert, who now sat placidly at the edge of the lawn. Why hadn't he thought of it before? A dog would add life and energy to his house. He needed company. Someone—something to talk to. A dog would be ideal.

Logan stepped outside and closed the door quietly behind him, then strolled down the sidewalk. The Explorer was still parked haphazardly at the edge of the lawn. Jingling the keys in one hand, he reached for the door. It swung open at his touch. The interior lights didn't flicker.

With a frustrated growl, Logan remembered lunging out of the vehicle the night before and leaving the door ajar.

He'd have to come back later, when people were up and about, and ask for a jump start. The morning was too beautiful to waste. A brisk walk home would be a pleasure.

After several strides, he stopped. Claire and the kids might wonder why the truck was still in the yard. Spinning on his heel, he went back to the house. He left a brief note on the kitchen table.

The telephone jangled as he turned to leave, its shrill tone rivaled that of a fire alarm. He hesitated, but there was no sound of activity upstairs. He picked up the receiver.

"Pine Cliff."

"Who is this?" The male voice dripped with suspicion.

Logan swore under his breath. If he lived a thousand years he would never forget the sound of that voice. Charles Worth. Answering the phone had been a major mistake, and now Claire would pay for it.

He forced his words through clenched teeth. "The manager isn't available. Can I help you?"

After a stunned pause, Worth drew in a sharp breath. "My God."

"Can I take a message?"

"What the hell are you doing there?"

"Would you rather call back?" Logan asked quietly.

"One daughter wasn't enough?" Worth's tone dripped venom. "Last time was nothing, Matthews. I want you out of that house."

Still the charmer he'd always been, apparently.

"I'm sorry, you must be thinking of someone else." Logan quietly hung up the phone.

Continuing this conversation would do more harm than good. The years had not dimmed the old man's hatred. In fact, there had been an odd note of fresh anger—perhaps even fear—in his voice.

Logan didn't feel all that friendly himself, but he was no longer an inexperienced college kid confronting powerful lawyers and a vindictive, hate-filled man. If he faced off against Claire's father now, Claire would be the one to suffer most.

Logan turned to retrieve the note he'd left on the table. She deserved some warning before hellfire and brimstone descended.

After brief consideration, he wrote, *Your father called, but didn't leave a message.* Knowing that Logan had taken the call would be all Claire needed to know.

CHAPTER TWELVE

CLAIRE WANTED to curl up under the covers and die, but first, she needed to get the kids up, dressed, fed, and on the school bus. Surely the morning commotion would provide enough distraction until that moment when the house was quiet. If not, the children were going to witness the meltdown of a woman who had been supremely stupid the night before.

By the time the children left for school she felt slightly better. Finding one lost shoe, discovering that a drawer overflowing with pink and white socks held not a single matching pair and racing to flag down an impatient bus driver had put things in perspective. Now, with the morning checkouts gone and Fred busy installing better locks on the cabin doors, she was back in control.

Smoothing her beige slacks and adjusting the collar of her cream silk blouse, she gave herself a quick evaluation in the long mirror that hung over the sofa in the living room. Dressier clothes weren't as comfortable as her fleecy sweatshirts and worn jeans, but first impressions were important. The first security company sales representative, due any time, was going to see a woman who expected competitive prices and prompt, professional service. Very prompt.

Being in control—if only for these few hours— felt good. After the salesman left, she would be back to the uncertainty of trying to find out who was threatening her existence at Pine Cliff. And she would be left with ample time to ponder the embarrassing scene last night with Logan.

At the sound of tires crunching up the lane, she swept a hand through her hair and picked up the notebook and pen she'd laid on an end table, then strode to the front door. But when she stepped outside and shaded her eyes against the reflection of the morning sun on the lake, a police cruiser instead of an upscale sales-rep sedan was pulling to a stop at the end of the sidewalk.

Didn't the sheriff himself ever do these calls? Wayne Miller, of all the luck, had arrived, rumpled and short-tempered and apologetic for the delay.

When she showed him the rows of dead bats and the bloodied photograph, he did a double take. "Someone wanted to make this personal. Anyone you might suspect?"

Claire gave him a steely look. "The two you arrested out here a few days ago. I didn't hear about their release until yesterday afternoon."

He had the good grace to look uncomfortable. "I've already heard about that from the sheriff. I was headed out here, but got sidetracked by a speeder and then got called back into town. One thing after another..." He cleared his throat. "Any sign of forced entry?"

"None. But the blood was fresh when I first saw it, so I figure the guy was here sometime late yesterday afternoon. I don't lock my doors until night."

He picked his way through the attic with a clipboard and pen in hand, taking occasional notes. "Do you have a list of what was taken?"

"Nothing. At least, not that I can see. There's a television and VCR downstairs. Some jewelry on my dresser, some camera equipment still packed away in labeled boxes...it all seems to be here."

Miller frowned as he scribbled a few more notes. "Any property damage—vandalism, or damage to windows or doors?"

"Nothing."

"Know anyone who might have a grudge against you?"

"None!"

The deputy stopped writing and looked at Claire over his half-glasses. "You sure someone was here?"

Speechless, Claire stared at him, then dropped her gaze to the collection of little corpses on the bloodstained photograph on the floor. "You think I had kamikaze bats?"

A tic started jerking at Miller's right eyelid. "No.

Are you sure you don't know anyone who would
try to scare you like this?''

"Killing those animals and leaving a bloody photograph are pretty extreme tactics, aren't they?''
Claire swung one hand wide, encompassing the attic. "What about those opened boxes?''

The deputy clicked his ballpoint closed and
tucked it into his breast pocket. "Do you have anything of significant value that's packed away?
Something an acquaintance could be after?''

"Your department just released the two guys
who attacked me.'' Claire reined in her heating
temper. "Who would be more likely to arrange
this?''

"Ma'am, I'm taking the bloodied photo in as evidence. We'll photograph the scene and lift fingerprints off the surfaces you believe were tampered
with. We'll compare them to those of the two men
who were arrested out here.'' He reached for the
evidence field kit he'd left on an old chair. "A
match isn't likely, though. As you pointed out, the
time frame isn't right. Plus both of 'em are steady
guys, who've held long-term jobs down in the Twin
Cities. They say they came up to go fishing and just
got skunked. They claim they didn't touch you.''

Claire shoved a hand through her hair and paced
back and forth. "They're lying. And they're out
there somewhere. Can you check whether they left
the area?''

Miller rocked on his heels. "We can verify that

they arrived back in the 'Cities. Otherwise, you'll need to talk to the county attorney for further information on the case.''

She threw up her hands and suppressed the urge to scream. "So, unless we have a body or two lying around, you can't do anything?"

"If these fingerprints match, we'll have the suspects picked up right away. In the meantime, we'll start patrolling the area. Lock your doors and windows at night, and don't let anyone in.'' Miller opened the evidence case and sorted through several vials, then withdrew a soft brush and a container of black powder. "If you have any more problems, call right away." He nudged an open packing box with his shoe. "These boxes were all closed?"

"Even the ones I'd been sorting through. I sealed each of them afterward to keep out dust."

He gave her a satisfied nod. "Then someone ripping open the tape would have left some good prints."

Thirty minutes later, Claire stood on the front steps of the house and watched the squad car pull away, then tipped her face into the sun and closed her eyes.

Soon a new security system would be installed in the house. By the end of the day, Fred's new dead-bolt locks would be installed. From now on, she would watch over the children and Pine Cliff like a hawk. The thought of unknown prowlers sent icy waves of fear down her spine.

Concentrating on her family's safety would be a welcome diversion from the trickle of embarrassment that still lingered over Logan's abrupt departure this morning. He hadn't waited to say goodbye. And his note was terse and unemotional.

At nine o'clock, the phone rang. Setting aside the stacks of bills and discarded paper, Claire took a sip of lukewarm coffee and picked up the phone. The caller started speaking before Claire could say "Pine Cliff."

"Why is Logan Matthews in your house?"

"Dad?" Nothing in Logan's note had suggested that her father had recognized his ex-son-in-law. Claire's heart sank. Her father's phone calls were invariably long and adversarial, and this one would be both, in spades.

"I can't believe you'd be so irresponsible."

Gripping the receiver tighter, Claire pinched the bridge of her nose between a thumb and forefinger, warding off the first throbs of a headache that would start at any moment.

"Excuse me?"

"Is he there now?"

"No, he's not." Claire massaged her forehead with her fingertips. "This is really not your—"

"The safety of my grandchildren and daughter are my business, Claire."

Silently Claire counted to ten, then lied through her teeth. "I appreciate your concern."

She picked up one of the children's pencils on the table and began sketching cartoons on a napkin. Scowling faces. Snarling wolves. Warlords with beaklike noses that hung to their knees.

"You know what Matthews's after."

"Look, *Dad*. Logan is simply a neighbor." Claire rested an elbow on the table and dropped her forehead into her palm.

"Was he there all night?"

The pencil in Claire's hand snapped. This was not his business, but she wouldn't give him the satisfaction of hearing her hedge about it. "Yes, he stayed. And I was thankful, because—"

Now there's another topic to start. One word about those poor murdered bats and her father would have five armed guards hired and heading for Pine Cliff within the hour, with orders to bring her back to New York.

"—because I was worried about some noises outside. Just raccoons, probably."

Her father swore. "You know he married your sister for our money," he said flatly.

Claire snorted. "I hardly think he's after mine. As you well know, I don't have any. He, on the other hand, seems to be doing very well."

"At marrying women for money and then moving on when he's taken them for everything they're worth?"

"He's an architect, okay? Look, I really—"

"Logan Matthews is a bastard. I made sure our lawyers bled him dry in that divorce. Stay away from him, *and keep him away from my grandchildren.*"

Again, it came to this. Orders, veiled threats. Claire rose from her chair and took a deep breath. "Frankly, I don't see a problem with being civil to my neighbors."

"You have no idea what could happen." His voice lowered, and if Claire hadn't known him so well, she might have thought it held a distinct note of anxiety. "You're playing with fire."

I love you, too, Dad. Claire tactfully ended the conversation and hung up, her fingertips lingering on the cool plastic of the receiver as she recomposed herself.

Looking at the collage of children's drawings, school-activity announcements and sticky notes on the refrigerator, she wondered what it might have been like to have a father who cared for her as much as he cared about profit and loss.

He was wrong about Logan, but too stubborn ever to reconsider. She was going to find out exactly what happened fourteen years ago, and confront him with the truth. She suspected that her family owed Logan more than just an apology for the past. And like it or not, the Worth family was finally going to pay its debt.

SHE HAD JUST FINISHED showering after cleaning up the bats in the attic when the sales rep she'd been expecting showed up. He toured the house and took notes, then gave his sales pitch on security systems and left her with a stack of literature and a rough estimate. His promise of installation within two weeks sounded good—but one week would have been better. Perhaps the next sales rep would offer a more timely job completion.

After grabbing a quick tuna sandwich, she went up to the attic once more, surveyed the scene and wondered where to begin.

From far below, she heard a distant, "Yoo-hoo!," which could only be Mrs. Rogers on one of her daily quests. Hardly a day went by without the portly lady knocking at the door.

Claire dashed down the attic stairway and shoved up the sash of a window in Jason's bedroom. "Up here," she called out. "What can I get for you?"

"Can I come up?"

"I'm working in the attic, if you don't mind the dust."

Mrs. Rogers puffed her way up the two flights of stairs to the attic. "Quite the excitement this morning. A police car! Is everything all right?" Breathing heavily, she plopped into a dusty Queen Anne chair and fanned herself with one hand.

"Fine," Claire said with a cautious smile. "Did the cruiser wake you?

"Nope, I'm quite the early bird." She leaned

forward, anticipation twinkling in her eyes. "So why was he here?"

Claire hid a smile. This sweet old busybody had charm to burn. "I thought I'd heard something during the night. It was nothing, really."

Mrs. Rogers pursed her lips. "It must be terribly spooky in this big old house at night, all alone."

"Alone?" Claire rolled her eyes, then bent over to start sorting through a box. "With three kids and their pets, I'm hardly alone."

"A woman on her own certainly has her worries, though." The older woman looked at Claire over the rims of her glasses. "Without someone to protect her, I mean."

"Protect me from what?" Claire gave her an innocent shrug to stave off further questions, then picked up another box and set it by the stairwell. Mrs. Rogers waggled an eyebrow at her. *Good grief, I'll bet she saw Logan leave this morning.* "Why, Mrs. Rogers. You're checking up on me."

"Please, just call me Flo."

Finding another two of Brooke's boxes, Claire picked up one and shoved the other across the floor with her foot. Three down, a thousand to go. She blew a dangling curl out of her eyes. "You don't need to worry, Flo. The deputy didn't see anything to worry about, but he promises to return right away if I call."

"If you say so, dear." Flo pushed herself up out

of the chair and looked around, her intent gaze landing on the boxes Claire had stacked nearby. "What on earth are you doing here? Moving in or out?" She leaned forward to peer at the labels. "Who is Brooke?"

Someday I'll be a lonely old woman, too, Claire reminded herself. "Brooke was my sister. She and her husband were killed about six months ago. I'm sorting through their things, trying to figure out what to keep, I guess."

She spied a stack of boxes marked Brooke on the other side of the room and started lugging them to the growing collection. "Neither of my parents wanted to deal with her belongings."

With an almost pathetically eager smile, Flo stepped to the center of the attic and lifted her hands. "The breeze changed as I was coming over to visit. You know how it can drop twenty degrees in a minute? It's too nippy for much of a walk. I'd be happy to help."

Most of the boxes were too heavy for the elderly woman to move. Finding anything to substantiate Brooke's claims about Logan's cruelty during their marriage or Jason's parentage was too personal to share, and heaven only knew what they might stumble across that could be luring intruders into the house. "I do appreciate your—"

"Please? I'd love to help. I've cheated at solitaire all morning, and it does get a bit dull when one always wins.'' Flo's face fell. ''But of course I don't want to be in your way…''

There'd probably be no harm in having her check a few of the boxes. ''You wouldn't be at all. Thanks.''

Claire moved a few boxes marked Clothes next to Flo's chair. Using a small penknife, she slit the bands of tape sealing them shut.

''Most of Brooke's and Randall's clothing will be going as Goodwill donations, except for anything special that the kids might want…''

Flo settled back into her chair, her eyes gleaming with satisfaction. ''Anything you say, dear.''

Claire continued sorting. With each opened box, more memories of her sister returned. And more questions. Randall had been some sort of a contractor. Perhaps he'd done well at one time, but their bank accounts had been nearly empty when they died. The designer labels in these boxes would have cost the earth. How could they afford to spend money like this?

Outside, the sky darkened, then raindrops pattered on the high rafters above. Illuminated by dust-yellowed lightbulbs, the attic seemed almost cozy, a perfect setting for nostalgia. Except for the recurring memory of the bloody photograph and those poor little bats.

And the thought that someone, some stranger,

had been up in this very room. Claire shuddered, suddenly thankful for the company of another adult.

By noon, Claire had poked through a small percentage of the boxes, and most of them were sorted and stacked in opposite sides of the room. She hadn't touched any of the ones that had been opened by the intruder the day before.

Rubbing the small of her back, Claire yawned. "Ready to quit?"

Flo peered around the fortress of boxes in front of her. "Whenever you want to, but I'm still game. I'll keep at this, if you have other things to do."

A large collection of clothing was now neatly arranged around Flo's chair in "Keeper" and "Goodwill" stacks. And Claire had heard a play-by-play of 1922 through 1936 of Flo Rogers's life. It was definitely time for a break.

"Let's call it a day. Can I buy you some lunch? I think we have some lovely leftovers from last night."

"I may just go back to my cabin and rest a bit, dear." Flo rose stiffly to her feet. "It's nice being useful. Will you let me come back when you start again?"

"Of course." Claire glanced over her shoulder at a stack of boxes she'd set to one side. They held Brooke's and Randall's personal papers, including the contents of the desk at the condo.

She could only search those when she was alone.

THE SCHOOL BUS bumped and jostled its way down the lane, moving slower than ever before. Jason rubbed one sleeve against the steamy window and peered outside.

It was still raining, darn it. That meant Aunt Claire probably would be in the house, instead of working outside. That made everything a lot harder. He needed time alone.

She wasn't so bad after all. She really did try to help, though the twins needed her a lot more than he did. He was beyond needing a substitute mom's hugs and kisses. And he didn't want her prying into his business.

If she saw him, she would ask questions. Lots. She knew how to give a guy a look that made it awful hard to lie, but she would never believe the truth. He'd tried to tell Grandmother, and she'd gotten so mad that the veins on her forehead had popped up like angleworms under her skin and her face had turned red. She'd called him a liar, and said he was no better than his dad.

No one would believe him. Bad guys and death threats were in the movies, not in real life.

The strangers were getting more careless now. He'd seen them from a distance, at dusk. He'd heard the sounds of arguing, though he could only make out a few of the words.

All he had to do was figure out what they were

after, and make sure they got it...without letting them know he'd helped. Then maybe they would finally go away and Pine Cliff would be safe.

Before anyone else had to die.

was a kindred spirit. With a few weeks of practice, maybe Logan could train him, at least in some manner.

Damn. Logan wasn't up for a chuckle just now.

Come on, Marcy urged, in his head. *He needs to unwind. Do it! You can do it, you idiot, just wave*

CHAPTER THIRTEEN

GILBERT HAD FOLLOWED him home. Logan surveyed his yard—a generous term, perhaps, for a carpet of pine needles studded with rocky outcroppings and bisected by a sandy lane—then looked down at the chastened dog lying at his feet.

He'd been home for a couple hours, and in that brief time Gilbert had turned the entire area into something resembling a county landfill. At a stern "Bad dog!" the mutt had belly-crawled across the sea of chewed and scattered garbage, then flopped upside down against Logan's shoes.

Maybe it wouldn't be such a good idea to get a dog, he reflected, looking down into those sorrowful eyes. He could end up with a garbage-guzzling fur-ball like Gilbert and regret the impulse forever.

"Guess we'd better get you home," he said, looping a piece of rope through the dog's collar. "Your little friends are going to worry."

The first time the dog had come to visit, he'd barked at the gulls and created general havoc. By now, he'd apparently figured out that the gulls were impossible quarry and that the trash cans were a lot more fun. But despite the aggravation, the old dog was a likable mutt. With a few weeks of obedience training Logan could have him listening to commands—

But in a couple weeks Logan would be back in Saint Paul. Sometimes it was hard to remember.

"Come on, buddy." Turning north, he strode toward Pine Cliff, choosing the woodland path where the footing would be easier for an old dog's arthritic joints, instead of following the shoreline. Chipmunks crisscrossed in front of them. Squirrels chattered above. The light rain had settled the dust and pine needles, leaving a springy carpet underfoot. Ribbons of sunlight streamed through the overhead branches.

He wondered whether Claire would be pleased to see him. He figured not. After last night's debacle, a casual, friendly relationship was probably out of the question now. He'd seen that stunned look on her face when the child's cries had interrupted them.

She'd clearly never meant to go that far. Never with him.

But he had reasons to go back—his Explorer was still there and Gilbert needed to be returned. Claire might as well get used to the fact that he would be checking up on them constantly, staying there at night for as long as he could. She and the children were in danger. They needed him whether she liked it or not.

Five minutes later, he and the dog sauntered past

the first few cabins of Pine Cliff. From the corner of his eye he saw a flash of white. He spun around. Fred waved at him from the deck of a cabin.

"Howdy," the old man called. "See ya got that durned dog again. What did he do this time?"

Logan retraced his steps and propped one foot on the bottom step of the deck. "Garbage. Think I dare let him go?"

Fred slowly shook his head, the creases of his leathery cheeks deepening. "Only if you want him back. Nice of you to return him."

"I had to come after my truck anyway." Logan reached down to scratch Gilbert's head. "Have you seen Claire?"

"Not for an hour or so." Fred gave Logan a broad wink. "Quite a gal, don't you think?"

Fred might imagine himself a matchmaker, but it just wasn't going to happen. "I'm planning on sticking around a while," he said casually, wondering if Claire had told Fred about the dead bats and bloodied photograph in her attic. "She's been a little nervous about prowlers." He nodded toward the house. "Noticed anything unusual lately?"

Fred pushed the bill of his cap back and scratched his head. "Nothing I can recall. Window's broken up at the house this morning, but she says it happened when she was moving a ladder. I'll keep an eye on things, though."

"You saw her break it?"

Picking up a bundle of linens and a mop bucket

at his feet, Fred shook his head. "Happened 'fore I got here."

Logan had left Pine Cliff by 6:00 a.m. Fred started working around eight. Claire sure as hell hadn't been moving ladders around while trying to get three kids ready for school.

Giving Fred a noncommittal nod, Logan tugged on Gilbert's makeshift leash and headed for the house.

Gilbert balked at the sidewalk.

Logan hauled him along anyhow.

The dog sat down. Then flopped onto his back, forepaws crossed over his nose.

Logan scooped him up, and looked toward the house.

Something wasn't quite right. It took a moment to register. Blinding sunshine glinted off the windows facing the lake, yet one window was as dark as the gaping mouth of a cave.

As he drew closer, he saw bits of glittering light along the bottom of the window frame. Most of the glass was gone, the wooden sash fractured. Something had gone through that window with a great deal of force.

As he rounded the back of the house, he saw Claire sitting on top of the picnic table, her legs crossed beneath her, with a slip of paper gripped in both hands. Her face looked white. If it hadn't been delivered by airborne brick through her window, he would do five laps of Pine Cliff's boundaries naked.

"Thought you might want your dog back," he said mildly, his gaze pinned on the paper in her hand. "Early mail delivery?"

Claire's chin jerked up. She gave him a dazed look, as if he'd appeared out of a cloud of smoke, and began folding the paper in half, then into smaller and smaller squares until it was nearly the size of a postage stamp. For a moment he expected her to swallow it, like evidence in an old espionage movie.

"Gilbert was—uh—at your place again? In the trash?" she asked tonelessly, her face still white as snow. "I'm sorry. I'll send Jason to take care of it."

Logan untied the length of rope from Gilbert's collar and snapped him to his tie-out chain. "No problem." He lifted the rope for her inspection. "He's usually not an easily returnable dog, but at least he's learning to heel."

"Good." Staring at the wedge of lake visible between the house and trees, she rolled the square of paper in her closed hand. "I mean, thanks." She swiveled at the approaching rumble of a school bus.

"Too bad about that window."

"Uh…yes. I was careless."

"You didn't really break it, did you?"

"Um…" She looked away.

"What's in that note, Claire?"

She turned back and gave him a haunted look. "Nothing."

"Right. Let me see it."

Her gaze snapped up to his face. A long moment passed before she finally extended her arm and offered the scrap of paper. Her eyes filled with resignation, she slipped off the picnic table. "I sure hope you're one of the good guys, Matthews."

Logan took the folded note, curling his fingers over it as he watched her cross the broad lawn and head down the gravel lane to meet the bus. Her blond hair gleamed in the sunlight as she ran, her faded jeans lengthened her long, slender legs and skimmed the enticing curves above. He wished she was running toward him instead of away. But in those few words she had revealed just how much she trusted him.

Logan unfolded the note in his hand.

You're a fool to stay here. Think twice about who you trust.

With a growl of irritation, Logan fought the urge to crumple the note and throw it far out into the lake. No wonder she'd said what she had. Who would want her gone, and why? Of course, he had, but that had been before... He shook his head. There were so many things they needed to discuss. But now she had the twins bouncing along at her side, and soon Jason's bus would be pulling in. Hardly the time.

Logan started across the lawn after her. The sky

above was a clear, crystalline blue unmarred by the faintest wisp of a cloud, the lake looked as smooth as a mirror. A beautiful day to go out on the lake. Maybe he could convince her to leave the twins with Jason and Fred, and go with him. The solitude of the lake would be ideal for a conversation, and she couldn't escape so easily.

Claire and the twins settled on a long wooden bench overlooking the water, and from the excited bobs of the girls' heads, she was receiving a full report on their day at school. The three blond heads bent closer together.

Logan's heart turned over at the scene. They looked so right together and so peaceful, yet someone was stalking them, trying to drive them away. What the hell was going on?

He should have come back right away this morning. He could have brought his laptop and the Wickham blueprints. He should have been here when that bastard broke the window. Maybe he could have gotten some answers.

The early-morning sun and soft breezes had deceived him into imagining that dangers existed only in the darkness of night. He had gone home, and someone had come back.

Logan would simply have to move in.

CLAIRE'S MOUTH fell open. "That's going a bit far, isn't it?"

Logan pitched a rock across the smooth water

and counted four skips before it finally sank. "You need me."

"Thanks, but we'll be fine."

"Minutes ago you were behind the house, studying that slip of paper like it was your death sentence."

"I overreacted." She studied the damp toes of her sneakers, as if searching for the right words. "This is all the stuff of some stupid television show, not what happens in real life. Who—besides you—" she made an attempt at a smile "—would care whether I stayed here or not?"

"Someone who isn't afraid to enter your house. Someone capable of more than just a few idle threats. Have you called the sheriff about that note?"

Claire glanced at Annie and Lissa, who were digging through the rocks at the water's edge looking for agates. She lowered her voice. "The dispatcher said someone would pick it up today and check for fingerprints. I think the sheriff believes I'm a lonely woman who sees villains lurking in every cupboard."

"Didn't he see the photo and the dead bats?"

"Yes, but nothing was taken, not even stereo and camera equipment left out in plain sight. No one was hurt, no damage done. He thinks I've been the victim of a prank."

Squealing, Annie ran across the rocky beach and

up onto the wave-smoothed granite shelf to Claire's side. "Look! It's an agnette!"

Claire bent over to inspect the stone closely. "By golly, you're right. A pretty one, too."

"Can I go back to the house and get a basket in case we find more? Please?"

Claire hesitated then saw Jason's school bus pull in. He waved as he got off and started loping toward the house. "All right," she said to Annie. "Come right back, okay? I'll stay here and keep an eye on your sister."

Logan growled in frustration as she slipped away from him and joined Lissa who was crouched over a pile of smooth gray rocks. At the sound of footsteps, he turned around.

"Gonna storm," Fred drawled, stopping beside Logan to scan the clear blue sky. "I can feel it. A good nor'easter."

Claire looked up from the pebbles the child had poured in her hands. "It's beautiful today," she protested, surveying the horizon. "How can you tell?"

"Fred knows," Logan said. "He's better than the Weather Channel."

The little girl looked up at Fred. "You can tell? Like with a crystal ball?" she asked, awestruck.

Fred shoved the bill of his cap up with a forefinger. "You ever hear of the *Edmund Fitzgerald?*"

The child looked mystified, but Claire softly

hummed a few bars of the popular song about the wreck and then she nodded.

"Back in 1975. Coulda gone out on the lake in a canoe. Pretty rare—just like today." Fred closed his eyes, remembering.

Logan had been just a boy, but he would never forget the raw fury of the lake blasting at the cliffs, sending waves over the cabins and onto the lane well beyond.

"The wind switched just like that—" Fred snapped his gnarled fingers and Lissa jumped. "You could see the darkness on the horizon—just a strip, but you could see it coming."

"Like a tornado?" Lissa asked, her worried gaze now fastened on the lake.

"Worse. 'Cause it's not just one place. Temp can drop forty degrees in minutes. You seen them big ships in Duluth? Seven hundred feet and more, but a bad storm can sink one so fast she can't call for help. Ninety- to a hundred-mile-an-hour winds—"

"Our house will be safe if a storm like that ever comes again," Claire said, giving Fred a pointed look. *"Right?"*

"Oh, right. You betcha." Hunkering down on his heels, Fred dug through his pockets until he came up with a roll of mints, then offered them to Lissa. "The cabins and house have been here for a good fifty years. Just stay inside if we ever have any bad weather, and you'll be fine."

Claire shooed the child toward the house, then

looked back to Fred and Logan. "Please don't scare the girls with those tales. They won't sleep at all tonight."

"Yes, ma'am." Fred touched the bill of his cap again.

"These aren't just stories," Logan said. "You've seen how the temperature can drop when a breeze switches direction. The lake can go from duck-pond smooth to twenty-five-foot waves faster than you'd believe. Come November, those waves can go over the rooftops."

She glanced at the horizon. "This is the most incredibly beautiful place I've ever seen. It's hard to imagine the kind of violent storm you're describing."

"Believe me, it happens. And when it does, you'd better be inside."

"Of course," she murmured. "I've got to catch up with the girls. I promised we'd go to town after I got the dishes done."

She turned and strode across the broad sweep of smooth granite, then darted up the sharp bank next to one of the cabins and disappeared behind a stand of pines.

Logan watched her go, willing the tension out of his muscles. He skipped another rock across the water without testing its balance. It sank on the first hop.

"I'm worried about her."

Fred shrugged. "They'll be fine as long as they stay in the house."

"Not about the weather. I know I already asked, but have you seen any suspicious strangers around here?"

"Nothing." Fred gave him a blank look. "'Course, we've got those Sweeneys in cabin eight, but they seem harmless enough. No one else around that don't belong." Fred frowned. "I'll keep an eye out, though. Right now, I'd better finish my work and get back to town before the weather changes."

So she wasn't telling Fred her problems. Watching him collect supplies from the old golf cart parked along the lane and then disappear into a cabin, Logan wondered if she had suspicions about Fred being involved or if she simply wanted to spare him any worry.

From what Logan had seen so far, Fred had a light workload. She had taken the old guy under her wing just as she had taken in the children, intending to protect and nurture them all.

Someone needed to be taking care of *her*.

He was halfway up the sidewalk leading to the house when he heard a commotion from somewhere on the main floor—the kitchen, he guessed. Hearing a cry of "Oh, no!" and a duet of sobs interspersed with "I wanted to help" and "We couldn't stop it!," he broke into a run and took the porch stairs three at a time.

The moment he opened the door, something damp and fluffy covered his running shoes.

Bubbles. Masses of bubbles flowed from the sides of the half-closed door of the dishwasher. In front of it, a mound of bubbles reached the girls' ankles. The kitchen floor was covered.

"You weren't even gone ten minutes, Lissa!" Claire gasped, looking dumbstruck. "What on earth happened?"

Annie scooped up an armload of foam and tried to shove it in the sink, but most of it clung like drifts of whipped cream to her arms and clothing. "We wanted to help so we could go to town."

"I started the dishwasher, just like you do," Lissa wailed. "I put in some dishes and some soap and closed the door. And when I turned it on, we got bubbles."

"Lots and lots," Annie added. "The kitchen will be really clean now, won't it?"

"It certainly will." Claire lifted the bottle of liquid dishwashing soap from the counter. "I'll bet you used this instead of the dishwasher soap."

"Looks like fun," Logan offered from the doorway. Claire shot him a dark look and he grinned in response. "Need some help?"

"Any ideas?" She nudged at the foam with her shoes. "A mop and water would make it worse. Shoveling would take forever. And if I did get it all outside, the detergent would kill the grass."

"I guess I'd just move out," Logan offered.

"Trust you to make that suggestion. Girls, see if you can catch Fred before he leaves, okay?"

Logan waded through the ocean of white to Claire's side. Her light scent sped through his senses. He wondered what she would do if he tossed her down into that bed of foam and kissed her until they were both senseless.

"What perfume are you wearing?" he asked, searching for distraction. He shoved his hands into his pockets.

She gave him a wary look. "Beautiful."

"It is. My secretary would like it."

Claire cocked an eyebrow.

"She's seventy-two," he added. "I can never figure out what to give her at Christmas."

Claire's eyes widened, and then she laughed. A pure, high sound he could listen to forever.

"It's *called* Beautiful. My first image of your secretary was of a woman in leopard-print leotards, draping herself across your desk to take dictation."

Logan thought for a moment. "Not for the last few years. Her rheumatism flares up when she doesn't wear all of her clothes."

Claire chuckled and met Logan's gaze. She stilled. Her lips parted, a look of confusion and pain filled her eyes. "I—"

"Don't," he whispered, drawing closer. "Just be still."

The girls would return any second, but the opportunity might never come again. This was his chance to talk. To straighten everything out. Instead, he found himself leaning over, brushing a puff of foam from her cheek. Then he kissed her gently.

Her palms pressing hard against his chest, she gave him a skeptical look. "You don't want this type of relationship, remember?"

Logan flinched. Her words were light, but her eyes revealed a depth of hurt that tore at his soul. "I'm sorry. I didn't mean for it to go that far."

Claire gave a short laugh, but her eyes looked suspiciously bright. "Mercy. That was clear enough."

"Dammit, Claire. It was a mistake."

"This is progress," she retorted. "Now I was just a mistake. Go home, Matthews."

"Claire—" But how could he explain? "I'm sorry. Chalk up last night to a man being overwhelmed by a beautiful woman, a man who let things move too fast." He gently rested his wrists on her shoulders. "A man who now wonders how the hell he managed to stop."

Her wry smile didn't quite reach her eyes. "Thanks for that, anyway. You're right, of course. Neither of us want any sort of personal relationship. It was a mistake."

You're wrong, Claire. We both want it too damn much, and we need to talk about it. Without volition, Logan's hands moved slowly, very slowly down her arms. He didn't intend to linger at her wrists, to feel her pulse throbbing beneath his fingertips. But when it quickened, his breath caught in his throat.

He could no more have discussed anything at that moment than he could have walked the surface of Superior. He kissed her cheek. Another light kiss—almost platonic. A promise to control any errant desires at all future encounters. Yet without conscious decision, he felt his lips move, forming the words he'd never intended to speak. He wouldn't go further.

Yet his hands slipped lower until they cupped her bottom and lifted her closer. The feel of her arms around his neck was heaven.

I want you, he thought.

"Yes," she murmured, her breath soft and enticing against his ear.

Had he spoken aloud? Had she? Reality and fantasy merged as he felt her hips cradling his own, felt the soft heat of her breasts against his chest.

"The girls—" Trembling, she looked past his shoulder.

Logan lifted his head and turned toward the windows. *Damn.* The twins were coming up the lane with Fred between them. From their animated gestures, he guessed their description of the dishwasher disaster was more than a little exaggerated.

Grasping the edge of the counter with one hand, Claire stepped out of Logan's arms. She slipped, flew backward. Logan caught her shoulders and pulled her close, twisting his own body beneath hers. They landed on the floor in a blizzard of foam.

Claire stared down at him in shock. And then she started to laugh, laughter that seemed to come clear from her soul. The feel of her warm hand at the side of his face felt as though she were laying claim to his heart.

"Not quite what we had in mind," she murmured. "But close enough."

A slam of the back screen door and the sounds of footsteps broke the moment in a flash.

"Good a way as any to deal with this mess, I'd say." Fred's voice sounded as loud as a foghorn. "You've got some little people out here on the steps who love to help, though. Right, girls?"

Claire pulled away sharply and rose to her feet, sweeping foam from herself with agitated movements. The deep blush in her cheeks spoke volumes.

Logan bent to kiss her, and for the audience behind her, he gave her bottom a gentle swap that sent foam flying in all directions. Fred and the girls laughed and surged into the room.

Logan couldn't help smiling. Even though his future was no longer clear. He no longer knew where he was heading or who he was. A loner or a man falling in love with a woman who was totally wrong for him.

So why did he feel so good?

CHAPTER FOURTEEN

THE WIND CAME UP surreptitiously, like a prowler easing through the pines along the shore. Near the house, poplar leaves shivering in a gentle, waterfall cadence had nearly lulled Claire to sleep.

With a start, she shifted in her chair and rubbed her eyes, then lifted her wrist. It had been six hours since Fred had gone to town for foam cutter, dispatched the masses of bubbles, and then left for home. Logan had stayed for supper, and then gone back to his house for his laptop and some files. But that had been an hour or two ago. Surely it shouldn't have taken this long for him to return.

The stack of papers on her lap slipped. Collecting them into a neat pile, she put them back into a small box next to her chair and stood up. It would take time to make sense of what she'd found.

The wind came a little stronger now, whining through the window frames of the old house and rattling the gutters. *Midnight in the attic, the stuff of childhood nightmares and horror movies.*

Shaking her head at such nonsense, Claire tugged at the string hanging from a lightbulb overhead. The vast attic turned dark as pitch save for a glow at the bottom of the stairs. From outside came the growl of an engine. Logan?

Nudging aside the unseen objects in her path, she felt her way across the floor toward a window. Standing on tiptoe, she peered outside.

The security light on the laundry building illuminated a patch of grass and a short stretch of the lane running past the cabins. Farther down, parked behind wind-tossed branches, the dim headlights of a car blinked like strobe lights. Judging from the distance, it was probably parked at the Sweeneys' cabin.

They were strange people who kept odd hours, and hauled bulky objects in and out of their cabin. They were the most likely suspects at Pine Cliff, though both of them seemed harmless enough. Picking up the box of papers by her chair, she slipped downstairs.

By the time she reached the kitchen, branches were scraping back and forth against the house with an eerie scrabbling sound, like bony fingers trying to tear away the siding.

Superior's waves sounded high and fierce; the house shook as walls of water slammed against the vertical granite cliffs along the shore.

Pulling back a lace curtain, she looked toward the cabins to the south of the house. Sheets of rain shimmered down the glass, obliterating the view. Lifting the sash, she rubbed at the wet screen with her hand. Wind-driven rain blew in, feeling like ice crystals thrown against her face.

Two tiny pinpoints of crimson glowed far down the lane. Grew smaller, then disappeared. *The Sweeneys are leaving—in a storm—at midnight.* Who came to the rugged, wild beauty of the North Shore for a month, kept their cabin's window shades closed all day and then went sight-seeing after dark?

Tomorrow, she would call the sheriff's office. It might be useful to know if the Sweeneys had prior records of any kind.

Shivering, she turned on the radio and scanned the channels. Amid the static only a few words came through well enough to hear. A severe storm was moving in, just as Fred had predicted. The first nor'easter of fall was well on its way.

It was going to be a long, long night.

AFTER TWENTY MINUTES of poring over old documents, Claire stood up, yawned and went to the counter for another cup of coffee. From behind her, she heard hushed voices as two sets of small, slippered feet approached.

"The wind is loud," Annie whispered.

"It's Fred's storm," Lissa announced. "We think we should be with you, in case you're scared."

Claire turned and smiled at the girls, who stood pressed shoulder to shoulder as if providing each other with moral support. "It's just a little wind and rain. Do you want to lie down on the couch for a while?"

Hugging herself, Annie shivered and nodded. "It's scary up there. Like ghosts are howling in the trees."

As if in response, the wind grew louder and the sound of waves crashing against the shore grew deeper, like the rumble of thunder. Claire felt the floor vibrate beneath her feet seconds after each wave hit.

She gave both girls a hug. "It's noisy, but we're safe and snug in here. This house has withstood storms for over fifty years."

The cabins had seen their share of storms as well, but the occupants were probably fearing for their lives. "I think I should go and tell our guests they're welcome up here, if they'd like," Claire murmured. "If I leave all the lights on, will you two be okay for a few minutes with Jason?"

Lissa furtively glanced around the shadowed room, then back at Claire. "Maybe we should come, too."

Another set of footsteps came down the stairs and into the room. "What a storm!" Jason said, his voice filled with awe. A bolt of lightning exploded close by, filling the room with blinding light. The lamps flickered. "Cool."

Excellent timing. "Could you stay here with the girls? I should go out and check on our guests."

Jason shrugged, a fair imitation of masculine nonchalance. "Sure."

After flipping on all the living-room and dining-room lights, Claire pulled on a yellow slicker hanging by the door. "Back in a few minutes," she called over her shoulder.

The wind tore the door out of her hand when she turned the handle. Fierce rain hit her face like a volley of ten-penny nails the moment she stepped outside.

The screaming wind and unearthly booming of waves against the shore sent a shiver of fear down her spine. She resolutely continued down the rain-slick sidewalk toward the closest cabin, where a dim light shone through the bathroom curtains. There was no answer when she pounded on the door.

"Hello, anyone here?" she called out before pounding on the door again with her fist.

After a few minutes, another light switched on inside, and an elderly man opened the door two inches and looked out at her. "Whatcha want at this hour?"

A burst of wind blew her hood off, sending icy rain down her neck and back. Claire shuddered. "Looks like a bad one," she shouted. "Do you want to come up to the house?"

"Hell, no. Me and the Mrs. always hope we'll have some good weather like this when we come. Love it. We've been sitting here just listening to waves.'' He gave her a hopeful look. ''Think it will keep going through tomorrow?''

''Not a clue. Don't forget—you're welcome at the house if you change your mind.''

''These cabins have been around as long as me. I'm not worried.'' He shut the door with a bang.

Bone cold, Claire trudged back out onto the lane and headed for the next cabin. The Sweeneys were gone. Mrs. Rogers had left for Duluth that afternoon. And nobody in any of the remaining cabins felt it necessary to come up to the house.

Apparently, people loved this place as much for the drama of Superior's storms as they did for its breathtaking scenery. Wishing she felt as calm as her guests, Claire wrapped her slicker tightly around herself and stumbled through the darkness toward the house.

Lightning flashed. Once, twice, then in a series of firework displays lighting the sky from one end of the horizon to the other. Only then could she make out the ferocious waves, one after another, rolling in and smashing against the cliff face in front of cabin six, sending a wall of black water and white spray fifty feet or more into the air.

Lightning hit along the shore with a deafening crack, illuminating the resort in an eerie blue light that cast each detail into sharp relief.

Claire cautiously made her way across the drenched lawn. Her hands felt numb. Her socks squished like ice-water sponges in her shoes. Just a little bit farther...

Another burst of lightning exploded, this time hitting a tall pine at the far edge of the lawn. Claire's ears rang. The impact nearly knocked her over. A sharp scent of ozone filled the air. For that endless moment, the landscape was as light as day—revealing a cloud of brown bark and dust.

With a sharp crack, the top of the tree hung in the balance for a split second, then crashed to earth.

The lights in the house flickered. Went out.

Smart girl. You could have been hunting for candles, instead of disturbing a slew of perfectly content people.

Claire felt her way along the sidewalk, reaching for the wet branches of the bushes that skirted the house. Another lightning burst helped her find the first step leading to the porch.

On the door, she discovered an unfamiliar, slender object that protruded several inches, with a scrap of white blowing wildly beneath it.

It could have been there for hours. It could have been placed there while she'd been outside.

With shaking fingers, Claire reached forward and ran her fingers over the object. *A knife.* Tugging, then rocking it back and forth, she managed to pull it out of the wood and catch the sodden flag caught on its blade.

Probably just a perfectly innocent note from the Sweeneys, telling her that they were headed up the shore for a day or two. But the knife suggested otherwise. She carefully folded the note once and slipped it into the pocket of her slicker.

Back in the dark warmth of the kitchen, she automatically felt along the wall for a light switch before realizing her foolish mistake. Of course, the electricity was out.

"Kids—are you all right?"

"Over here," one of the twins whispered from the couch.

Claire ran a hand along the kitchen counter as she walked through the kitchen. Just past the sink, there should be a flashlight in a drawer…unless one of the kids had lost it.

The drawer was empty, of course. Her first discovery as a new mom had been that flashlights, scissors and cellophane tape disappeared faster than prime parking spaces in New York.

Pulling a chair next to the counter, she climbed up and retrieved three squat candles and the kerosene lantern from the darkened ledge above the cabinets.

"Here, Jason. Grab these."

Jason reached up to take the candles and set them on the kitchen table. Claire brought down the dusty lantern and eyed it uncertainly. "Know anything about these things?" she asked. "I do have some matches."

Jason took it from her, adjusted the wick and

struck a match. The room glowed with warm golden light. Claire beamed at him. "Way to go."

"Scouts," he muttered, a faint wash of pink flooding his cheeks.

"I can't tell you how happy I am that you joined, sport." Claire shoved the chair back into place at the table. "Okay, guys. Time to get to back to sleep."

Once the girls lay back on the couch and Jason settled into the recliner in the living room, Claire brought out the wet piece of paper and knife she'd taken off the back door.

Get the picture yet, lady? If you don't leave, you or those kids could get hurt.

"Get the picture?" The message sounded like dialogue from a grade-B movie with second-rate actors. Claire didn't know whether to laugh or shudder.

But whatever this person's intellect, he—or they—had already trespassed in her house, tampered with her washing machine and killed a dozen innocent little bats to deliver a gruesome message. It didn't take intelligence to be dangerous.

She reached for the phone, her anger rising. This time, the sheriff was going to make her his first priority.

The phone was dead.

Claire held the receiver in her hand and scanned

the kitchen. Her bravado began to slip. Someone could be out there, peering in the windows. Enjoying her growing awareness of danger. The hairs at the back of her neck prickled. Goose bumps rose along her arms. Her heart picked up a faster beat. *Where was Logan?*

She would not give in to her fear. Stalking across the room, she checked all the window locks and pulled the curtains closed, then double-checked the dead bolt on the door. It wasn't likely that anyone would stand out in a fierce nor'easter, watching her through the sheets of rain pouring down the windowpanes.

Whoever it was, he was probably gone for now, satisfied with his night's work and eager to get out of the storm himself.

Claire poured herself a cup of lukewarm coffee and settled at the kitchen table with a box of papers and files she'd found in the attic. Dimming the kerosene lamp to avoid disturbing the children, she began to read, trying to ignore the uneasy premonition curling through her midsection.

The first few folders had come from Randall's desk. Her father's accountant had collected the business-related documents but had missed these. Randall had been a construction foreman for a large firm, and there were pages of calculations, material and labor estimates, and copies of bids.

Claire whistled softly over the bids for a mall. A smaller shopping complex. A six-story office complex in White Bear Lake. Working for a company like this one, Randall should have been doing very well. So why had their condo been mortgaged to the hilt? Brooke's elegant, brand-new furniture had been purchased on credit, and most had been reclaimed by stores when the estate was settled. The family bank accounts had been nearly dry.

She flipped through more files, hesitated, then went through again, taking notes. Nothing struck her as irregular. By the time she reached the last folder, her eyes burned from trying to focus in the dim, flickering light. There were just a few bulky envelopes left at the bottom of the box.

Thunder rolled through the house, rattling glassware in the cupboards and awakening Gilbert, who looked up at her and whined. Sleep would be impossible. She stood up to gather the papers and files strewn across the table, tapped them into a neat stack and reached for the final contents of the box. One envelope, heavier than the rest, slipped from her grasp and landed on the floor with a thump barely audible over the howling wind and sharp cracks of thunder outside. The flap broke open, revealing a white, embossed cover.

Curious, Claire removed the envelope. Her excitement rising, she lifted the other envelopes from the box.

She'd found the children's baby books. She settled back into her chair and eagerly opened the first one—Jason's. A lightning flash illuminated the room for a split second. A deafening crack of thunder shook the house.

"Sullivan?" Annie's sleepy voice rose as she called for the cat. "Sullivan?"

Claire slipped quietly into the living room and knelt by the couch. "She probably went to her favorite spot for the night," she whispered. "Do you two want to go back up to bed?"

Casting a wary eye toward the windows facing the lake, Annie sat up and scrunched the afghan around her shoulders. "I like it better down here tonight."

"That's okay, sweetie. Lie down then and go back to sleep. Sullivan is just fine."

Annie nestled back into her afghan, her head at one end of the long couch and Lissa's at the other. Lissa's eyes were open and filled with worry when Claire bent down to give her a good-night kiss.

"Sleep tight." Claire stroked the little girl's cheek.

"Did Sullivan go outside? She'd get wet and cold. And the waves might grab her."

Claire shook her head. "No, she wouldn't have gone out. Cat's don't like to be out on a night like this. She's curled up somewhere in the house, warm and toasty."

"Are you sure?"

"I'm sure." Claire gave Annie a kiss, pulled the afghan up around her shoulders, then tiptoed away.

Back in the kitchen, she closed and fastened the

flap of the little pet entrance in the back door, then sat down to read. The embossed covers of the baby albums promised tantalizing glimpses into the past. Her pulse quickened with anticipation. Cradling Jason's book in her lap, she angled the pages toward the lantern.

He'd been eight pounds, three ounces. Twenty-one inches. On this page was the hospital bassinet card with his name and particulars. On the next, an impossibly tiny footprint, curved and wrinkled, crowned with an arc of eraser-size toe prints.

Claire thought of the size ten shoes Jason always left just inside the back door, and ached for the years she'd missed in his life.

First words. Inoculations. Several carbons of well-baby exams. At the back of the book she found a large envelope. With shaking fingers she eased the flap open and withdrew photocopied hospital records. Jason had been circumcised. He had Type AB− blood, while the delivery records listed Brooke as Type A−. Suddenly the question that had haunted Claire for days came tumbling forward.

She shut her eyes. Logan—tall, capable, strong, with that sensual grin and a way of looking at her that sent her hormones racing. Jason, with his strong jaw and arching eyebrows. They both possessed sharp intelligence. Artistic talent shone in Logan's architectural designs and in Jason's intricate pen-and-inks.

The possibility seemed greater than ever. The time frame made it possible, and subtle similarities kept adding up. How would Logan respond when she shared her suspicions with him—stunned silence? Joy? Disinterest? Or with raw fury at not being told of the possibility years ago? If her suspicions proved false, would she have then hurt him even more?

"Suuuuulllivan!"

The soft, faraway voice broke into her thoughts. Claire shut the book and slipped it back into its envelope. Taking the lantern with her, she stood at the living-room doorway and peered inside. A tangle of empty afghans lay on the couch. Both girls were gone. Jason stirred in the recliner, squinted against the dim light.

"Morning?" he mumbled, more asleep than awake.

"Not for a long time," Claire whispered. She went back to the kitchen. There had to be flashlights somewhere here. Drawer after drawer yielded nothing. Reaching above the refrigerator, she blindly searched its dusty surface.

Bingo.

Setting the lantern back on the kitchen table, she turned on the flashlight and headed toward the living room and the flight of stairs. The girls were searching the house for the silly cat, and in the darkness they could take one misstep and get hurt.

The screen door slammed.

Claire whirled, raced back to the kitchen.

"What's going on?" Jason shuffled in behind her, rubbing his eyes.

The heavy oak door was ajar. The screen door whipped back and forth, crashing against the side of the house with each swing. The girls had gone after their cat.

And they were outside in the worst storm Claire had ever seen in her life.

SOMETHING WAS WRONG.

They weren't answering the phone. He'd tried five times. It was after midnight, but Logan had no illusions about anyone being able to sleep through a night like this one. With the spray of wild waves hitting his topmost windows and the wind howling, only the dead could be asleep.

He had visions of accidents at Pine Cliff. Lightning strikes. Fire. The prowler. He'd planned to be away less than an hour. He'd never expected to find a skylight in his own house broken by a fallen tree limb and a veritable flood in the spare bedroom. Damage control had been a challenge without electricity to illuminate the process or help vacuum up the water. Lashing down a wind-whipped tarp on the steep, slippery roof, in the dark, had taken even longer. Finally done, he'd grabbed his laptop and files, jammed them into a waterproof case and headed for the Explorer.

A massive old pine tree blocking the lane had missed his truck by inches.

An inexplicable sense of urgency slammed through him. He couldn't wait until the storm died down, or until he could clear the road. Ignoring the wind that howled and clawed at his slicker, he raced out into the night.

CHAPTER FIFTEEN

THE WIND BIT her face like a winter-hungry wolf. Incisor-sharp rain slashed her flesh. Nearly blinded by the storm's fury, Claire stumbled down the steps and screamed the children's names until her throat ached and her lungs burned.

The wind howled in return, mocking her weak effort. She had three children out here now. Jason had rushed past her at the door, a thin jacket in hand. He shared her gut-deep fear for his sisters, but now he'd added to her terror.

One false step and the children could plunge over a cliff. There, Superior's waves would slam them like driftwood against the rocks, or suck them deep into an icy graveyard.

The wind lunged at her from unexpected angles with a ferocity that nearly knocked her to the ground. She bent low and struggled forward, stumbling, falling to her knees. The weak light of the old flashlight faded.

With the security lights out, only an occasional burst of lightning illuminated her surroundings and kept her on course. *Please God, let them be safe. Please God, let them be safe…*

Without warning, she rammed into an unseen corner of one of the cabins. Freezing rain poured down her face and into the collar of her coat.

Feeling her way along the side of the cabin, she reached the edge of the steps and leaned forward to grope for the rustic pine railing. Ahead, maybe fifteen feet or so, the scrubby grass underfoot would lead to a steep bank rimmed with wild raspberry vines. From there a path descended to the broad granite shelf that ran below most of the cabins.

But if she was one cabin farther than she thought, she could be nearing the edge of a sheer drop-off.

"Jason! Lissa! Annie!" She could barely hear her own words above wind wailing through the pines. The earth shook in counterpoint to the sound of massive waves colliding against the cliffs. The force vibrated up through her shoes.

A distant flash of lightning out over the lake revealed the path she sought. She slithered down the muddy bank. Mammoth waves hit the rocks and soared skyward, flinging icy spray into her face. Lightning revealed the turbulent water beyond, and the ghostly pale outline of a building close to the shore.

Thank God. I'm near the boathouse. Ahead, there should be a downward twist of the rocky path. She could get even closer to the shore.

"Jason! Girls!"

Only the wind and the waves and the pounding rain replied. She cautiously toed her way forward, holding up an arm to defend herself against the waves breaching the ten-foot drop below.

Like a sign from above, lightning flashed again and revealed a small, dark figure sprawled near the water's edge. *Jason?*

Both relief and fear flooded through her as she scrambled down the crude, weather-carved steps worn into the rock. The rough granite ripped her jeans, tore at her flesh.

It took forever to reach him. It took a heartbeat. Leaning over to shelter him from the surging waves, she ran her hands over his back and legs, and battled the impulse to sweep him up into her arms. "*Jason!* Can you hear me?"

A shudder wracked his thin body. "C-Claire?"

"Sweetheart, are you hurt? Can you move your arms and legs?" She hovered closer, willing her own warmth into him as she glanced out over the black fury of the lake. Sudden terror speared her heart. "Were the girls with you? Have you seen them?"

"I c-couldn't find them." A spasm of coughing shook him.

Thank God. If they'd been with him, they would have been far too close to the surging waves. With luck, maybe they'd found their way back to the house.

One of Jason's hands, curved near his face, clenched and released. "My arm hurts so much!"

"I know, honey. Let's get you home. Can you stand?"

He coughed again, then inch by inch, he struggled onto his hand and knees.

Breathing another prayer of thanks, Claire slid her arms around his chest. He moaned. She lowered her grip to his waist as he lurched to his feet. "Keep going! You can do it!" she shouted into the wind.

He straightened, cried out, then sagged weakly into her arms. Bracing him against her side, she began moving slowly toward the steep bank leading to the lane. The ascent would have been treacherous for her alone. Helping Jason up would be nearly impossible unless he fought with every ounce of strength he possessed.

"Jason?" She looked down, willing him to hear her. "We've got to make it up this slope. Understand?" *And if I can get you home, I can go after your little sisters.*

Wobbling along beside her, he stumbled over an uneven place in the rock and cried out again.

At the bank, Claire reached out and felt the muddy surface rise steeply above them. It was as slippery as soapsuds on vinyl, with jagged rocks speared up through the mud. Boulders waited below. "We've got to go up here," she shouted at him. "There's no other way."

Jason shuddered. More alert now, he cradled one arm with the other. He might have said something to her, but it was impossible to hear over the crashing waves and howling wind.

Straining every muscle against his weight, she urged him up the steep surface. For every six inches up, they slid at least three inches back.

Suddenly, Jason's foot slithered off to one side and he fell against the bank. "I can't," he sobbed. "I can't!"

"You can. We're almost there."

The waves were coming up higher now, washing over the granite shelf behind them. Sheets of freezing rain battered them both. Claire felt the boy's sobs wrench his body, wished he were small enough for her to carry. And where were the girls? Their terror must be unimaginable. Claire struggled to think of a way to bargain with God. *Please, keep them safe.*

Peering upward, eyes clenched against the rain, she saw a dark form silhouetted against the dark sky.

"Claire! Is he okay?"

Logan. With a sob, she reached up, willing him to be real. He clasped his hand around hers. His skin felt warm, his grip was iron-hard.

"Can he make it up? Does he need a stretcher?"

Never in her life had words sounded so wonderful.

Jason would be safe. She could go after Annie and Lissa.

"The girls," Claire shouted. "I've got to find them!"

"Got 'em. They're in the house."

Claire nearly collapsed with relief.

A crack of lightning and long roll of thunder obliterated Logan's response, but she instinctively knew that he had protected them well. In a heartbeat, she knew what she had to do.

Logan was an honorable man, a man to count on. Tonight she would tell him of her suspicions about Jason's birth. If he was Jason's father, the boy would be in good hands.

Jason huddled against her, guarding his arm. Claire gently urged him forward. "Come on, kid. The Lone Ranger's here," she shouted. "Let's get rescued."

AT THE HOSPITAL, Claire expected to see swarms of injured people and frantic medical staff. Instead, the building was relatively quiet. After filling out endless forms and answering a thousand questions, she'd been taken to one examination room and Jason to another, where Logan was keeping him company.

"Most people stay inside in this weather," the emergency-room nurse said with censure in her voice, looking over her half-glasses at the scrape on Claire's forehead. "You people are lucky."

"Jason—"

"He's doing fine. The X rays came back a few

minutes ago, but I'm not sure if the doc has read them yet.''

''I should be with him!''

''You will be in a minute.'' The nurse clucked her tongue as she applied antibiotic cream to Claire's wound. ''He's down in the ortho room—''

''What?'' Alarm skittered through her.

Surprised, the nurse looked up. ''Oh, sorry. We put all the fractures—er, people with fractures—in there.''

Claire moaned. ''I knew he was in pain. He must be so frightened.''

''You've only been away from him for ten minutes.'' The older woman patted Claire's hand. ''Your husband is with him. The little girls are doing just fine with Cindy down at the admissions desk.''

Her husband? Logan would certainly contest that. ''I need to get back to him.''

''You're all set.'' Her gray curls bobbing, the nurse put aside her supplies. ''You were a little shocky when you came in, but other than a few bruises and scrapes you're okay.''

Claire escaped the cubicle and hurried down the hall to the room where Jason lay. From farther down the hall she heard Lissa and Annie giggling with an admissions clerk who was apparently having a slow night.

LOGAN GLANCED UP at Claire's approach and gave her a reassuring nod, then turned back to Jason and the ER doctor.

"So," Dr. Olsen was saying, "we have some paperwork to fill out, and then you guys can relax until the surgeon gets here. Not the way you planned to spend the evening, right, champ?" He squeezed Jason's hand and nodded to Logan.

"*Surgery?*" Claire darted a worried look at Jason, then glanced up at the IV hanging by his gurney.

Dr. Olsen draped his stethoscope around his neck and picked up Jason's file. "The X rays show a fracture just above the elbow. Sometimes we can fix these with closed reduction-alignment of the bones by manipulation, but this one might need surgery. Either way, he'll need a cast."

"That sounds serious!" Logan heard the raw fear in her voice.

"Everything should go fine, though I'm a little concerned about the amount of swelling." The doctor took a few steps toward the door and lowered his voice. "The ends of the bones are a bit close to an artery. We've typed and crossed him as a precaution."

Claire's grabbed for the back of a nearby chair, her face pale. "My God."

Logan put a comforting arm around her shoulders and drew her close to his side. "He's going to be okay, Claire," he said gently.

"Of course he is." The doctor shuffled through

the papers in his hand, then withdrew a lab report. "An excellent orthopedic surgeon is on his way in. We'll have to put Jason under general anesthesia, so he doesn't feel anything, and to relax the muscles enough to try a closed reduction. If that isn't possible, we'll go ahead with surgery. His vitals are fine, and we don't believe there are any internal injuries."

Logan watched as Claire took a deep breath, then exhaled slowly to regain her composure. Her concern and love for the boy couldn't have been more clear if Jason had been her own child. Logan felt his own tension ease. Everything was under control.

"The anesthesiologist will be in shortly to go over the consent forms with you, Mrs. Matthews."

"I'm Claire Worth, Jason's aunt and his legal guardian."

Logan contemplated her faint blush with a flicker of amusement. *Mrs. Matthews.* And then a flash of awareness streaked through him. He remembered the night he had joined them all on the lakeshore, her smooth skin gilded by the pulsing glow of a campfire...her sultry laughter...

"You're special, champ," the doctor was saying to Jason. He glanced down at the lab reports in his hand, then gave Jason a wink. "Not too many people have your blood type."

Jason gave him a wan smile. "What kind is it?"

"AB−."

Jason's eyes widened. "Is that bad?"

"Nope—just extra special."

Logan's heart skipped a beat. He felt frozen in time and space, as if he were watching the people in the room from a different dimension.

Somehow, he'd felt a strange connection from the first moment he'd seen Jason on the shore. That undeniable pull had grown a little stronger with each passing day. And now he knew that Jason's unusual blood type matched his own. Certainly not conclusive evidence, but a clue nonetheless. Especially if Brooke had been anything other than type O.

He shot a glance at Claire. She was staring right through him, a mixture of dread and guilt sweeping across her face.

"Tell us, Dr. Olsen," Logan said, keeping his voice low and even. "Just how rare is that blood type?"

"Less than one percent of the population is AB−." The doctor looked from Logan to Claire, then coughed discreetly. "Perhaps we should step outside. There's a lounge down the hall."

Fighting for control, Logan moved to the gurney and ruffled Jason's hair. "Don't worry, kid. We're going to have a long, dull talk that would put you to sleep. I've always been fascinated with blood typing. We'll be back in a few minutes."

How he'd managed a normal tone of voice, Logan didn't know. The furious pounding of his heart thundered in his ears. The Worths had done it. He thought they'd done their worst years ago, when they'd turned their wealth and power, full force, against him.

Yet all the while, they'd been quietly doing something far worse. They'd stolen his son. And from the guilt on Claire's face, she'd known it all along.

Once they reached the lounge, Claire turned to face the doctor. "Logan was my late sister's first husband. There's a chance he could be Jason's father," she murmured. "Are there tests you can order?"

"Er, yes." He gave Logan a curious look. "We could draw blood for DNA testing tomorrow, before Jason is discharged. We would need small blood samples from both you and Jason, of course."

Logan gave him a curt nod. "The sooner, the better. How accurate is the test?"

Dr. Olsen pursed his lips. "Testing can exclude paternity if two or more tests are negative. If there's a match, the probability of paternity would be above ninety-nine percent. I'll go write the orders and leave them at the nurses' station." He left the room, leaving Logan and Claire to face each other.

Cool as iced tea on a hot day, she'd neatly turned the situation into a simple fact-finding mission, devoid of emotion. From the remote expression on her face she might have been considering an addition to her stock portfolio. Not one ounce of remorse played across her features.

"He's mine, isn't he." Logan stated flatly.

"I honestly don't know. During the last week or so, I've come to wonder." Frowning, she twisted the gold bracelet on her wrist. "I have no proof."

Logan gave a sharp bark of laughter. "Come on, Claire. This really isn't a major revelation, is it?"

"What?"

An urge to ram a fist through the wall stormed through him. Instead, he clenched both hands at his sides. "Quite a secret for you and your family to hide all these years."

She paled. "You believe that?"

"I believe your father and sister created a smoke screen with all of those accusations during the divorce. Now I know why they wanted me out of the picture as fast as possible."

"You're crazy!"

"Yeah—crazy enough to expect basic honesty from a family that has none." He moved closer, until he made her back up a step. "If Jason truly is my son, then your family robbed me of years I can't ever regain. He's thirteen, and I don't even know him."

Anger flared in her eyes. "We don't have *any* answers yet. And even DNA testing has a margin for error."

"Brooke and I separated in February. Exactly when is Jason's birthday?"

"The end of this month—September 25."

"Certainly makes it possible, don't you agree?"

"I—I guess so."

"Is that why the family got a court order to keep me away?" Logan stalked a few paces down the hall, then came back to Claire. "There was no need for it, believe me. I never wanted to lay eyes on Brooke or any other Worth again, and they knew it. So why would they bother?"

"I was fourteen at the time, Matthews," Claire snapped. "I wasn't privy to all the fine details. She must have been afraid of any further contact."

"The only thing she ever feared was finding an imperfection in her appearance." He looked at Claire closely. Anger glittered in her eyes, while her jaw was set at a stubborn angle. "My God. You believed everything she told you."

"Brooke was my sister."

"And she wasn't always honest. How could you be so naive?"

"She remarried right after your divorce. Her new husband could have been Jason's father."

"True, but take a good look at Jason, and tell me you believe that."

"Brooke wouldn't have kept the truth from you all these years!"

He gave her a scornful smile. "Doesn't it make you just a little curious, about how a devoted, innocent wife could snag another husband within weeks?"

"I—"

"Grow up, Claire. Take a good look at the past."

"If Jason is yours, then surely you would have had *some* idea about the possibility of a pregnancy," Claire persisted.

"The question here is why no one told me, not whether or not I have ESP. Brooke knew. Your family would have known. Her new husband couldn't have been *that* stupid. I had a right to know."

Claire stared back at him, then said softly, "Maybe Brooke was afraid of your influence on her child."

Logan took a long, slow breath. Then another, to calm his racing heart. He'd known about Brooke's tales years ago, how she'd used them as leverage to enlist her father's support. The thought that Claire believed those stories made his insides clench. "I never, ever touched her in anger."

"But verbal assault and unfaithfulness are painful, too," Claire retorted.

How well he knew that. At the idealistic age of twenty-two he'd been on the receiving end, not her darling sister. After the humiliation of hearing Brooke's unfounded accusations in court, and the loss of half of Pine Cliff to her in the settlement, he'd sworn that he would never again be unable to afford the best legal defense.

That vow had made him the most goal-driven student in his graduating college class.

"It's very probable that Jason is my son," Logan said coldly. "When I have proof, I'm going to pursue custody." He ignored the look of raw pain in Claire's eyes. "You and your family have stolen too much of his life already."

"I do believe there's a chance you're his father," Claire said slowly, looking Logan straight in the eye. "But I swear to you that I didn't know about this before. None of us did."

Right, Logan thought savagely. *You didn't "know" until you were caught.*

THE HALLWAY of the hospital, stark under the bright fluorescent lights, provided little comfort. The girls had each curled up on a brown vinyl couch and fallen asleep. Claire sat in a chair between them, nervously watching the door to the surgical area.

Her muscles protested as she stood up to retuck the blankets over each child, then settled back in her own cold, vinyl-upholstered chair and pulled a blanket around her shoulders. She'd been shivering for the past twenty minutes, but the heaviest of blankets wouldn't touch the soul-deep cold that had settled around her heart.

Logan sat alone farther down the hall. Not once had he glanced in her direction. From the side, he looked as impassive as marble. Her skin still burned from the last searing look he'd given her before they each retreated to their own corners to wait, like boxers anticipating the start of a fight.

Her ears still rang with his accusation. *You knew*.

Not for a moment had he accepted that she'd only just begun to question Jason's parentage, or that she'd planned to tell him. She'd been such a fool. The fact that Logan refused to believe her broke her heart, but the effect of this on Jason and the girls would be devastating.

Ten minutes later, the surgeon and anesthesiologist appeared through the door with surgical masks draped around their necks. Claire stood up, her heart racing and knees weak. The surgeon approached her.

"Ms. Worth?" He rubbed the muscles at the back of his neck. "Jason came through just fine. It took a fair amount of manipulation, but we were able to reduce the fracture without doing surgery. He's in recovery right now."

Relief flooding through her, Claire extended her hand. "Thank you so much. When do we take him home?"

"We'd like to keep him until morning." The surgeon took her hand for a moment and gave her a comforting smile. "There was quite a bit of swelling, and his hand looks a tad mottled. The nurses will do frequent circulation checks during the next few hours, and keep me posted."

"And if there's a problem?"

"It's possible that we'll need to replace the cast, but that's a simple procedure."

"Everything went okay?"

Logan had come up behind her. His voice resonated against the fine hairs at her nape, sending a shimmer of awareness through her.

The surgeon nodded. "He'll be out of commission for a while, but he'll be fine."

The doctors strolled away swapping football scores. Claire turned to face Logan. "I'll stay with him tonight."

"No, I will." He held up a hand when she started to speak. "The twins will sleep better in their own beds. And I think I deserve a little time alone with him."

He looked hurt and angry, hardly in the mood for logical discussion. "Okay," she said finally, after a long hesitation. "I'll be back in the morning to pick him up."

"No."

Alarmed, Claire took a step toward him and touched his arm. "We have absolutely no proof yet. You don't—"

"I'll bring him back to you in the morning." A small muscle in Logan's cheek jerked. "You don't have to worry. Unlike your family, I can be trusted."

Anger flickered in his eyes, and his white-knuckle grip on the back of the chair beside him would leave dents in the plastic. But Claire knew his word was good. "It's not that. I'm like his mom, now. I should be—I need to be—here."

Logan stalked a few yards away and then swung back to her. "I was never able to be there for him, was I? Do you have any idea how that feels?"

The words caught in her throat at the deep pain in his eyes, the intensity in his voice. *One night.* She could give him that. "All right. As soon as the blood tests come back, we'll know where we stand, okay?"

"I think you've always known." He raked her with a look of pure disgust. "Was it amusing, playing me for a fool?"

She took a deep breath. "I want you to promise that you won't talk to Jason about this until we know for sure."

"I wouldn't do or say anything to hurt him. But if the tests are positive, I'll fight you forever for him," Logan said softly. "The influence of your family is the last thing I want for my son."

His words hit her like a slap across the face. "Fathering a child doesn't make you a daddy, Logan. I'm not so sure that you're a perfect influence, either."

Claire turned and went back to the twins. Tucking the blankets around their shoulders, her heart ached as she thought about the future. If Logan somehow gained sole custody of Jason and took him away, the girls would be devastated. They didn't deserve to face another loss in their young lives.

Reassured that they were warm enough, she walked to Jason's room to await his return from recovery, her heart heavy. There was only one possible decision. If Logan proved to be the boy's father, she would do everything to maintain an amicable relationship. Shared custody, perhaps. The twins needed their brother just as he needed them.

If Logan refused that, she would fight him through the courts. There was nothing more important than family. If it took her last dime, the children were not going to face losing each other.

CHAPTER SIXTEEN

THE MARQUIS DE SADE would have been pleased. Even he couldn't have devised anything less comfortable.

In disgust, Logan threw off his covers and fought the temptation to shove the hospital cot into the hallway. Throughout the night, either his head or his legs had extended well beyond its frame. The horizontal support bars had creased every bone and organ he had.

Intentionally poor design, he decided grimly. One that would discourage hospital guests from staying more than a single night unless under contract with a good masseuse. But then again, his thoughts would have precluded sleep no matter where he spent the night.

Shaking the kinks out of one knee, he hobbled over to Jason's bed and sat on the edge. The sleeping boy looked so young, so vulnerable. *His son.* Logan lightly stroked his cheek.

If the blood tests were positive, how would Jason feel when he found out the identity of his real father? Logan settled his hand softly on Jason's shoulder and contemplated the child's possible reactions. Confusion, maybe. Perhaps he'd feel a deep sense of betrayal by the parents who'd raised him, and anger over the abandonment of the father who'd disappeared.

Turning away, Logan moved to the window, leaned against the cold marble sill and stared at the boy, the only child he would ever have. Jason had been raised in a complete family, with sisters and parents and togetherness. A real family.

Something Logan had never had. Hell. He'd never even met his own father. What would he know about parenting? Claire was right. A long-forgotten moment of passion had not transformed him into a daddy.

He crossed his arms in front of his chest feeling hollow inside as he looked at the photograph of Jason and Brooke on the bedside table. Jason had insisted on bringing it along to the hospital as some sort of talisman, apparently.

That Brooke had been capable of such a selfish and cruel deception shouldn't have surprised him. That her family would stand beside her and hide the truth was a fact of who and what they were. But Claire's secrecy stunned him.

He thought about the few times he'd held her in his arms. She'd responded to him totally. There had been nothing but honest desire in her eyes.

Honest, hell.

She'd been capable of telegraphing deep and honest emotion, without a shadow of guilt over the secret she'd kept about his son's paternity. She was every bit as devious as her sister. The thought slammed into him with the force of a hit-and-run, the image chilling him to the core.

There was no way he could allow her even partial custody of his child, no matter what Brooke had specified in her will. This time he could afford the best lawyers.

Rising to his feet, he moved back to Jason and gently stroked his dark blond hair. "I'm here for you, son," he whispered. "If I'd known, I'd have been here for you from day one. I don't know what I can do about the twins, but I do know there's no way you'll be raised by another Worth."

JASON WILLED his eyes to stay closed when he heard Logan speak. Choked back his response.

His arm hurt, keeping him half-awake. He'd wanted to call for the nurse, but the woozy effect of the anesthetic seemed to come and go. And just when he'd been ready to reach for the call button, something held him back. The thought of a big syringe, maybe. Or the unexpected presence of a man in his room.

It hadn't taken him long to figure out who it was, even without opening his eyes. Some weird sixth sense maybe. Or just the way the man moved—easy and quiet. Somehow, Logan's presence wasn't a surprise.

But the words Logan whispered hit him like a

high fly ball to the head, sending memories swirling through his thoughts. His dad had never been like the fathers his friends had, the kind that played baseball and wrestled on the floor and beamed with pride when their sons made a home run. His own dad had rarely showed up for anything. And nothing Jason ever did had been good enough. Randall's words had become a familiar litany running through his thoughts. *Stupid kid…you little bastard…*

A feeling of hope flickered in Jason's chest. If Logan was his father—

But Logan's voice sounded angry, and his words rasped through Jason's thoughts like a dull saw. Custody? Away from Claire? Away from his sisters? He suddenly felt dizzy. He let his mind spin off into the mist, to a place where the words could float harmlessly away. It's just a dream…it's just a dream…

Except it wasn't. For some reason, Logan was angry with Claire, and planned to take him away. Could Logan force him to go? The thought was terrifying.

No matter how much he'd tried to avoid his aunt at first, she was his family now. He needed her as much as his sisters did. He didn't ever want to leave. He squeezed his eyes shut, but a fat teardrop escaped and fell onto the pillow.

And he couldn't leave, not now. Especially not until he made sure his family would all be safe.

This time you have to do something, he told himself fiercely.

Because he hadn't done anything earlier, his parents were dead and his sisters and Claire were in danger. Shutting his eyes, he prayed harder than he ever had in his life.

Then he remembered a stormy afternoon last winter. A drive on icy streets, and a small bank outside of Minneapolis. One that his mom had never stopped at before.

He opened his eyes and thought about the framed photograph by his bed, remembering her words. *Make sure you keep this always, honey. It means more to me than you'll ever know.*

LOGAN HOVERED over every nurse who came in that night, watching them check the warmth and color of Jason's hand, frowning over their shoulders as they checked his vitals. For every reassurance they offered, Logan thought of a dozen ways everything could go wrong. By morning he was emotionally drained.

Bleary-eyed, he slipped away for a quick shower in the parents' lounge down the hall. Even while pulling on the same clothes he'd worn all night, he felt recharged after standing under the cold, stinging spray for a few minutes.

Jason was awake and propped up against a cloud of pillows when he returned, his casted arm elevated on extra pillows at his side.

The boy eyed him warily over a breakfast tray of oatmeal and apple juice. "You're still here," he said finally, his tone tinged with accusation. "Where's Claire?"

"She took the girls home so they could have a good night's sleep, and I stayed here with you."

Jason stirred the lumpy cereal with a spoon, banking the lumps against one side of the bowl and then the other. "My dad never did anything with me," he said finally, his gaze fastened on the cereal. "He was never home much. But he was still my dad." He looked up, a sheen of tears in his eyes. "Wasn't he?"

Logan stared at him. *Not now. Not without proof.* But the look of fear and worry on the boy's face demanded an answer. An honest one. "He had the privilege of being your father in every way that mattered," Logan said carefully.

A single tear slid down Jason's cheek. "My mom and dad fought a lot, and I heard them talking," he mumbled. "I guess I always sorta knew."

"Knew?"

Jason looked up, his eyes gleaming with defiance. "He thought I wasn't good enough. He never thought I was his."

Pain arrowed through Logan's heart at the revelation. Pain, followed by an unfurling sense of certainty and joy. "He said that?"

Looking away, Jason nodded. "Not when Mom was around. She stood up to him even when..."

His voice trailed away. "He was better with the twins."

Words weren't necessary to convey the life Brooke and her son had led. Years of anger and hurt slipped away, leaving bittersweet memories of the woman Logan had once loved and a feeling of impotent fury at the man who had treated Jason and her badly. Logan cursed under his breath. It was too late to make Randall pay for his sins. But he could now make things right for his son.

"So, you think you're my dad?" Jason gave an offhand shrug as if the answer didn't matter, but the tremor in his voice gave him away.

Logan sat on the edge of the bed and reached for Jason's hand, searching for the right words. "If I were your dad, there could never be a man on earth more proud of his son."

"But you think you are?"

"This isn't the right time to talk about it." The look of pain and longing in Jason's eyes was more than Logan could take. *Please God, let it be true.* "I was married to your mom," he added cautiously. "But we were divorced before you were born."

Jason sat up straighter, guarding his arm. "You're an architect, and you draw really cool buildings."

"Thanks."

"I'm good at art."

Logan thought back to the wonderfully creative

pen-and-ink sketches on Jason's bedroom walls, and felt a surge of pride. "Yes, you are."

"Both of us have wavy hair."

"Yes, but—"

"And you have a cowlick in the same place."

"Yes, but other people—"

"And Claire says you're even more stubborn than me."

Logan fought a smile. "Does she?"

"I know you probably think I'm saying this 'cause my other dad is gone. But that's not it." He sniffled and took a deep breath, as if trying to fight his emotion, but another tear slipped down his cheek. "I always wished I had a dad who could love me as I am." He looked down at his cast. "And I—I wish it was you."

Careful to avoid Jason's arm, Logan wrapped him in a hug and breathed in the scent of him, wishing he could call back the years. Then he stood and turned toward the windows, blind to anything that lay outside as he fought to control his emotions.

He'd bet his soul that the DNA tests would be positive. His heart couldn't be so wrong. But with that certainty came a crushing sense of loss. He'd never had the chance to hold Jason as a baby, never had a chance to see him take his first steps or to hear his first words.

"If it's true, would you make me leave?"

"What?" Logan pulled up a chair and straddled it next to Jason's bed.

"I heard you say you wouldn't let me be raised by the Worths."

"So much for residual anesthesia," Logan muttered. "I didn't realize you were awake."

"I can't leave. Lissa and Annie need me. And Claire..." Jason hesitated, his eyes searching Logan's face. "I need your help."

"I'll do anything I can."

"I know who's after Claire. I've got to help her, or she'll end up dead just like my mom. Please, can you take me to Minneapolis?"

CLAIRE PACED the kitchen floor for the tenth time, pausing to peer out the windows every time she passed by. The girls had slept late, and were now quietly watching cartoons in the living room. Five guests had checked out, Fred had stopped at the house for his list of duties for the day and Igor had somehow appeared by the refrigerator once again.

She'd called the hospital hourly throughout the night for condition reports on Jason, and knew the doctor had released him a half hour ago. How long should it take to get home, twenty minutes? Thirty?

Had Logan taken him?

From his favorite place in front of the sink, Gilbert watched her pace back and forth, with one eyebrow cocked.

"I never, ever should have left the hospital," she muttered, trying to quell the anxiety rippling through her midsection.

Gilbert thumped his tail.

"Five more minutes and I call the police."

Gilbert bared his teeth in a goofy dog grin, and thumped his tail harder.

Claire sighed. "You're right, it was a dumb idea. But where are they?"

The phone rang. She caught it on the fly, and felt her heart still at the sound of Logan's voice.

"Claire, I want you to be really careful. Do you hear me? Keep the girls inside, and lock the doors."

"Where are you? Where's Jason?"

"Don't worry, he's fine. We're just leaving the sheriff's office, and should be home in twenty minutes."

Before she could respond, Logan hung up.

THE SHERIFF'S OFFICE? Claire sat at the kitchen table with the phone in front of her, barely aware of her father's voice on the speaker. Every few minutes she paced to the windows and looked out at the driveway. *Logan, where are you?*

With the phone's speaker function turned on, her father's voice followed her throughout the room. He was in the middle of one of his get-back-to-civilization lectures, but she couldn't have repeated a word he said if her life depended on it.

At a light tap on the door, she jumped to her feet and spun around. Logan and Jason were standing outside.

She darted across the kitchen, unlocked the door and caught Jason in a careful hug as soon as he stepped inside. "Honey, you look so tired! Are you hungry? How is your arm?" She looked up at Logan and lowered her voice. "What's going on?"

Static erupted from the telephone speaker, as if Charles had walked too far from his desk with a portable phone. "Claire, who is that?"

She pivoted, and searched the keypad of the phone for a way to switch it from speaker to the receiver, then gave up in exasperation. "Jason and Logan are here, Dad. I've got to go."

"You let Jason go off with him? That's the final straw, Claire. I'm on my way."

"I'll call you back later." She reached forward to hang up.

"I'm going to charter a flight to Duluth and arrange for a rental car. I should be at Pine Cliff by early evening."

Oh, no. Claire faltered, her hand hovering above the phone. *"Today?"*

"I've got grave concerns about my grandchildren."

Not now, of all times. Logan shook his head silently, warning her to head off the visit. "Next week would be a lot better, Dad. We'd have more time to—"

"This isn't a social trip."

She gave Logan a helpless shrug, knowing that

nothing would dissuade her father once he'd made a decision. "Would you rather stay in a cabin, or with us? I'm afraid the house isn't quite ready for guests."

"Cabin," Charles snapped.

"Done. And Father," Claire added, her voice firm, "we're all just fine up here. This trip isn't necessary. But while you're here, we're going to discuss the truth about Brooke and Logan, because you've been wrong all these years. I'll make sure he joins us for supper."

For the first time in her life, she heard her father falter. "Dammit, you have no idea what you've done, Claire."

"You're wrong, Dad. I finally know who to trust. It's time to finally make things right, don't you think?"

Charles hung up. A loud dial tone filled the room.

Claire pressed the speaker button, then gave Logan and Jason a wry smile. "Close family, right?"

Jason hung back, looking uncertain. "Maybe I should just go upstairs," he ventured, cradling his cast with his good arm. "So you can talk?"

"You're a part of this, kid." Logan gave him an easy smile. "Unless you're getting tired. Do you want to lie down? Do you need any more Tylenol?"

Jason shook his head and sat down, propping his cast on the kitchen table.

Logan turned back to Claire. "Did you mean what you said to your father?"

"Of course." She'd come to trust Logan, had given him her heart. Now she hoped he would never know. She'd fallen in love with the one man who could never fall in love with her, a man so betrayed by her family that he would never forgive them. His harsh words at the hospital had made his feelings painfully clear. "I'm so sorry for what we've done to you—for what you've lost because of us."

He moved so fast she almost didn't see him coming. He gripped her shoulders and turned her to face him fully. His eyes darkened to the color of Superior at nightfall, his voice lowered. "I'm not leaving until this is all settled. You, me, Jason...and what happened to your sister."

Claire stiffened. "Brooke?"

"But first, I need your permission to take Jason to the Twin Cities. We can be back by late evening."

"You want to go clear down to the 'Cities?"

"It's important, Claire. Jason knows where Brooke left some documents, but can't remember the name of the bank...he isn't even sure which suburb it's in, but he thinks he'll remember some landmarks once he gets back home. You and the kids are in danger until we can nail Hank and Buzz for good. Jason has already given the county sheriff a statement.''

''But *today?* Jason just got out of the hospital! His arm—''

''He'll be fine, I promise. He'll be more quiet in a seat belt than he would be roaming around the house, and he can keep the cast elevated on a pillow, just as the doctor said. If his hand changes from a healthy pink, or tingles, or his arm becomes more painful, I'll have him back at the hospital right away.''

''But—''

''I wouldn't do this if it wasn't important. If we go now, we can find the bank before it closes. He's got a safe-deposit key.''

''*Jason* does?''

Logan stepped back and retrieved the duffel bag he'd left by the door, then withdrew the framed photograph of Jason and Brooke. ''He remembered his mother telling him to keep this always, that it was more important than he'd ever know. The key was inside the back of the frame. It has a box number on it, but it isn't in the original bank packet, so there's no way to identify which bank it's from.''

''Don't you need identification to get into the box?''

Logan nodded. ''When we find the right bank, I'll call the Minneapolis police. Since you're

Brooke's executor, they may be checking with you. At least we'll know where the evidence is."

He reached into the back pocket of his jeans and handed Claire a small manila envelope. Brooke had written Claire's address on the back, followed by a terse message.

If anything happens to me, give this to your aunt Claire, and tell her where we went the night we bought your Minnesota Twins coat. She'll know what to do.

Claire sank into a chair next to Jason's, and curved her arm around his shoulders. "My Lord."

"Your old friends Buzz and Hank are probably getting desperate, from what Jason says. The sheriff is putting out a bulletin for their arrests, and will be keeping a close eye on Pine Cliff. He can't hold them long without hard evidence, though."

"Jason, honey, are you sure you can handle this?"

Jason's expression turned bleak. "I have to. I could have saved my mom's life, but I was too afraid. It's all my fault!"

Logan pulled up another chair and sat down at his other side. "That's not true. Your mom and dad died in a car accident."

"It wasn't an accident," Jason said fiercely. "Some guys came one night and threatened her.

They said she had evidence that could send them all to jail, and they wanted it back. They said they would kill her if she didn't cooperate. I—I was upstairs, but I heard everything.''

Claire held back a sob rising in her throat. ''Did you see who these people were?''

''N-no. Mom and Dad had a terrible fight after they left, because she wanted to go to the police. Dad knew I must have overheard. He told me that he and Mom were in big trouble, and that no matter what happened, I had to keep quiet. If I ever said a word, and the police got involved, his partners would come after me and the twins. Two days later, Mom and Dad were dead.''

''Honey, you couldn't have done anything to stop it.''

''I should have called the police,'' Jason said brokenly. ''I should have told them, no matter what Dad said.''

Claire hugged him tighter, then lifted his chin with her hand so she could meet his gaze. ''The plans were probably in motion from the night of that argument at your house. Don't feel responsible for something you couldn't control.''

Jason's gaze skittered away. ''I—I knew those guys were up here, snooping around. I figured they would find what they wanted and go away. I even looked through the boxes in the attic myself, thinking I might find something they might want. Business stuff, or something.''

Claire gave him a quick, reassuring hug. ''It will all be over soon.''

Logan stood. ''The sheriff will be cruising the area until we get back.''

''Go, then. Drive safe.'' Claire's heart turned over as she watched Logan and Jason go out the door. ''I love you both,'' she added softly.

But they were already gone.

CHAPTER SEVENTEEN

CLAIRE WAS STANDING at the door when Logan drove in that evening. The moment he pulled to a stop, she ran down the sidewalk. As soon as Jason stepped out of the car, she enfolded him in an embrace.

Logan stared at the boy—his son—held so securely in Claire's arms. A sense of peace washed through Logan's heart like a healing rain, a balm for the wounds he'd carried for far too many years.

Over the top of Jason's head Claire studied him, her eyes dark and luminous. "Were you successful?"

"Thanks to Jason." Logan looked down at him. "How are you holding up, kid?"

"I'm beat," he admitted, stepping back. "I'm going to bed. Is Grandfather here yet?"

"His charter flight arrived a while ago, but he still has to drive up here. You and the girls can see him in the morning." Claire reached out to touch his forehead. "How are you feeling? Is your arm hurting?"

"It's okay. Logan gave me some Tylenol an hour ago."

"Sleep tight, sweetie." She leaned forward and gave him a quick kiss on the cheek. "I'm so glad you're back safe and sound."

Once Jason disappeared into the house, Claire turned to Logan. "How did everything go?" She'd hidden her fear from Jason, but Logan now heard a tremor in her voice.

"Jason remembered where he bought his new jacket that day, and after he recognized a motorcycle shop at an intersection, we found the bank. Brooke rented a safe-deposit box a few months before she died."

"But she didn't keep any records of it."

"She wouldn't have wanted to leave a paper trail for her husband to find."

Claire shuddered. "He was an awful man."

"She left a letter to you, along with an audiotape of phone conversations, photocopies of bids and contracts, and a stack of invoices. Enough evidence to put Randall and his buddies—including Hank and Buzz—in prison for a good long while. They had quite a scheme going—construction kickbacks, substandard materials, some extortion on the side. They defrauded the state of Minnesota and a number of private companies."

A look of stunned disbelief filled her eyes. "But Randall and Brooke were nearly broke when they died."

"I think some of Randall's schemes were starting to unravel, and the guys involved were probably getting desperate toward the end. Payoffs, bribes—who knows. The investigators will have a field day with this case.

"Based on Jason's statement—" Logan lowered his voice "—the police believe there's a good chance Brooke and Randall were murdered."

Claire stiffened. "Oh no." Her eyes filled with grief. "Brooke couldn't have been a part of all this. She was awful with money. She couldn't even balance a checkbook!"

"She was trapped. As Randall sank deeper and deeper, he dragged her in. You need to read her letter."

"Where is all the evidence now?"

"We gave the Minneapolis police everything Brooke hid in that box. They issued a statewide bulletin for the arrests of everyone involved. They've already got Hank and Buzz—Gerald Thompkins and Willie Black—in custody."

"And those two were here at Pine Cliff. I just wish I'd known what they were after! My God, what if they'd hurt the kids?" Claire shut her eyes and drew a shaky breath.

"Willie Black has already confessed to their activities up here. They made the anonymous phone calls, searched the house and damaged the washing machine. He and Thompkins killed those bats. They wanted to frighten you away."

Claire frowned. "The sheriff said they weren't released in time to have done it."

"Apparently the time of release was recorded incorrectly. The sheriff's office was short-staffed at the time, and someone made an error. The lawyer who posted their bail was involved, and lied about taking those two back to Minneapolis."

"Do you have Brooke's letter?"

Logan searched his back pocket. "They let me have a photocopy, but they kept the original."

Claire sniffled, and managed a smile. "It must have taken some convincing for them to let you have a copy."

Logan shrugged. "A little." A sense of deep compassion filled his heart as he handed it to her. His voice grew rough. "I'm sorry. I know this is hard."

"Let's go inside, where there's better light." In the kitchen, she clutched the letter and closed her eyes briefly, then groped for a chair and sank into it. She scanned the contents of the letter, then dropped her hands to her lap.

"She was too terrified to go to the police," Claire whispered. "Randall threatened to harm both her and the kids if she didn't give back the evidence."

Logan reached for her hand and held it between both of his.

"Once she decided to blow the whistle, the others figured that both she and her husband were liabilities, especially after she refused to cooperate. Brooke's documents revealed a lot of influential

names, and not one of them would want to be im-
plicated, much less face the possibility of prison.''

Claire lifted the letter again, and read aloud the
last paragraph.

I hope you've gone to Pine Cliff with the
kids, Claire. The manager tells me that Logan
is planning to build soon, next to your property. You'll be safe with him nearby. He didn't
deserve what happened between us. Jason is
his son, and I will always regret not telling him
the truth. Make things right for me, please.
Tell him? I've made far too many mistakes in
my life, and I might not have time to fix them
all. Please tell my kids I'll love them with all
my heart, forever and ever.

Brooke

She smoothed the letter against her lap, as if trying to feel a connection to her sister.

''You read all of this?'' she whispered, looking
up at Logan. He nodded. ''Does Jason know you're
his father?''

''He guessed in the hospital, but he hasn't read
the letter.'' Logan swallowed. The next words were
the hardest he'd ever had to say. ''I thought you
should decide when to talk to him, and how much
he should know.''

Claire pulled back and gave him a startled look.
''He should know the truth.''

"Thank you for that." Logan hesitated, trying to find the right words. "I'm sorry for all I said at the hospital. I was cruel, and I was wrong, accusing you like that." He took a deep breath. "I won't fight you for custody of Jason."

She winced, as if he'd slapped her. "What?"

"I'll agree to shared custody, visiting rights—the lawyers can work it out. He needs a stable, loving home. With his sisters, and with you."

Claire's eyes brimmed with tears. "Is that what you want?" she asked softly. "Is that all?"

"I want what's best for the kids, and for you."

She swayed, and he reached out to steady her. "Are you okay?"

She gave him a watery smile. "Just fine."

From outside came the sound of an approaching car. Claire went to the window. Her face looked as pale and fragile as porcelain, but then she straightened, as if summoning an inner reserve of strength. "My father's here."

Together they walked out to meet him, but Logan had never felt more alone in his life.

CHAPTER EIGHTEEN

CLAIRE POURED three cups of coffee and set them on the table. Charles, looking more haggard than she'd ever seen him, shifted in his chair, then loosened his tie. Away from the empire he ruled with an eagle eye, he no longer seemed as intimidating.

Maybe it was because she'd finally managed to grow up.

Avoiding eye contact with Logan, Charles glanced around the room. His gaze settled on a large manila folder on the table.

She snagged the folder and slid it over to him. "Photographs."

He shrugged. "I'd rather not."

"No, look at them. They're beautiful photographs of the North Shore in the moonlight." She managed a smile. "Some guests gave these to me this morning when they checked out. I had no idea the Sweeneys were nature photographers. With the odd hours they kept, I thought they were involved in some of the troubles we were having."

"Troubles?"

From the glint in his eye, she knew what was coming next. "Before you even start, I want you to know that the kids and I are staying here,'' she said simply. ''Nothing you say will change that.''

Charles stood abruptly. ''That won't do, Claire. You have obligations now. You must come back to New York. The kids will have only the best—''

''We know about Jason,'' Claire said quietly.

He stared at her for a long moment. ''You just couldn't leave well enough alone.''

Logan swore softly under his breath. ''Hell of a statement there, Worth. Your interference led to more trouble than you can imagine. Randall despised Jason, and he involved your daughter in—''

''Stop,'' Claire said. ''Both of you. Dad, sit down. There's a lot you don't know, and it's time you found out.''

Two pots of decaf later, she reached across the table and took her father's hand. His shoulders weren't as square as they'd been before she'd told him everything.

''You did what you thought best,'' she said quietly. ''But now it's time for honesty. Logan deserves an explanation, and an apology from our family. Mine alone isn't enough.''

Charles sighed heavily. ''When Brooke eloped with Logan, it nearly broke my heart. She needed a marriage to someone successful, who could afford to take care of her well. Running off with a penniless college student was the dumbest thing she could have done. When she said she was miserable, and told me Logan had married her for our money,

I was furious.'' He shot a glance at Logan for the first time all night. ''Any man who tried to get at my money through my daughter, or hurt her in any way, deserved every bit of punishment I could deliver.''

''I loved your daughter, and never asked for a single penny from you,'' Logan retorted. ''All I wanted was a life here at Pine Cliff. But then she met someone else. Apparently she thought he could give her a lot more than I ever could.''

Charles shook his head sadly. ''She jumped into a second marriage before the ink was dry on her divorce papers, and that piece of slime was in my face from the moment they married, wanting me to back his wild schemes. I told him he'd never see a nickel, and that's the last we ever saw of either him or Brooke. I tried many times…''

''Randall was a controlling, abusive man,'' Claire said. ''He didn't deserve Brooke, and he wasn't a good father. Logan would have loved his son with all his heart, but you took that chance away from him.''

Charles stood up heavily, his face grim. He stared at the photograph of Brooke and Jason still lying on the counter. Finally, he raised his eyes and met Logan's gaze. ''I always tried to protect my family. Maybe too much. I thought I was doing the right thing by keeping Jason from you. But my interference and pride meant that I never met any of my grandchildren until this fall, and maybe even led to

Brooke's death. If I'd agreed to Randall's business deals..." His voice broke. "I don't expect forgiveness. God knows I won't ever forgive myself."

He turned away and trudged to the door. "Which cabin key?" he asked gruffly, looking up at the rack.

Claire crossed the room and laid a hand on his arm. "No, Dad. We need to finish this."

He didn't look at her. *"Just give me a key."*

She handed him one, then watched him open the door. Maybe tomorrow she could talk to him again, make him understand.

"Wait." Logan stood and set his coffee cup down, then crossed the kitchen to where Charles stood. "Because of your family's secrets, I lost all of Jason's childhood. If not for seeing Claire again, I might never have even known about my son. I can't begin to describe how empty and angry that makes me feel."

"I—I'm sorry." The expression in Charles's eyes turned bleak. "I've lost a child myself."

Logan's voiced gentled. "Jason already has guessed the truth, and I hope he'll be a part of my life from now on. I don't want him to ever feel torn between your family and me, or to feel he has to choose." He extended his hand and looked Charles in the eye. "It's time to move ahead, don't you think?"

Charles hesitated for only a moment, then he took Logan's hand and held it fast. "I was wrong about you.'' With that, he stepped out into the night.

His stride seemed far less purposeful than usual, his demeanor far less imposing. "He should have stayed here at the house,'' Claire murmured.

Logan came up behind her and rested his hands on her shoulders. Awareness shimmered through her at his touch, sensitizing her skin.

"Your father needs to be alone for a while. You'll see him tomorrow.''

She turned into Logan's embrace and looked up at him, absorbing the scent of his aftershave, the strength of his jaw, the quarter smile that sent a little shiver of excitement through her whenever he was near.

But the raw pain in his voice and his harsh words at the hospital had played through her thoughts over and over, a litany defining just how impossible any hope for the future would be.

He'd said he would leave custody to her. He hadn't said he wanted to stay. And why would he, with all that had happened in the past? She closed her eyes and saw the years ahead stretching on and on, the casual encounters with him through Jason. Each meeting would feel like salt on an open wound.

She studied the lean, tanned planes and hollows of Logan's beloved face, the eyes shadowed by dark lashes. She wanted to thread her hands through his thick, dark-honey hair, to pull him close until she felt his mouth on hers. The thought made her skin tingle, her heart contract with sorrow.

And then, in a heartbeat...she realized his eyes had darkened to the shade of November storms.

The shade of desire.

"Come with me?" he whispered, his voice a vibration beneath her fingers.

A flash of vertigo spun through her, until she realized he'd swept her up into his arms and was carrying her through the house, up the stairs. Burying her face against the curve of his neck she inhaled the scent of sandalwood and pine, and that unique, clean scent of his soap.

At the top of the stairs he strode into her bedroom. Quietly shut the door. Locked it. His face was a breath away from hers, his eyes dark and deep and hungry. "I want you," he said, brushing a kiss across her forehead. "So very, very much."

The fans of his lashes lowered as he shifted, then let her slide slowly down the length of his body. He was all hard muscle and welcome heat, his arousal undeniable beneath the flannel-soft denim of his worn jeans. The intensity of his gaze beneath his lowered lashes drew her like a magnetic force. His breathing grew shallow, faster as his hands drifted from her shoulders and down the curve of her spine.

"I want to see all of you, with the moonlight on your skin and nothing else," he said. His voice rasped like a brush of sandpaper against her flesh.

Her clothes melted away beneath his touch, his mouth hot and urgent on each new expanse of skin, until she stood naked and trembling before him.

"Not fair," she managed to say, trailing a hand down the front of his shirt. But where his hands had been deft and sure, hers shook too much to open a single button.

"Let me," he said, one hand at the back of her neck, the other at the top button of his shirt.

With excruciating care he unfastened that first button, kissing her hot and hard, tracing the edges of her teeth until she moaned and opened to him, welcomed the warm force of his tongue deep into her mouth. The kiss went on and on until she was dizzy with need. The erotic dance of his tongue against her own was almost more than she could bear.

"Please," she said, wanting to rip his shirt away and tumble him backward onto the floor, wanting to hold him there for an eternity of wild, drugging kisses, wanting to feel his flesh burn against her own. Deep inside, her hunger grew.

But he held her back, his free hand moving slowly to the second button of his shirt. And then the next, his dark gaze never leaving hers.

The shirt fell open. With a sigh she ran her fingers through the dark silk hair on his chest, feeling the heavy beat of his heart beneath her palms, testing the expansion of his chest with each breath he took. With one fingertip she traced the dark streak that disappeared into the unbuttoned V of his jeans. At the contraction of his muscles beneath her touch, she experienced a surge of feminine power.

She lifted her hands to his shoulders, curved them over the heavy muscle, then swept the shirt back until it fell away.

"Oh my," she whispered.

He watched her as she explored and touched and savored, but now, one corner of his mouth tilted into a smile. He slid one hand behind her and coaxed her backward, onto the soft eyelet coverlet of her bed lit only by a broad ribbon of moonlight streaming through the window.

Her senses intensified, taking in the warmth of the bed and the nubbly feeling of fabric beneath her, the intoxicating scent and heat and image of the powerful man who rose above her.

With deliberate care he bent lower, covering her mouth with his own, his lips soft against hers, his tongue making love to hers while his hand stroked the length of her body with infinite gentleness. His fingers traced the undercurve of her breasts, first one, then the other, with such tantalizing sweetness that she arched into his palm, begging for more. His hand drifted lower, to trace the dent of her navel, and then lower still.

She cried out, wrapped one leg against his, trying to drag him closer to her. Needing the weight of his body. Needing him.

"Slow down, honey, or this isn't going to last,"

he said against her ear. His breath sent shivers down her back, made her toes curl.

"I want to hold you tight." He traced the rim of her ear with his tongue. "I want to stroke every part of you." He kissed the tender skin below her ear, then farther back, to the exquisitely sensitive nape, cupping the back of her head to gain a better angle.

Claire closed her eyes, savoring each moment, trying to separate each sensation so that she would be able to remember it all later. But the sensations grew until they blended into a wildfire of wanting so strong that she could no longer wait.

And though she'd wanted to remember it in detail, from the moment he entered her, she could only feel and respond and give herself up to the sheer beauty of it all. This was Logan, her beloved Logan. Cradling his face with both hands she took his mouth with the desperate hunger of one who had been starving her whole life, giving herself to him heart and soul, until they both shattered in a moment of primitive, all-consuming joy.

A long time later, his head cradled against her breast, Claire stared at the curve of his long, muscular body in the moonlit darkness, and wondered why she'd ever thought once would be enough. If he stayed in her bed from now until eternity, it would never be enough. Tears formed, hot and prickly, beneath her lashes for what she'd discovered and what she'd lost.

Logan stirred, raised one hand and cupped her breast. Instantly the nipple grew sensitive, hardening in eager response.

She wanted his mouth there. She wanted it all, again and again until both of them were too exhausted to speak.

But she knew what Logan wanted, and it wasn't anything long-term. He'd made that clear. And if Claire had discovered that making love with him drove her beyond rational thought, today she'd also discovered that she had more strength than she'd ever realized.

She wouldn't make this difficult.

"Thank you," she said, drifting her hand over the sleek hot satin of his skin.

He growled deep in his throat, edged closer until he was behind her, then pulled her backward against his chest into full body contact. She sighed with pleasure.

It took a moment before she remembered what she'd wanted to say. "You make this so difficult…"

"Hmm?"

"I appreciate so much that you'll let the children stay together, with me. I can't tell you how much that means to all of us."

She felt his eyelashes flutter open against the back of her neck.

"Huh?"

"And this—this experience with you—was simply incredible. I appreciate this, too."

"You *appreciate* it?"

Claire slipped out of bed, winding the sheet around herself. In another second her tears would be making serious tracks down her face, but she could hold on just a bit longer.

He launched out of bed.

Startled, she stepped back. "Is there a problem?"

Logan had never felt such soul-wrenching emotions. Love and burning desire for her overwhelmed him. Every moment had been almost painful in its beauty.

And she was brushing him off as if he'd just delivered cold pizza to her door.

He'd been thinking *forever*.

She'd politely thanked him for a nice time.

Logan grabbed his shirt, shoved his arms in the sleeves, then jerked on his briefs and jeans, unable to speak.

He stood near the door, shirt open, jeans unsnapped, his heavy, dark blond hair hanging over one eye. With his legs spread and hands clenched at his sides he looked like the embodiment of every sexual fantasy Claire had ever dreamed, from the tanned expanse of muscular chest to the flat, ridged belly, to the dark passion in his eyes.

And then he was gone. Out the door and out of her life as abruptly as he'd appeared. She had the sudden vision of him holding her heart in his hand, testing its weight and balance, then flinging it out across Lake Superior. Caring no more about it than he might have cared for a pebble he'd skipped over the waves.

. With lifeless fingers she picked up her scattered clothes, an aching loneliness crushing her heart.

She stopped. Stared at the crumpled clothing in her hands. Looked up at the dresser mirror on the wall. The woman staring back at her looked desolate, alone.

She stood taller. These past months had taught her that there was nothing she couldn't do, nothing she couldn't face. She would not give up her future without a fight.

Lifting her chin, she flung open the bedroom door. And ran into a wall of warm flannel.

Startled, she stared up into Logan's pensive face. And then she laughed. "We have got to stop running into each other like this," she murmured. "Signal lights, or..."

"I couldn't leave," he said.

"I couldn't let you."

"But I need more—more than just this."

"I do, too."

"I need you when I go to sleep at night. I need to know that you'll be there every morning." He took a deep breath, slid his hands up her arms and rested them on her shoulders. "When I'm ninety-five I want your rocking chair next to mine. You're a part of my soul, Claire. When I walked down those stairs, I knew I'd left behind every part of life that mattered. I love you, honey. Marry me?''

''Yes,'' she said. She reached up, cradled his face in her hands. Her eyes filled with warm tears.

He backed her into the bedroom and shut the door. The clothes in her arms slipped to the floor, along with the sheet she'd worn. Stepping closer, she breathed in the warmth and essence of the man she'd loved since childhood. The man she would love through all eternity.

She felt the glow of the stars and the moon radiate through her, felt the joyful blessing of the angels above. And knew that she and Logan had found heaven on earth.

Somehow, forever would never be enough.

EPILOGUE

"SHE'S MORE BEAUTIFUL than a princess," Annie breathed.

The shower of sequins and tiny beads on Claire's ivory wedding dress sparkled in the spring sunlight. She held a delicate bouquet of flowers that matched the ones woven through her silvery-blond hair. Behind her, Superior's waves glittered, and seagulls swooped low.

Jason, as best man, and Logan wore matching dark blue tuxes. With another six months of growth, Jason was fast approaching Logan's height, and anyone could see that they were father and son.

Lissa poked her sister in the side with an elbow. "Grandma's crying. I bet she wishes she got to wear a dress like that, instead of that old green one."

Nodding sagely, Annie edged over a few inches and patted Gilbert's head. Clipped and groomed, with a big pink bow on each ear and a look of supreme embarrassment in his eyes, he flopped to the ground and curved a paw over his nose. His gaze never left the couple standing with a minister out on the rocky promontory overlooking Superior.

Smoothing the skirt of her frothy pink brides-maid's dress, Lissa looked over the small crowd gathered along the shore. Fred, dressed up in a suit, was smiling from ear to ear, Mrs. Rogers, at his side, had started sniffling before the ceremony ever started. Grandma and Grandpa had stood apart, un-til Grandma started crying, and then Grandpa had moved closer and put his arm around her waist.

In a few moments the ceremony ended with a long…very long kiss that finally broke when the crowd started to cheer. A blush rising on her cheeks, Claire looked up into Logan's eyes and locked her hands behind him.

"I love you," she whispered. "Forever and al-ways."

"Longer than that," he murmured.

How life had changed.

They'd decided to live in Logan's new home, and were turning the old Victorian at Pine Cliff into a bed-and-breakfast. Mrs. Rogers had been instru-mental in that decision—she'd begged for the op-portunity to stay on as an employee, much to Fred's delight.

Claire's mother was still coolly distant with most everyone on the planet, but Logan had developed a tentative friendship with Charles after that first shaky truce.

And best of all, Claire and the children no longer had to live in fear. Buzz and Hank's confessions had led to the convictions of the rest of Randall's cohorts. Hank was now appealing his conviction for first-degree murder, but would probably end his days behind bars, while Buzz faced five-to-ten.

Logan slid a look at the friends and family gathered to celebrate the best moment of his life, then lowered his mouth to his wife's for another kiss. She melted against him, soft and warm and unbearably desirable, and he nearly forgot where he was until he felt a small hand tug on the hem of his coat.

"Cake!" pleaded Annie.

"It's time to eat!" Lissa added.

Laughing, he released Claire and swept both bundles of ruffles and lace up into his arms. With his son and wife at his side, he stepped forward into the crowd.

With the soft lap of waves against the shore behind him, the scent of pine in the air and the people he loved around him, he knew he'd come home at last.

HARLEQUIN

SUPERROMANCE®

From July to September 1999—three special
Superromance® novels about people whose
New Millennium resolution is

By the Year 2000: CELEBRATE!

JULY 1999—*A Cop's Good Name* by Linda Markowiak
Joe Latham's only hope of saving his badge and his reputation is
to persuade lawyer Maggie Hannan to take his case. Only Maggie—
his ex-wife—knows him well enough to believe him.

AUGUST 1999—*Mr. Miracle* by Carolyn McSparren
Scotsman Jamey McLachlan's come to Tennessee to keep the
promise he made to his stepfather. But Victoria Jamerson stands
between him and his goal, and hurting Vic is the last thing he wants
to do.

SEPTEMBER 1999—*Talk to Me* by Jan Freed
To save her grandmother's business, Kara Taylor has to co-host a
TV show with her ex about the differing points of view between men
and women. A topic Kara and Travis know plenty about.

By the end of the year,
everyone will have something to celebrate!

HARLEQUIN®
Makes any time special™

If you enjoyed what you just read,
then we've got an offer you can't resist!

Take 2 bestselling
love stories FREE!
Plus get a FREE surprise gift!

"Fascinating—you'll want to take this home!"
—**Marie Ferrarella**

"Each page is filled with a brand-new surprise."
—**Suzanne Brockmann**

"Makes reading a new and joyous experience all over again."
—**Tara Taylor Quinn**

See what all your favorite authors are talking about.

Coming October 1999 to a retail store near you.

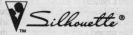

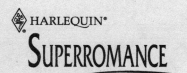

HARLEQUIN®
SUPERROMANCE

COMING NEXT MONTH

#858 TALK TO ME • Jan Freed
By the Year 2000: Celebrate!
When Kara Taylor left her husband on their disastrous first anniversary, she figured she'd just call her marriage a bad experience and move on. Sure, Travis was handsome and charming and wonderful, but they were mismatched from the start. He was a true outdoorsman, and she was the ultimate city girl. Success mattered more to her than it did to him, so who would've thought that nine years later he'd be the only person who could save her business?

#859 FAMILY FORTUNE • Roz Denny Fox
The Lyon Legacy
Crystal Jardin is connected to the prestigious Lyon family by blood—and by affection. And she's especially close to Margaret Lyon, the family matriarch. Margaret, who's disappeared. Whose money is disappearing, too. At such a critical time, the last thing Crystal needs is to fall for a difficult man like Caleb Tanner—or a vulnerable young boy.

Follow the Lyon family fortunes. New secrets are revealed, new betrayals are thwarted—but the bonds of family remain stronger than ever!

#860 THE BABY AND THE BADGE • Janice Kay Johnson
Patton's Daughters
Meg Patton, single mother and brand-new sheriff's deputy, has finally come home to Elk Springs. It's time to reconcile with her sisters—and past time to introduce them to her son. And now her first case has her searching for the parents of an abandoned infant. But Meg can't afford to fall for this baby—or for the man who found her. No matter how much she wants to do both....

#861 FALLING FOR THE ENEMY • Dawn Stewardson
When crime lord Billy Fitzgerald, locked away in solitary confinement, arranges to have prison psychologist Hayley Morgan's son abducted as a bargaining tool, Hayley's life falls apart. To ensure her son's safety, Hayley has to rely on Billy's lawyer, Sloan Reeves, to act as a go-between. Trouble is, he's the enemy and Hayley is smitten.

#862 BORN IN TEXAS • Ginger Chambers
The West Texans
Tate Connelly is recuperating from near-fatal gunshot wounds. Jodie Connelly would do anything to help her husband get well—except the one thing he's asking: divorce him. Maybe the Parker clan—and Jodie's pregnancy—can shake Tate up and get him thinking straight again.

#863 DADDY'S HOME • Pamela Bauer
Family Man
A plane crash. An injured woman. A courageous rescue. All Tyler Brant wants is to put the whole thing behind him. But the media's calling him a hero. And so are the women in his life: his mother, his six-year-old daughter and Kristin Kellar—the woman he saved. If only they knew the truth....

Starting in September 1999,
Harlequin Temptation®
will also be celebrating
an anniversary—15 years
of bringing you the
best in passion.

Look for these
Harlequin Temptation® titles
at your favorite retail stores
in September:

CLASS ACT
by Pamela Burford

BABY.COM
by Molly Liholm

NIGHT WHISPERS
by Leslie Kelly

THE SEDUCTION OF SYDNEY
by Jamie Denton